He moved his power was able to see his fa His eyes seemed almo so that she could see

Hugh stared intentl all the perfection of h in, great grey pools of temptation; the warm velvet of her skin, which seemed to invite his touch; and the mouth— such a mouth!

She knew he would kiss her, and she knew she would not protest. It was beyond her power to stop him. His lips came to hers, gentle at first, searching, and she felt her mouth respond as if of its own volition, in answer.

Louisa Jordan was born and educated in Bristol. She started writing children's stories for pleasure at an early age and then graduated to adult fiction in her twenties. *The King's Man* is her first published novel and her first venture into historical romance. She now resides in Vienna, Austria, with her husband and writes full-time.

For my parents,
Jean and Alan Pennington—
always there.

THE KING'S MAN

Louisa Jordan

MILLS & BOON LIMITED
ETON HOUSE   18-24 PARADISE ROAD
RICHMOND   SURREY   TW9 1SR

First published in Great Britain 1988
by Mills & Boon Limited

© Louisa Jordan 1988

Australian copyright 1988
Philippine copyright 1988
This edition 1988

ISBN 0 263 76152 5

Set in Times Roman 10 on 12¼ pt.
04-0888-70171 C

Made and printed in Great Britain

CHAPTER ONE

THE SOUND of the horses, saturated and exhausted as they trudged wearily into the cobbled courtyard, had made Bethan's heart beat wildly, but through the thin aperture of her window she could see that none of the three men was Edward. The strangers were the King's men, and they too seemed as exhausted as their mounts. The rain that had abated during the night chose to return with a new fury, and she heard the men curse and run to the door of the house as the heavens opened. The pounding of fist against wood seemed to echo angrily through the warren of time-worn passages.

Quickly Bethan unbraided her long dark tresses until they hung freely, cascading to below her waist like a waterfall. Carefully and with practised ease she gathered them once more into two heavy sections, splitting each into three and then braiding them again so that the two ropes hung richly down on either side. Satisfied, she stood up and stepped out of her thick woollen night-dress and warily approached the pewter bowl sitting so innocently on the oak chest next to her bed; it was filled with freezing water. Gingerly she splashed and rubbed herself, and laughed as tell-tale goose-pimples covered her skin and her full, well-formed breasts rose and firmed in protest at the sudden chill. A deep green gown, the rich colour of silken moss, lay across the wooden rungs of a chair close to the door, and padding softly across the rush-laden floor she pulled the garment swiftly over her head, slipping a heavy cotton underskirt beneath. Finally, she reached for a small brown glass bottle filled with water of roses—it was her own recipe, from her own garden, and the delicate heady scent never ceased to delight her as she dabbed it lightly on her neck and wrists. Smoothing her skirts, she moved quickly to the door, anxious to find out why King Henry's men should venture into their little part of Somerset.

Bethan walked quietly along the narrow passage, and as she neared the top of the wide staircase she heard the familiar voice of her aunt Matilda instructing the men where they could dry out and refresh themselves. Pausing, she looked down upon the three strangers who stood just beneath her; they seemed to loom over her aunt like giants, the crimson of the King's colours now stained black with rain, and their hair so wet that it lay flat and lifeless against their damp skin. When one of them suddenly looked up as though he felt her gaze, Bethan started, feeling a deep flush invade her cheeks as she stared into fierce black eyes. There was no warmth in them: they were cold, searching. For a moment she was unable to unlock her stare, and then her aunt's voice called her attention.

'Bethan—good morning! As you see, we have visitors.' Matilda gestured towards the three men. 'Hugh D'Savoury, Edwin Marshfield of Kent, William Penley of Redruth—my niece, Lady Elizabeth Astwood.' They bowed their heads dutifully and Bethan found her gaze returning fleetingly to the flaxen-headed one. So he was

'Hugh', but the name seemed too gentle for one with such a forbidding countenance. Matilda continued, 'They have come to oversee the dissolution of the abbey and were caught in the sudden downpour.'

Bethan could not mistake the soft warning note in her aunt's voice, and felt her face freeze. The King's henchmen who had come to oversee the distribution of the spoils would be a more accurate description. How dared they! How could her aunt allow them in the house! Anger made her eyes blaze as she looked once more at the leader of the three. As if he had wasted too much time already, Hugh D'Savoury turned away, following Aunt Matilda down the panelled corridor to the parlour, where they could dry themselves before journeying on.

When she was sure that the door had closed safely behind them, Bethan rushed down the wide wooden staircase and into the hall to confront her aunt. But before she could do so, the older woman put a finger to her lips and ushered Bethan into the long room where the table lay set with the early morning fare.

'Bethan, you must not show your feelings so plainly! All could see the fury in your face at the presence of these men!' She would not let Bethan speak, and resolutely continued, 'Whatever their duty, whatever they are asked to do, is by order of the King. The King, child! We cannot question it.'

'How can the King destroy the abbey and make the friars, the good fathers, homeless? They have done nothing, nothing!' Bethan's eyes filled with angry tears as she thought of dear Friar Dominic who had always been her friend and counsellor since childhood. What would happen to him?

'Our good fathers had done nothing, Bethan, but it seems that there are other houses of God that have used their position to corrupt, to steal, to abuse all their vows—and also the power they wield—and that power is a mighty one, as you know.'

'Why doesn't the King merely close down the bad houses? Why does he insist on closing them all—destroying them all?' Bethan persisted stubbornly. 'It cannot be right. I cannot believe that God has given him his blessing! It is a wicked thing, Aunt—a blasphemous thing!'

'Child, child—hush!' Aunt Matilda was horrified at her outburst. 'In the wrong hands, your words would become treasonable...and with the King's men under our very roof! Never say such words again—*never*! Do you hear me, Bethan?' Her words trembled with a fear long suppressed. Too many had died already for defying the King: good Bishop Fisher and Thomas More's executions still hung heavy like dark shadows, making her old heart pound with disbelief. Fisher had been the King's mentor and councillor—an intimate member of his household—yet that had not saved him. The frail old man, withered with age and emaciated from months in the Tower, had seemed like a fragile shadow as he faced the block. It was said that after the headsman had done his work, the severed head affixed to London Bridge remained startlingly lifelike for days, its incorruptibility proof of the slain bishop's holiness. And More—the shock of his execution was the scandal of Christendom.

Matilda drew in a breath sharply, and her shaking hand reached up to her throat in remembered terror.

Immediately her niece looked shamefaced as she saw the distress in her aunt's face. Why could she never hold her tongue! 'Forgive me. It is the thought of poor Friar Dominic—he is so old, so old.'

Matilda nodded her head wearily in understanding. 'I have been assured that many will be found places in the new houses which have been reorganised by the King; some will even receive pensions.'

'Yet what of the terrible things we have heard?' Bethan continued, as she remembered the frightening talk that had seemed to hover on everyone's lips. 'Pillagings, burnings and beatings? It cannot all be lies.'

'Bethan,' Matilda said slowly and with great care, 'as some have abused the power of God, so some abuse the power of the King, and they shall suffer the consequences. I am afraid, child, that life is not always fair, always just—you must try to come to understand and accept that.'

Bethan looked into her aunt's kindly face and then turned her eyes to the great fire that burned with such ferocity in the centre of the room. 'I shall never come to accept injustice, or injury to the innocent,' she said firmly, almost as if she were making a vow, and then added, 'But please do not be concerned that I shall allow my wilful tongue to run away with me while King Henry's men are in the house—and, of course, I shall be civil to them. Perhaps they, in their turn, will be kinder to those they must chastise.'

Matilda sighed heavily as Bethan moved past her to the window. These were hard, difficult times, and she had no real answers for her sweet but passionate niece. And how could she tell her that the King frightened her? His actions seemed like those of a desperate man: the isolation of poor dear Queen Catherine, the scandal of the divorce and the conniving Bullen woman, and his anger with a Church that would not do his bidding, and now the resulting destruction of the monasteries. It was as though he would shake the very fabric, the very core, that was England. She sighed again, sweeping back a strand of tired whitening hair into her coif, and moved closer to the fire. Indeed, how *could* the King be head of the Church—surely it was blasphemous? Aunt Matilda shook her head sadly. Where would it all end?

The rain continued all day, beating mercilessly down on the already saturated land, filling the house with premature grey shadows so that torches and candles were lit far earlier than usual. Bethan knew that Edward would not come. He hated the wetness—how the damp seemed to creep into his bones—but somehow she had hoped he would attempt the journey. Today her heart was heavy and she needed his gaiety. In May they were to be married, four long months away! It was an age, an age! Sighing, she returned to her tapestry. It was of the house, Astwood House, in summer, surrounded by the luxuriance of pink dog-roses, marigolds and hollyhocks; she could almost smell the plump opulence of the flower-heads, hear the soothing hum of bees. But suddenly the door of the parlour opened, and she was shaken abruptly out of her reverie to find herself looking into the face of Hugh D'Savoury. It was handsome, she admitted reluctantly, but lacking in compassion, in mercy. She stood up.

'Forgive me, Lady Elizabeth, I seek your aunt,' he said quietly, but his voice was firm, as if expecting immediate obedience.

'My aunt is resting. This weather gives her joints great pain, but she will be down for supper this evening.' Bethan could not keep the sharp edge out of her words.

'I am sorry to hear that.' Hugh paused for a moment, sensing her dislike. 'I am also sorry that I and my men must inconvenience you further. Since the rain seems likely to continue, we shall have to stay the night.'

'Yes, we had expected that, sir,' she replied coldly. 'Perhaps tomorrow we may hope for better things, as I am sure that the King's work cannot wait.'

A thin, mocking smile broke the set of his face, and Bethan felt anger stir within her.

'One must always obey the King, lady,' Hugh said quietly, allowing his eyes to sweep over the indignant, but lovely, girl before him.

'Always, sir? Like sheep?' Bethan returned contemptuously.

'We are all sheep—merely some more than others.' He would not take her bait, but how he wanted to strip her of her audacity, to laugh. And, God in heaven, she was not much more than a child!

'And some are wolves in sheeps' clothing who prey on poor helpless old men!' She knew she was allowing her temper to get the better of her, but he was so insufferably complacent!

'And some should not judge others without knowing all there is to know,' he retorted, and that irritating smile still lay unperturbed on his lips.

'You play with words, sir, as you play with people's lives. I find it contemptible!' Bethan's eyes blazed with fury.

Hugh seemed to grow serious quite suddenly, and she wondered whether her words had had some effect. 'Perhaps,' his tone was almost solemn now, 'I may say just one thing?'

There was no amusement in the dark eyes, no mockery now, and Bethan felt her face soften in anticipation of his penitence, and then she replied gently, 'Yes, sir, you may. What is it?'

All at once the wide sensuous mouth broke into a broad, teasing grin. 'You are most enchanting when you are angry!' He bowed then, too low, and she was outraged.

A new fury swept through Bethan as she watched him stride arrogantly towards the door; she had been so easily outwitted, and he had known all the time. How dared he patronise her!

Aunt Matilda had gone to great trouble to create a more than usually agreeable supper table; it was not often she had the opportunity. It reminded her of the days when her husband had been alive, before the smallpox had taken from her not only him, but Bethan's parents. Now it seemed a lifetime ago, sixteen long years—high summer, 1520, when England seemed at peace and the young King and his wife were at the pinnacle of their

happiness. She shook her head in wonder. Bethan had
been just a few months old; now she was grown and
would soon be wed. It did not seem possible. Her old
shoulders heaved with a long sigh, but then she moved
closer to the table and endeavoured to cast the shadowy
memories aside, for it would not do to look miserable
this evening. Proudly she surveyed the table's heavy
burden: two huge rabbit pies, a suckling pig, a side of
salted ham, a plump glistening duck, a great piece of
freshly set cheese surrounded by newly-baked bread, and
in the centre an enormous earthenware bowl, its belly
full of steaming thick onion and leek broth steeped in
herbs. The potent smell teased her nostrils and made her
mouth water almost unbearably. On the carved oak table
against the wall were the sweetmeats, custards and
latticed pies—gooseberry, blackberry and apple—accompanied by bowls of preserves, highly spiced pickles
and two huge jugs of thick cream. Aunt Matilda smiled
to herself, thinking it would be so good to have some
hearty masculine appetites at her table, but then her
forehead creased as she thought of Bethan—pray God
she would not say anything out of turn! Absently her
hand moved to a platter which sat not quite straight,
and then she turned as the soft creaking of the door
called her attention. Hugh D'Savoury walked slowly into
the room. He was a commanding and most attractive
man, she thought, and Bethan came into her mind again.
If only things were different! But then, of course, there
was Edward—sweet Edward. What was she thinking of!

'Good evening, my lady. Your niece told me you were not well, and I hope that you feel improved?' Hugh's voice sounded full of concern.

'Why, sir, thank you,' she replied, smiling. 'Yes, my old bones do not plague me quite so much, but I am afraid they will complain as long as this weather stays with us.' She reached for a large jug and poured him some warm ale.

'This weather also forces us to stay longer under your roof,' Hugh said quietly, and took a sup of the rich golden liquid.

'I thought as much—it could be no other way,' Matilda responded easily. 'This rain allows neither man nor beast to move. The lower meadows are flooded, so my headman tells me, and most of the sheep are stranded.' She sighed, and then looked to the table. 'But let us not talk of such things. I hope, this evening, we may forget the world outside and enjoy ourselves for a few short hours.'

'Of course,' he replied, returning her smile. 'You have gone to much trouble, and my mouth is already watering at the sight of such a table!' Hugh said warmly, sensing her pleasure, and then turned towards the door as his companions entered.

Matilda filled their tankards herself, and watched, satisfied, as all three men stood around the blazing hearth, knowing that they were glad to be dry and warm at last and in a house that appeared, at least, to accept them openly.

Bethan heard the deep murmur of their voices and laughter as she reached the bottom of the staircase. Her anger from the earlier meeting with Hugh D'Savoury had not abated, but merely simmered beneath an outward appearance of calm. She knew she must hold her tongue. How many times had her aunt told her! Taking a deep breath, she entered the room. She was not aware of the effect she had on the company as she stood slightly awkwardly in the doorway. The amber light of the fire seemed to add a soft delicious glow to her already lovely features, and her hair, hanging free now to denote her virginity, shone like a raven's wings, framing the firm roundness of her young body like a cloak. She was beautiful.

Supper began, tankards were replenished, and the pewter goblets were filled with rich plum-coloured wine. Initially Bethan was determined to remain aloof and be only distantly polite, but she found very quickly that the warmth and practised wit of the King's men drew her out, all except Hugh D'Savoury, who seemed to take more interest in her aunt. This irritated her, the more because she had no desire to have the attention of such a shallow individual, and yet her aunt appeared to be quite charmed by him!

The heavy wine made Bethan's cheeks burn, for she was not used to such generous quantities, and when the pounding on the main doors first started she thought it was the distant sound of thunder heralding more rain, but the door opened and she saw Edward, drenched and annoyed, standing in the doorway.

'Edward!' she exclaimed.

'Pray do not let me intrude on such jollity!' The sarcasm in his voice could not be missed, and Bethan had no idea why she should suddenly feel so guilty.

Aunt Matilda quickly rose from her seat. 'My boy, my boy, this is an unexpected pleasure! Let me rid you of your wet things, and then you must join us.'

Several minutes elapsed before Edward reappeared and he was introduced to the strangers. Eyeing the King's men suspiciously, he sat possessively close to Bethan.

'You obviously have business in these parts, sir,' he said pointedly to Hugh. Matilda sighed inwardly, knowing the peace of the evening was over. Dear Edward was not known for his diplomacy.

'Obviously, sir,' Hugh D'Savoury replied, but not taking the young man's bait.

Not put off, Edward continued, 'I see, so I must guess... What would bring the King's men to a remote little backwater of the west country in these difficult times of ours? I fear it must be this monastery business, if I am not much mistaken,' he said triumphantly and reached for his goblet.

Hugh smiled thinly. 'We are on the King's business, sir, and tomorrow we leave the hospitality of these two gracious ladies, so neither you, nor they, need trouble yourselves about our presence—or our business—further.'

But Edward was determined to pursue the inevitable course of his questioning. He did not want his sweet Bethan to be impressed by these swaggering braggarts of the King, especially this Hugh D'Savoury who had such a slippery tongue and who was quite clearly endeavouring to conceal something. 'Your destination must be the Abbey of St Julius and St Clement, only three leagues from here.' There was no reply, and ignoring the sudden silence that had descended on the table, he went on, sure that he had hit the right target. It was like a hunt—and how he loved the chase! 'I would have thought it too insignificant to be of interest to the King, hardly worth the blink of an eye...' He paused for a moment, savouring his words. 'Although I hear the Abbot has a cellar that houses artefacts of great value.'

Hugh slowly reached for his tankard and took a long sup of ale, as if he had not heard Edward's remarks, and then finally he spoke. 'Nothing is too insignificant to be of interest to the King, sir—and you do well to remember that—as you will overtax yourself with so much concern for our duties. I am sure there is enough to interest you here, in this "little backwater", as you so kindly put it...'

Edward grew crimson at the barbed insult, and at the thinly veiled contempt on the face of the King's man, as if he were some stupid young puppy! He felt the tremor of Bethan's hand as it lay beneath his own and heard her taut, nervous sigh. As if *he* had caused this uncomfortable scene, as if it were *he* who was the stranger and not they!

'Please, gentlemen—let us talk of lighter things...' Matilda's forced gaiety broke into the quiet, and she gestured anxiously to the side table laden with sweet puddings. 'And see, we have not yet tasted my good tarts!'

The tense atmosphere dissipated slowly and all, save Edward, breathed more easily. An effort was made to resume the pleasant warmth the company had found earlier, but now it remained stubbornly aloof, like a thing apart. The evening suddenly seemed protracted, but at last came to an end with the King's men retiring early, followed very shortly by Aunt Matilda.

'Be sure you two are not long, or I shall send Dickon to you! And, Edward, your room is made up as usual.' She smiled, and then moved awkwardly towards the door, adding conspiratorially, 'Make sure you kiss goodnight before you reach the upper landing!'

Bethan laughed softly, and both bid her aunt goodnight. As soon as the door was safely closed, Edward brought her cool hand up to his lips. 'God in heaven, I thought we'd never be left alone! Those damnable, arrogant King's men sicken me!' He paused, and Bethan could see the fury waiting in his eyes. 'How dare they stalk our county, preying on the good men of the abbey—they are nothing more than thieves! I cannot think that the King knows all that goes on; he surely cannot.'

In an attempt to mollify him, she said gently, 'But my aunt says that most of the good friars will be sent to larger houses and some will even receive pensions.' She waited for a moment, allowing her words to penetrate Edward's anger. 'These seem to be honourable men, Edward—I am sure they will do their duty.'

'Perhaps, perhaps, but I do not trust them. I have heard too many dire tales to believe that they all do their duty without lining their own pockets first.' He sighed dramatically, and then turned to Bethan, who sat so invitingly close. 'In any event I have you, and I could see the envy in their eyes, particularly the fair one's. He thought himself so clever!'

'Please, Edward, do not talk like that,' Bethan murmured, surprised and hurt at his words. 'He has shown not the least interest in me.'

Edward brought his face close to hers, letting his lips brush her ear. 'Oh, my sweet Bethan, you are so innocent, so naïve! Do you not know desire when you see it in a man's eyes?' She felt her face flush and then the touch of Edward's elegant finger as he tilted her chin, drawing her lips up to his searching ones. 'Do you not see it in mine, sweeting?' he whispered. For a moment in the crush of his embrace Bethan felt as if she could not breathe, for his mouth seemed to swallow her, covering her lips and face mercilessly. His hands developed a life of their own as they crept so stealthily over her body—it seemed not like her Edward at all!

'Edward! Edward, please stop! Aunt Matilda will wonder where we have got to.'

He said angrily, 'Why stop? Why? You do not usually find my kisses offensive.'

'Your hands were asking for more than kisses, Edward,' Bethan retorted firmly.

'We are not children, Bethan, but lovers about to wed, and I am a man, with a man's needs,' he pleaded.

'Is that all, Edward? Is there nothing else?' Suddenly she, too, was angry.

Realising his mistake, he grasped her hand. 'Forgive me, forgive me! Do I have to remind you of my love? Have I not said a thousand times how much I love you?'

He could see her face begin to soften. 'Are we not to marry in only a few short months?'

There was silence as she stared into the striking blue of his eyes awash with the golden hues of the firelight. She let his words take hold and seep into her, then slowly her lips drew into a gentle, relenting smile. 'Forgive me, too, Edward. I did not mean to be angry with you. Perhaps it is all the wine I have drunk—and this day, too. It has been such a day, and I do not like these King's men, either, or the thought of what they must do.' She gazed into the dying embers of the fire. 'You know that Friar Dominic is like a father to me—the father I never knew.' Her voice trailed off into a whisper, and he saw tears start to fill the great grey pools of her eyes.

Seizing his reprieve, Edward brought her to him, stroking her dark silken hair, murmuring sweet words and caresses into the soft shell of her ear. She was so beautiful—and she was his!

CHAPTER TWO

IT WAS LATE, well past dawn, when Bethan awoke. Already she could hear the morning sounds filter through her narrow window, hear young Walter the stable-boy whistling as he tended the horses and the rhythmic thump of someone somewhere chopping wood. Her head ached, and as she rose a faint feeling of nausea swept over her. Never would she drink so much wine again! She moved slowly to the window and took long breaths as she looked out into the grey sea that was the sky. The rain had ceased at last, but the leaden clouds were still heavy, still filled with the promise of a storm. She hurried with her toilet, anxious to stretch her legs and let the sweet fresh air sweep the ache in her head away. Slipping a heavy mantle about her shoulders, she quietly made her way down the creaking stairs. There would only be Aunt Matilda to contend with, for she had heard the King's men leave earlier through a fog of sleep, followed by Edward. Her aunt would not miss her for a little while, busy about her housewifely duties, and surely it was not so much to ask—to be free for a short time; free of questions and the cloying suffocating walls of the house.

The stout side door cried out for oil as Bethan opened it and stepped out into the waterlogged courtyard. Cursing softly, she realised it would take days for the water to soak away. She trod carefully to the stables down a short footpath, now a quagmire, that ran the length of Astwood House. The warm safe smell of horse-manure and fresh hay invaded her nostrils as she finally reached the first door, and she smiled as the horses whinnied at the sound of her approach. They would be so restless after being shut inside for so long, but at least she could take advantage of this halt in the bad weather to exercise Tallow.

By the time Bethan had reached the end of the broad track that led into the field path, her hair, which had been so neatly tied about her head, had fallen and now streamed out behind like so many dark ribbons. Irritably she swept it back, and then bid Tallow make haste down the curve of a hill in the direction of the abbey. The abbey: it had been in her mind all the time. If the King would not oversee his own men, then she would!

The ground was almost impossible and poor Tallow's hooves were soon coated in thick slimy mud, but Bethan would not turn back. Everywhere she could see the past fury of the rain and wind, how bowed were the tall trees and the beaten, tilting fields. The water—pools of silted brown water filled every hole, crevice and shallow. She gave Tallow her head, knowing that she would avoid the path for the safety of the verge when it became impassable. When she reached the shoulder of the next hill, she felt quite weary with concentration and paused to take in the familiar view. It seemed an age since she had breathed such pure air! The crest rolled down into a small wooded valley. Any spare grassland was choked with dead twigs, bracken and rotting leaves, the flotsam of the storm. She skirted the saucer of the hill and decided to reach the abbey from its lip and Darwent Point.

She walked Tallow slowly as she neared the spot from which she would see the building she loved so well. It was then that she saw the smoke—black and thick, rising like a wrathful devil's finger from behind a dark expanse of trees. It was the abbey! It could only be the abbey! Her heart hammered against her ribcage as she spurred Tallow into a canter and then into a gallop, ignoring any danger to either of them. At Darwent Point, she saw all she would ever need to see. The fire was raging through most of one wing of the ancient building, plumes of ebony smoke billowing from each aperture, meeting and joining to lie as a sodden black cloud above the abbey. She saw men running, some on fire, some obviously injured, perhaps even dying. Fear rushed into her throat and she could hardly breathe. As she bade Tallow down the side of the hill, tears poured into her eyes and down the hot pink of her cheeks, and the hollow words, 'He lied, he lied!' seemed to echo in her ears.

The slim tapering hand that had started the fire wiped frightened droplets of perspiration from a deeply furrowed brow. It had started so fast, so furiously. He remembered the first spark, the first bright hungry flame leaping forward as it devoured all in its path. Guilt and fear swept through his body as he thought of the unfortunates who had been studying so earnestly in the scriptorium. In the fervour of their plans, they had forgotten the scriptorium, had forgotten that it lay so close to the cellar door and the abbey treasures and relics—

but he had warned them. Why were a few old books and scrolls worth saving, worth risking their lives for? His teeth clenched as he recalled the old man. He had seen him, seen the telltale torch in his hand, seen the guilt in his eyes, and he had had no choice but to kill him. It was as though the knife in his hand had possessed a life of its own.

As Bethan neared the burning abbey, she realised the scale and ferocity of the blaze—nothing would save it, nothing in heaven or earth! She jumped quickly from Tallow and ran to a thin young friar who crouched nursing an injured brother, his bloodied face covered with the filth of damp soot.

'Father, have all been accounted for? Is anyone left in the abbey?' Even as she spoke, she realised that at this stage no one could answer her question, but the voice of fear made her ask and would not be quieted.

'Only God knows. The fire happened so fast, spread so quickly.' He paused to wipe grime and sweat from his weary eyes. 'One moment I was studying, bent over a scroll in the scriptorium, and then it seemed that the room was suddenly full of smoke.' He looked to the burning building, tears in his eyes. 'The flames consumed all, the foul smoke seeped into all, choking and blinding. It was a miracle that I got out with my life.' He crossed himself with a strange urgency, and then his lips broke into a bitter smile. 'And the rain has ceased—ceased! I think Satan mocks us...'

Bethan touched his shoulder gently in understanding. 'But how did it start? Have you any idea at all?'

'The King's men arrived early this morning, before Prime. There were a dozen or so—impatient, insolent men. Our Abbot tried to subdue them by filling their bellies with food and ale, but it was a useless gesture—they were after bigger game, as we all knew.' He stopped, to make the injured man beside him more comfortable, and his voice continued flat and empty. 'The leader split the group into twos and threes, and very carefully, very skilfully, they stripped each cell, each room. It was during this turmoil that the fire started. The King's men left very quickly then—I heard their cowards' voices and the thunder of horses as they rode into the protection of the forest—no doubt with their spoils. What cared they for the screams of their fellow men? What cared they if the abbey were razed to the ground?' She heard the edge of hysteria in his voice and then he turned away, trying to calm himself, his head hanging in grief and shock.

The complacent face of Hugh D'Savoury seemed to dance before Bethan's eyes and a terrible anger began to swell within her, but gently she said to the bruised man, 'Forgive me, but I must ask one more thing.' She paused, almost afraid. 'I cannot see Friar Dominic among the injured. Did you see him at any time?'

The young man did not move for a moment, only his lips gave a faint quiver, but slowly he shook his head. 'I do not remember seeing him. There was no hope, with the filthy smoke turning the air to blackness.' He wiped his mouth with a knuckle. 'I recall, often at that time he would stay after Prime, long after most had gone.'

'In the Chapel of St Clement,' Bethan added, her words dropping like dead things from her mouth. Within the burning abbey, the Chapel of St Clement lay at the heart—a heart that now burned.

Dense clouds of acrid smoke still soiled the air, invading defenceless lungs and throats. Bethan coughed and tried to shield her face from the fumes, but still she drew closer. Friar Dominic must lie injured somewhere. He could still be alive! Even through the filthy haze she could see the fatal fascination of the blood-red inferno, hear the sound of its roaring and the groan of ancient timbers as they succumbed to the torture of fire.

'In God's name, are you mad?' The voice seemed to scream at her out of the roar of the flames. A strong hand grasped her shoulder, and she was turned abruptly about to confront Hugh D'Savoury's searching and angry face staring down at her from his horse. She felt dazed, and then suddenly both her anger and grief seemed to erupt inside her.

'Do not touch me!' Bethan pulled sharply away from him, her eyes as fierce as the burning flames. 'Where were you—sir—when your murdering dogs broke the peace of this gentle place? This house of God!' There was no expression on his face as she gave further vent to her anger. 'You who would charm your way into Godfearing folks' homes—you with your fine words of kingly duty!' She could feel her whole body tremble with emotion as she turned to the burning ruin that had once been the abbey she loved. 'Is this what the King commanded? The slaughter of innocent men—the destruction of an ancient and holy place? It is all true what they say, all true! I wanted to believe otherwise, but it is all true...' Weeping, she turned from him and searched blindly for her horse as tears blurred her vision. Tallow had wandered well away from the disturbingly frightening smells and sounds of the fire, her chestnut head now bent low as she nibbled at the long grass on the edge of the abbey grounds.

Hugh's eyes followed the distraught girl. He was unable, he knew, to stem either her anger or her sorrow. This was no time to mollify such a wilful creature or to attempt futile explanations. He had other, far more pressing, duties. Bethan Astwood would wait—there would be time enough for niceties.

Spying Tallow at last, Bethan ran to her and fleetingly, as if for comfort, she brushed her cheek against the warm gentle neck before she mounted. She directed her to the short path through the thick wood that surrounded the abbey lands, but immediately regretted it as her poor horse began to flounder through the glutinous mud of the much-used track. She had to pull Tallow on to the verge, to the safety of the turfy ground of ferns and bracken, and then slowed to a halt. She wiped her cheeks, chiding herself for letting Hugh see her cry, but then she thought of Friar Dominic and her tears started anew. Home! She must get home. Since the usual path was out of the question, her progress was painfully slow as she picked her way through the dense undergrowth. When, at last, she reached the end of the woodland, the sky had turned an ominous grey, and huge droplets of the promised rain began to fall. Soon she was drenched, her hair hanging like black ropes down her back. Lightning lit the sky, followed quickly by the smack of thunder that made her nerves jangle. She tried to comfort herself with the thought that the storm would quench the fire, but in her heart she knew it was too late.

Saturated, and hunched over the broad neck and shoulder of her faithful Tallow, Bethan finally reached the outskirts of the Astwood lands and saw with relief a glimpse of the stout walls of the house. Tallow seemed to sense the nearness of home, and moved more surely, more swiftly, on the familiar ground. The courtyard had almost disappeared beneath the onslaught of more water from the heavens, but Tallow's sure steps took Bethan safely to the shelter of the stables, where she slipped down at last. Wearily she reached for a length of coarse wool and quickly rubbed Tallow down. Young Walter could finish grooming her later. She almost slipped as she crossed the flooded courtyard; cursing and holding back a sob, she fell against the great wooden doors of the house just as they opened.

'My dear! My dear, let me help you!' Aunt Matilda's kindly voice was so reassuring, so warm, that Bethan felt her tears come to the fore again. 'Where have you been? I have been so worried, and then this storm began...'

Bethan did not reply, merely allowing herself the luxury of being taken to her aunt's room, where a great fire burned. Slowly each item of clothing was peeled from her streaming body, as she was dried roughly with thick cotton until her skin sang.

'To bed—and I shall bring you some mulled wine,' Matilda commanded, and disappeared with a serving-maid to supervise the brewing of her niece's cup.

The hot spiced wine warmed Bethan through, and she gave a tired smile to her concerned aunt as she sat beside her on the bed.

'Well, child, tell me,' Matilda said quietly.

Bethan waited a moment, collecting her thoughts, then slowly lifted eyes full of grief to her aunt's face. 'I had not intended to go to the abbey, but somehow I was compelled.' It was only a small lie! 'As I neared it, I saw the smoke.' Aunt Matilda's eyes widened. 'It was on fire.'

'God in heaven! Were any of the good brothers hurt?'

'Yes, Aunt—many...' Bethan looked away, feeling the weakness of the tears that seemed to plague her come again, and the name which had hovered on her mouth tumbled unchecked from her lips. 'Friar Dominic... I could not find Friar Dominic!'

'Oh my child, my poor child!' The plump arms of Aunt Matilda encircled her, and for long minutes she rocked her niece gently in her arms, the lines of her face somehow etched deeper now as she was aware of her own inadequacy. If only her dear parents had not died so young; if only Bethan had known even a little of her father, but she had only been a babe. Matilda sighed. Life seemed to be made up of 'ifs'. She stroked the sweet dark head gently. And now she was hers, this head-strong passionate child. Protectively she held her more tightly, as though by doing so she could shut out the pain.

Gradually Bethan composed herself, and with her head against her aunt's shoulder, she told what she knew of the King's men and her meeting with Hugh D'Savoury. 'He lied, Aunt; he lied! I shall never forgive him, never!'

'Hush, hush. We do not yet know all the facts.'

'He was *there*, Aunt, and he is one of the King's men,' Bethan said adamantly. 'There is nothing more to know.'

'He did not impress me as a dishonourable man, Bethan, but quite the opposite,' Matilda argued gently.

'He charmed you, Aunt. I saw how he flattered and cajoled you! Why, he is like a serpent, a hideous rat! Edward said as much,' she retorted, bringing her head up and staring fiercely into her aunt's surprised face.

'Yes, Bethan, he was very charming. Do you not think that I was unaware of that? Most men would not waste time on an old woman such as I,' Matilda's tone softly rebuked her.

Bethan blushed, ashamed, her lids falling guiltily over tear-bright eyes. 'Forgive me. That is not what I meant. I am so upset, dear Aunt, I don't know what I say.'

Matilda wiped the damp strands of hair from her niece's wet cheeks. 'No doubt we shall find out the truth soon enough. I shall send a note to Sir Victor, and ask him to look into the matter.'

Bethan's face visibly brightened. Sir Victor Courtenay was Edward's father, their nearest neighbour and once a member of the King's household. He would know what to do. Even as the sudden brightness lit her face, it was overcast by the memory of the fire. 'Do you think, Aunt... Do you think it possible that Friar Dominic escaped the flames? That perhaps he was elsewhere?' The glimmer of hope in her niece's voice touched the older woman's heart.

'I think it would be better if we waited. Wild assumptions will solve nothing,' she said, and patted

Bethan's hand. 'Now you must rest and sleep. I do not want my darling Bethan coming down with a fever.'

The storm abated as dusk drew near, and the heavy quiet was palpable, as though all living things held their breath at the longed-for but unheralded peace. It was the leaden silence that awoke Bethan, and she lay in the semi-darkness thinking on all that had passed. She tried to balance what her aunt had said with Edward's account, notwithstanding the words of the young friar to whom she had spoken. Nothing seemed clear, except that the King's men would seem to be responsible, and surely that would also point to Hugh D'Savoury?

His cold handsome features hung like a picture before her. She had felt the strength in him as he stopped her before the flames of the abbey, seen the blaze of anger in his eyes as she had so fiercely rebuked him, yet he had said nothing. Did that imply his guilt or his innocence? Irritably she turned her eyes to the glowing apple-wood that burned so hotly in the hearth, but it only served to remind her of the crimson colours of the King's men. Was it difficult to serve the King? She had heard the many stories surrounding King Henry's court; how poor Queen Catherine had been divorced in favour of the Bullen girl and now lay sick and dying away from all, even her own daughter, the only surviving child of the seven she had borne Henry. Was it really because of the wrath of God that he had had no living son? Even the Bullen girl had given him a mere daughter, but it was true that she was pregnant again. Perhaps if she gave the King a son, it would soften him, make him less ruthless. Bethan shook her head gently. It would be a hard task to satisfy such a tormented King. Feeling her own anger diminish, she sighed in exasperation and chided herself. She would not so easily fall under the spell of Hugh D'Savoury, even if it were proved that he had had no part in the burning of the abbey. She thought of Edward then, and their coming marriage. Only four months, and she would be mistress of Courtenay Manor, but her heart did not leap with its accustomed enthusiasm, and instead she felt a stab of doubt. She pushed back the coverlets, letting her feet drop to the floor, and cast her uncertainties aside. It was this dreadful day, and the tireless, miserable rain—it was enough to make any decent person's heart sore! Comforted, she pulled her aunt's nightrobe about her and decided to dress for the evening meal.

Sir Victor Courtenay arrived as Bethan and Aunt Matilda were about to have a quiet supper and retire early. He was a tall, strongly built man, and had once been most handsome—so her aunt had once told Bethan—but the smallpox that had killed her parents had left him horribly scarred. She always found it hard to look into the disfigured face and to hide her discomfiture at her future father-in-law's ill-starred countenance.

'I came as soon as I received your message,' he said, taking Matilda's hand. 'My lady, it grieves me to know how much this fearful tragedy has coloured your day and sweet Bethan's happiness.'

Aunt Matilda thanked him for his solicitude, and asked if he had any news.

'Little,' he replied, 'but it seems clear that the King's men lie at the bottom of it. Edward should arrive shortly.

He has taken the news very hard, and has been making his own enquiries.'

Bethan smiled gratefully. Dear Edward, how could she have doubted him? The sound of horses crossing the courtyard made all of them look to the door as Dickon, Aunt Matilda's head serving-man, came into the room.

'The King's men return, my lady.'

'You had best show them in, Dickon,' Matilda replied, and then looked anxiously to Sir Victor. 'Perhaps we shall hear a different story now.'

'I pray so, for their sakes. The King does not take kindly to evil business done in his name,' he said with some warning.

Hugh D'Savoury bade his men wait in the hall and then walked slowly into the room, his head high and his face set with determination. Bethan found her eyes searching for his, and as they met, she veiled her embarrassment with a façade of anger. Why did he vex her so? He was like a constant thorn in her side. The officer of the King was introduced to Sir Victor by Matilda, and as she poured him some warm ale, he spoke.

'First, I must apologise to Mistress Bethan for my lack of consideration in not seeing her safely home this morning. Under the circumstances, it was unforgivable.' His eyes held hers for a moment, and she nodded her head curtly in acceptance of his apology. He continued, 'Second, contrary to the rumour in the county, it was not the King's men who sacked and set fire to the abbey.'

Bethan saw Sir Victor lift one cynical eyebrow and then smile thinly, as if he had expected Hugh's words.

'Then who has done such a terrible thing?' Matilda asked. 'My niece tells me that one of the young friars said that the King's men were present when the fire started. I do not understand.'

'They were not the King's men, lady,' Hugh D'Savoury replied quietly, his words seeming to lie heavily in the air. 'I fear you must look closer to home for the culprits.'

'Do you deny the word of a man of God?' Sir Victor said, meeting the unrelenting stare of the other man.

'He was mistaken, sir,' Hugh returned.

The sound of another horse approaching the house made Matilda go to the window. 'It is Edward. Perhaps he has more news,' she said nervously, not liking the awkward and uncomfortable situation.

Edward looked surprisingly fresh, if a little dishevelled, from his foray. Once he had settled himself within the company and taken a goblet of wine, Sir Victor resumed his enquiry.

'My son, I have been told by this King's man, Hugh D'Savoury, that his men were not responsible for the burning of the abbey. Have you heard anything to substantiate this claim?'

Edward's smile was almost a leer as he looked to the man he had come to dislike so much. 'If he wishes to believe that, he is alone. The rest of the county are only too aware of the truth!'

'Do you say that I lie, sir?' Hugh's voice was filled with menace.

But Edward was enjoying his triumph. 'If not, then your brain is addled!'

Bethan felt her heart hammer. Why was Edward goading him? It could only make matters worse. She could see the terrible anger in the eyes of the King's man, and its ferocity frightened her.

'Enough, Edward!' ordered Sir Victor, and Bethan breathed a sigh of relief. 'We have yet to hear why he champions his men.' He turned to Hugh, who was standing icily controlled. For a moment, the air seemed to sparkle as they waited for him to speak.

'Sir, I do not "champion my men", as you so kindly put it.' He paused, staring directly into the scarred face of the man before him. 'I was due to meet the rest of my party at midday, after meeting with the Abbot. When I arrived at the abbey it was already ablaze, as Mistress Bethan will vouch. The men—whoever they may have been—had left some time before, once they had completed the sacking of the buildings.'

'Your men!' Edward added vehemently.

'Not my men sir!' Hugh retorted equally as vehemently. 'I received a message later in the morning that my men were stranded near Limpley Stoke, unable to cross the swollen Avon which has near burst its banks.' He let his words sink in, and then continued, 'They will not get here for two, perhaps three, days—and there are witnesses. Before reaching Limpley, they stayed with the Earl of Somerset's household near Bristol, and now stop at Bath Abbey.'

'How convenient!' Edward's sneer cut the quiet that had descended on the small group.

'Your insolence is beginning to become tedious, sir,' Hugh said coldly. 'Perhaps you also doubt the word of the Earl of Somerset, in which case you should practise your puppy accusations on him. I am sure he will be as amused as I.'

'Enough, enough!' Sir Victor broke in. 'If these men were not the King's, then who were they?'

'They must be county, sir, that is clear—men who know the district and the abbey. I believe the fire was a shield while the abbey treasures and relics were stolen, and that these men either planned the sacking or were hired by someone of note. There are many who would stand to gain from the ruin of the abbey.'

'Not least of all the King—and, of course, his men!' Edward persisted.

Slowly Hugh turned his head to the young man who stood so arrogantly in the shadow of his father. 'Do you speak treason, sir?'

Bethan closed her eyes in exasperation and fear. Never had she seen Edward behave so. What had come over him? She looked to her aunt for comfort, and saw that she was trembling.

'He speaks too hastily, sir. He is young and head-strong, and does not mean what he says,' Sir Victor intervened, realising that things had gone too far.

Matilda's gentle voice broke in. 'Please, let us all calm ourselves. The monstrous tragedy of the abbey has taken its toll on our tempers. Surely we should now look to the perpetrators of the frightful deed? I shall not sleep easy in my bed until this fearful matter has been settled.'

'Forgive me, my lady,' Hugh apologised, seeing her distress. 'You judge right.'

Sir Victor looked to his son, who immediately turned to Matilda. 'And I, too, apologise. It is difficult to keep calm when one sees the meaningless deaths of old men—and holy men at that.'

Matilda nodded her head wearily, and said, 'It has been a long day, gentlemen. Bethan and I will now go to our beds. Please keep us informed of events.'

'Of course, of course,' Sir Victor replied.

Hugh bowed his head formally and bid them goodnight. Bethan heard clipped words directed at his waiting men, then their footsteps and the echo of thunder as the great doors were closed behind them. Edward waited awkwardly as first Matilda left the room and then his father. Quickly he moved to Bethan, who seemed to linger by the fire.

'My sweet, I am sorry you had to bear witness to such unpleasantness.' For a moment she thought he meant the burning of the abbey, but quickly realised that he was referring to Hugh D'Savoury.

'Perhaps we should wait and see how things pass, Edward, before making rash judgements,' she said quietly.

'Do you doubt me, Bethan?' She heard the sharp intake of his breath. 'Would you set the word of that blackguard before mine?'

'Edward, I am tired. Things confuse me.' Touching his arm, she moved to the door. 'Please, I would go to my bed.'

'Bethan, why do you look at me so? All day I have been riding, searching, trying to find the dark truth so cunningly hidden at the bottom of this bloody business,

and now you treat me like some wilful child!' He looked
both hurt and angry. 'I won't have it, Bethan! It is not
just.'

Immediately she relented. He looked so pained, so
humiliated, and perhaps she had judged him too soon,
too harshly. 'Forgive me, Edward, it has been a long,
unhappy day, and your argument with Hugh D'Savoury
was too much on top of everything that has happened.'

'Do you not hear my words, Bethan? I was anxious
to get to the truth—the truth. And I shall not be fobbed
off by his clever story,' he said stubbornly.

'You cannot deny the word of the Earl of Somerset,
Edward,' she rebuked gently.

'Bah! He is probably hoping for a lion's share of the
spoils!'

'Edward! You must not say such things—please!' she
said, shocked.

'Come, come, Bethan, do not be so naïve! We all know
that the lands of the dissolved abbeys will be transferred
to the Crown and then sold off to those leeches who
perpetually surround the King.' His hands reached for
her shoulders, turning her to face him. 'And what of
the jewels, the chalices, pray?' he continued. 'All sent
to London, to the Jewel House—or the treasure-chests
of others. Even that is not all, my Bethan. They miss
nothing, these vultures, for there is still the lead from
the roofs and the bronze of the great and small bells that
have hung so safely for centuries in towers and belfries.
These are stripped and sold to the nearest lucky bidder!
Oh, my dove, can't you see what this Hugh D'Savoury
is trying to do?'

His words had receded almost to a whisper, a soothing, coaxing whisper. She felt his lips tickle and caress her ear. How he confused her! He pulled her close so that she could feel the hotness of his breath and his hands, moving so slowly, down to circle her waiting breasts. Doubt assailed her. Somehow, he was not her Edward any more; even his kisses seemed not to stir her as they used to. How had he changed? How had *she* changed? All this time her body seemed cold, unable to respond.

'What is it, Bethan? Why do you not return my fervour? Are you not convinced of my love?' She did not reply, and felt only relief that at least his words were not angry. He tilted her chin up so that she was unable to turn away, and spoke softly. 'I see the love plainly in your eyes—is it that you are so tired, then, sweeting?'

'Yes, that must be it, Edward.' She grasped thankfully at her reprieve; after all, it was not much of a lie. She kissed him lightly on the cheek. 'I am sure a good night's sleep will cure all.'

Slowly he walked with her to the staircase; in the warm glow of the candlelight he thought her more desirable than ever, if that were possible. The wedding seemed too far off, too distant, and he wondered how much longer he could stand the waiting. Perhaps he could bring it forward. He would ask his father.

Bethan watched his elegant figure disappear through the great oaken door and felt perplexed as she began to ascend the stairs. *Could* he see the love plainly in her eyes? If so, why did she feel so confused, so empty? She shook her head gently, and then the face of Hugh D'Savoury seemed to come suddenly out of the shadows as if to taunt her with some secret that only he knew. Guiltily she blinked his image away, and was glad all at once that her weariness was so heavy: it left little time for thoughts and fears she was, as yet, unable to understand.

CHAPTER THREE

FOR THE first time in many days a Tudor sun shone on the west country of England, the soft hills and vales of Somerset basking rich and dewy in its rare winter warmth. Bethan heard the harsh joyous caw of crows and shouts of birds released from the shelter of trees, and the bleating of sheep as they were brought in from the far pastures at last.

She ate breakfast alone; her aunt wisely staying in the warmth and comfort of her bedchamber as her wrists and ankles had swollen mightily from the damp. Once she had eaten her fill, the table was cleared and she retrieved her embroidery from the parlour in order to finish it. It was a pretty, engaging design, she knew, but her fingers seemed clumsy and, in any event, she was not really in the mood for needlepoint. Perhaps later, when the ground had dried out a little more, she would take Tallow out for some exercise. This made her think of yesterday, of the abbey and dear Friar Dominic. Although she tried to concentrate on her work, it was in vain, and, yielding at last to her whim, she put it to one side and stood up to warm her hands at the fire. Then she perched in the deep window sill, staring absently out into the courtyard and to the woodland beyond. It was warm for January, except for the sharp sting in the air, reminding her of the words of old Jenna, the apothecary's wife—'A soft winter is beloved by the plague.' Pray God they would have a cold snap to rid the air of the badness! The sound of a horse made her head turn, and she saw the unmistakable figure of Hugh D'Savoury riding slowly towards Astwood House. Hastily she moved away from the window, skipping quickly across the room to the firelight and her embroidery. Her face glowed nervously, and she wondered at the hammer of her heart. Angrily she chided herself— why did he effect her so?

The long sallow face of Dickon appeared round the door. 'Hugh D'Savoury is here, mistress.'

'Please send him in, Dickon,' she replied with pretended ease, and found her fingers trembling as she endeavoured to pull the needle through the thin weave of her tapestry.

Hugh stood in the doorway for a moment and allowed himself the luxury of looking at the lovely girl who seemed so intent on her needlepoint. Is she aware of her beauty? he wondered. The soft light from the fire played sensual tricks with the curves of her body so that a voluptuous silhouette spilled tormentingly across one wall. As she raised her head suddenly, he saw the wide-set deep grey eyes and the wonderful full red plumpness of her mouth, like a ripe luscious fruit. From the first moment he had seen her at the head of the stairwell, he had felt his body's urging, its desire. But he would return to London soon, to the court, and the familiar, generous body of Kate—empty-headed, sweet Kate. Her husband was a fop, weak and pallid, always dancing attendance at court, so that his bored, pretty wife grew irritated and frustrated. She had been such a safe, easy conquest! He watched the face of the girl before him turn questioningly upward, and the vision of Kate slid effortlessly away. This was no Kate, no plaything either, but Bethan Astwood did not fall into his plans. He could not afford a dalliance now, particularly with such a headstrong creature, and he certainly had not the time or patience for the subtle seductions a virgin always required—and which she so obviously was. Sighing inwardly, he supposed that that delightful and enviable task would go to that mollycoddled dullard, Edward Courtenay.

'Can I be of service?' Bethan asked, unnerved by his scrutiny.

'Forgive me for disturbing you. I had hoped to ask a few questions concerning your time at the abbey yesterday,' Hugh said, moving a little closer to the fireplace.

'Ah, yes.' Bethan felt a forced smile fix itself on her lips, then she bade him sit down and reached for a jug of mulled wine on a nearby table. 'What is it you wish to know?'

Hugh pulled a wooden stool nearer to the fire, so that she sat directly opposite him, perhaps only three feet away. He could see the curved darkness of the eyelashes that rimmed her eyes like velvet, saw the delicate cushion-soft earlobes half-hidden temptingly behind the curtain of her hair. Suddenly he realised that his thoughts were like those of a moonstruck boy! He laughed soundlessly; it must be the air, this over-pure country air. The sooner he returned to London, the better. He said, 'I would like to know exactly what you saw as you ap-

proached the abbey, and all that occurred until our unfortunate meeting at the last.'

Bethan saw a small smile on his face, and felt the beginnings of irritation. His closeness disturbed her, and
she found that she could not easily meet his eyes, so she
stared instead into the world of the fire and told him
what she had seen. It was only as she reached the part
which took in the whereabouts of Friar Dominic that
she faltered.

Hugh listened carefully, watching her intently. Her
voice seemed to lull his senses; he was too much aware
of her presence, her closeness and the soft woman-smell
of her. He realised all at once that she disarmed him,
and he, who was always in control, who always had the
ladies begging for his favours, was on dangerous ground.
The sudden pause in her story made him grow impatient, but particularly with himself, and his voice when
it came was too harsh.

'Well, mistress, I know that is not all!' he said sharply.

Bethan tried to fight her tears away, but she saw only
the flames and heard the unfeeling tone of the man before
her. How hateful he was! How could she feel so at-
tracted to him! Shocked at her own admission and the
uncomfortable scene, she stood, and only then did he
see the tears waiting in her eyes.

'Forgive me—forgive my clumsiness. I had no idea
my questions would upset you so.' He, too, stood, and
moved towards her.

'Please go. It is not your questions or your bullying
ways that upset me, Hugh D'Savoury, simply that one
of the good friars who was most dear to me was probably

burned to death in the fire.' Her eyes glistened with anger as she stared up at him. Unbidden, the tears pooled in her eyes and fell, and automatically he moved closer to her so that their bodies almost touched, his hand reaching gently to her shoulder. Bethan looked up into his face and for an instant thought she saw a flicker of regret, but this was suddenly extinguished by the sure blackness of desire—a lust that both repelled and drew her. Her heart pounded as she felt the pressure of his hands burning through to her skin—and the closeness of him, the terrible beautiful closeness of him.

But, all at once, his hand was gone and she was released. Hugh had moved quietly and swiftly away from her and stood looking into the fire. Shame, the colour of the red coals, burned her cheeks as she tried to collect herself.

'I am quite recovered now, sir. If you have finished with your questioning, I would like to be left alone.'

'I did not mean to presume, but neither did I wish to injure your delicate feelings. We King's men are not used to the sensitivities of women,' he said gently and then allowed himself briefly to look into her face where he could see the doubt, the confusion and—God in heaven, most tantalising of all—the innocence which beckoned to be plucked! He had almost, almost, given in to his old friend, Lust. But not with this girl, this country-innocent, and yet he was angry with himself. Had he not had scores of women? Why should she make him feel like a trespasser, a criminal? 'One final question, mistress, before I take my leave.'

'Only one, sir, for I grow weary,' she said, conscious only of the tremor in her own voice and the flush that still burned her cheeks.

'Who was this friar, the one you so cared for?'

'He was an old man, small and frail—Friar Dominic,' she replied.

'Thank you,' he said quietly, and then added, 'And thank you for your forbearance in this matter.'

Bethan watched him leave, watched the arrogance in his stride as he reached the stout wooden door, and then the sure heavy footsteps as they crossed the flagstones of the hall to the main doors. She waited in the sudden silence of the room until she heard the sound of his horse being led from the stables and the soft thunder of hooves as he rode through the courtyard and away from the house, until his passing lessened and then died away into strange nothingness. Only then did she breathe easily again. Staring once more into the fire, she could not help but relive the touch of him, still burning, making her senses reel. It was madness! She was betrothed to Edward—she loved Edward. Even as the thought gained substance in her mind, she felt doubt. Doubt. Bethan brought her hands close to the dancing flames, suddenly feeling cold. Edward would be a good husband, and he loved her. Hugh D'Savoury was a King's man and always a King's man, and everyone knew of their reputation for lewdness—it even surpassed their master's! Indeed, he was everything she had been brought up to fear, to despise, in men. Surely this was just a passing fancy? Once he had left the county, she would forget him.

It was an uneasy calm that finally settled upon her, and she noticed his goblet standing alone on the table where he had left it. She reached for her own, swallowing the last ruby drops gratefully, and then, as she passed the table, placed it with great deliberation just out of reach of the King's man. 'That is the closest we shall ever come, Hugh D'Savoury,' she said aloud, almost as if she recited a charm. Then she left the room; her aunt would be wondering where she was.

The day stayed fine, and Aunt Matilda improved much; by mid-afternoon she and Bethan sat together in the parlour with their needlepoint. She had heard her niece's story of Hugh D'Savoury's visit and wondered at the lines that wove themselves so stubbornly across Bethan's forehead. There must be more to this than she had been told! She pondered on Bethan's quiet and uneasy demeanour, pondered whether she should ruffle that carefully composed façade of calm. Before she could do so, they both heard the pounding of a fist on the great doors of the house.

Bethan felt her heart jump; surely it could not be Hugh again? But it was a messenger from Courtenay Manor with an invitation from Sir Victor to Bethan and her aunt to sup with him.

'Oh, Bethan, I am still a little weak and in no humour for the journey, and yet I suppose we cannot refuse.' For a moment Matilda allowed herself for once to weaken, and then said gently, looking into her niece's face, 'I cannot ask you to go alone, can I, my sweet child?'

Bethan felt her face grow pale. Not tonight, not when her blood seemed to have turned to water. 'Oh no, Aunt, please!' she pleaded, guilt and shame bringing the colour back to her cheeks.

Aunt Matilda sighed, but nodded her head in acquiescence. She had predicted her niece's reaction. 'Well, then it is settled.' She gave Dickon their reply, and shortly they heard the soft thunder of the great doors as the messenger left.

'I do hope Sir Victor will ensure that the fires burn heartily in every grate! It is always so cold, so draughty, at Courtenay Manor—the wind seems to scream down those long corridors! Sometimes I wonder at his finances, that he should be so sparing. The last time we stayed I could not help but notice that the draperies were almost threadbare in places, and the tapestries in great need of repair.' Then Matilda shook her head sadly. 'Perhaps it is simply that Sir Victor misses the shrewd eye of a wife—so sad that poor Anne died so young and he was left alone to bring up dear Edward.'

'What did she die of, aunt?' Bethan asked. 'Was it the smallpox?'

'Not that time, child,' Matilda replied, as remembered sorrow passed like a shadow over her face. 'Lady Anne died in giving birth to Sir Victor's second son. Poor mite, it lived only a few days and was buried with its mother.'

'Poor Edward,' Bethan added, her voice almost a whisper.

'And my poor Bethan,' Matilda retorted softly. 'You have not had the benefit of even a father's guidance and love.'

'Yes, that is true,' she replied, and then looked into the face she loved so well. 'But I have you, dear Aunt.'

Towards dusk Bethan and her aunt sat their horses and, chaperoned by a member of Sir Victor's household and their own, made their way to the Courtenay lands and manor. In recent times Sir Victor had sold much of the land, claiming that he had not the time or the inclination to tend it, but even so, there still seemed enough to leave his heir a substantial inheritance. One stretch of the boundary bordered on Astwood pastureland, another took in the leased land of the peasantry, while the longest stretch was taken up by abbey lands—rich woodlands and well cultivated fields.

It was a pleasant journey, the air dry and keen now, filled with the prospect of frost. Aware of the coming cold, Bethan turned to her aunt, who sat quite jauntily on an old grey mare called Tib.

'Aunt, what will become of the friars in this cold? Have they been taken care of?'

'Yes, of course, child. I understand they have been taken to the convent of St Agnes.' Seeing the concern in her niece's face, she added, 'Now, hush! We go to visit your betrothed for a pleasant evening. I am sure I see lines enough already from your constant frowning!'

'Oh, Aunt, that is not true!' Bethan cried, but there was uncertainty in her voice.

Relenting, Matilda said, 'Well, it will be true if you wrinkle your face in vexation much more!'

Bethan smiled and tried to relax a little, but the evening seemed to stretch out endlessly before her. She hoped Edward would sense her delicate mood and not demand too much. Sometimes she longed for something more, but whatever that might be seemed to have no form, no substance; like a bewitching dream, elusive and out of her reach. Throwing her dark hair back in exasperation, she comforted herself with the thought that it would be better when they were married, then her endless questioning and confusion would be bound to cease. She could not allow it to be otherwise.

They reached Courtenay Manor just as darkness settled. The sea of grass at either side of the long avenue leading up to the house already seemed dusted with frozen dew, and their breaths came white and thick as fog. The house glowed with pin-pricks of light, and several torches lit the ornately carved frontage to welcome the awaited guests. It was a huge building, U-shaped, encompassing a fine courtyard, far larger than Astwood House, and very old. The timbers and stone were now almost black with age.

As they neared the paved courtyard, Bethan looked up at the familiar crouching figures of the 'Courtenay Heads'—the stone gargoyles that never ceased to make her heart flutter uneasily. What a milksop she was becoming! Suddenly the heavy oak doors of the house flew open and Edward came running to greet them and to help them from their horses. She felt unexpected pleasure at the sight of him and was able, with relief, to smile easily at his beaming countenance as he lifted her down.

Quickly they were ushered into the warmth of the house—and it *was* warm, Aunt Matilda noted thankfully—with a host of candles and torches seeming to burn in every nook and cranny, lending a new lightness to old shadows. 'Why, your father has gone to much trouble this evening, Edward—the house is transformed!' she said, clapping her hands with delight.

'We do not entertain perhaps as much as we ought, and this time my father wished to make an especial effort for my future wife and her most charming aunt,' Edward replied coyly, as he supervised the removal of their outer garments, while Matilda smiled wryly at his undisguised flattery.

Lowering his voice, he continued speaking as they followed him down the panelled passage to the dining hall. 'I am afraid father insisted on inviting that infernal King's man, D'Savoury, this evening. Of course I tried to dissuade him, but he would not be moved. I believe he wishes to be kept informed of this abbey business, and so we must endure the company of this outsider yet again.'

'I am sure it will not be as unpleasant as you fear, Edward,' Matilda replied, trying to placate him.

'Well, I hope you are right, dear lady,' he said, but the look on his face said otherwise.

Bethan had been listening with half an ear, but as soon as she heard the name of D'Savoury, she felt a telltale flush rush up to invade her cheeks. God in heaven, he seems to haunt me!

The dining hall was aglow with the flickering crimson of two great fires, a quantity of rushlights and the

softness of many candle flames. Matilda's old nose
twitched pleasantly as the scent of fresh sweet herbs from
the rush-laden floor mingled with the delightful smell of
roasting meat. The fine oak table was set with all manner
of roasts: pork, pigeon, quail, a dozen delicately cooked
larks, venison, a swan served tail and all—enough for
an army, and such extravagance! But Bethan saw only
Hugh D'Savoury standing close to the fading gilt over-
mantel, his great shoulders turned against her. As the
door closed behind them, he looked up suddenly as
though they had startled him from some waking dream.

Once again the King's man was struck by her beauty
and caught his breath sharply—but this evening she had
excelled herself. The virginal white of her damask,
braided with twines of burgundy and gold, made her
skin glow the warm colour of honey as a narrow golden
girdle snaked twice about her waist falling in gilded
tassels to her thighs. She had coiled her hair in rich ropes
about her head, leaving raven tendrils to caress her neck.
Too perfect! It could not be so. He looked to her eyes,
and saw the fear there. Of him? For some reason it
amused him, and blatantly he allowed his eyes to fall to
the full breasts that peeped so provocatively from her
bodice. He saw her shame, and was amused still further
as her embarrassment turned to obvious anger.

Bethan felt fury stir within her. How dared he! Her
hand itched to slap his face! Did he think she was some
common tavern wench to be appraised and ravished with
his eyes? She felt with relief the familiar touch of Edward
as he guided her to her seat. She was placed next to her
betrothed, her aunt sitting at one end of the table and

Sir Victor at the other. Hugh D'Savoury sat opposite, now seemingly indifferent to her; his conceit was beyond belief! In any event, she would do her best to ignore him. However, as they settled and the fresh ale and wine were poured, Sir Victor spoke with unexpected solemnity, and Bethan's thoughts were distracted from the presence of the man who disturbed her with such effortless ease.

'Through the good offices of our guest, Hugh D'Savoury, news has come from the court.' He paused for a moment. 'His men reached the abbey grounds today, bringing with them the tidings that Queen Catherine is dead.'

She was still called Queen Catherine as though Anne Bullen had never been crowned, Bethan thought, and then turned sharply as she heard her aunt gasp, almost as if she felt pain. The elderly woman had loved the old Spanish Queen, and had never come to terms with the King's dispassionate banishment from court of his faithful and devout wife.

'I must yet continue, for that is not all.' Sir Victor took a sup of his wine. Bethan saw a crimson droplet held in the corner of his mouth like blood.

'The Bullen girl was delivered of a dead son but two days ago.' There was contempt in Sir Victor's voice and thinly veiled satisfaction; he had never liked or accepted the King's new wife—no more than a whore and a harlot—and indeed, he despised the way her insipid father Thomas had risen on the back of his daughter's good fortune while he himself, through a whim of fate, festered forgotten and out of favour in a country backwater.

'Lord save us!' Matilda cried, as if she could bear no more bad tidings. 'Surely she had not gone full term?'

Hugh agreed. 'That is right, my lady, but it is of little consequence now. The King, no doubt, is full of angry disappointment, and that does not bode well for any of us.' He reached for his wine. 'At least, now that the old Queen is dead, opposition to Anne should lessen, but I believe the King tires of her already. She tries him too much, and has not fulfilled her early promise. It is all too clear that the King has little time to waste in hopes and dreams; he knows that time is running out for him.'

'Thank God I have a fine and healthy heir,' Sir Victor said haughtily as he looked at his only son. 'I understand King Henry's impatience and his desperation, but perhaps he should temper his judgements with less haste and more charity.' He spoke the words as much for himself as for any other.

'The King is the King, sir,' Hugh retorted firmly, not liking the arrogance and vanity in Sir Victor's words.

'Of course, of course—and England must have an heir.' Sir Victor lowered his eyes, wanting to bite his loose tongue. It had cost him dear in the past; he must never let it do so again.

'England must have an heir,' Matilda repeated sorrowfully. 'And what misery it causes! Poor Queen Catherine, so alone, so neglected, and she loved him to the last, I have heard. It is a sorry state of affairs, and I wonder at its ending,' she finished wearily. She thought of Anne Bullen, bewitching, greedy, who had once held the King—and indeed England—in the palm of her ambitious young hand. But now the brilliance of her charms was at last fading and she would feel the full force of the King's disappointment. Foolish, arrogant child! She was surprised at the pity that surged suddenly into her heart.

'Come, come,' Sir Victor said somewhat sharply, 'we must not dwell on these bad tidings. It is God's will. Now, please, Lady Matilda, sup some wine and allow it to warm and cheer your veins.'

'Forgive me,' she replied, hearing the impatience in his voice. 'I am becoming a silly old woman.'

Before Bethan could gently rebuke her, Hugh D'Savoury intervened. 'Never a silly old woman, my lady,' he said kindly. 'Your words were well said, but please do not let the affairs of the court so upset you. They are almost a world away from your peaceful lives here.'

'Like the burning of the abbey?' Edward could not resist.

'Hush, Edward—we have had enough dark talk,' Sir Victor reprimanded. 'In any event, I intend to discuss the matter with our guest later.' As an afterthought he added, looking to the ladies, 'We shall find the culprits, never fear.'

Please God, Bethan thought. Then the kind old face of Friar Dominic came into her mind. And what of him? She looked at Hugh D'Savoury. Surely he would have news? At the very least that they had found his poor old body. Perhaps later, with the help of the wine, she would brave her own fears and ask. Perhaps there would be an opportune moment.

The evening was a pleasant one and Edward was more charming than he had been for a long time, caring and thoughtful, pandering to her every whim. Bethan wondered, and noted the sparkle in his eye as if he were playing some mischievous game, but as the rich wine began to seep into her veins she allowed herself to respond to him—it was so much easier than trying to understand the turmoil inside herself. Hugh seemed able to divide his time equally between Sir Victor and her aunt with amazing skill and charm. The King chooses his men well, Bethan thought.

'I think the Lady Matilda should perhaps be taken to her bedchamber.' Hugh's words were low, yet his voice cut through the chatter and sounds at the table. Bethan looked at him and then at her aunt, whose gentle grey head was nodding sleepily over morsels of honey-cake, a goblet of wine swaying precariously in her hand.

'I shall call my housekeeper and her husband,' Sir Victor said immediately, rising.

'No, no, sir,' Edward stayed his father. 'I would deem it an honour to escort dear Lady Matilda to her room.'

'Oh, Edward, how kind!' Bethan said softly, touching his hand. 'But you must allow me to assist you.'

Edward was not quite able to hide the smile of satisfaction that crept across his face. 'I would not dream of trying to persuade you otherwise, my sweet.' It had worked beautifully! For some time he had been looking for an excuse to be alone with Bethan, and now her aunt had provided the perfect one.

Sir Victor and Hugh stood up as the little group left the room. For once, no candle need be carried to light the way in Courtenay Manor: the house still glowed, still shone from the finest waxen tapers—like a woman whose cheeks burned with the fleeting and heady abandonment of too much wine.

Matilda's bedchamber was only two doors from Bethan's on the first landing. Edward waited impatiently outside as Bethan, ignoring her aunt's protests, helped her into her bed. He heard her warm voice bidding her aunt goodnight, heard her light footstep as she came close to the door, then she stood before him, smiling, and quickly closed the door behind her.

'She will sleep the sleep of the just tonight, Edward,' Bethan whispered.

He hardly knew what she said, only aware of her mouth, the way it moved, the way the wine had stained the full lips to a ripe ruby red. He must have her to himself a few moments, just a little time. Without thought, he pushed her into the shadows of an inglenook.

Bethan saw plainly the way of it, and a sudden alarming panic made her heart beat wildly. 'Edward, we must return! Your father will wonder at us if we tarry.'

Edward wanted to laugh aloud at that—his father would wonder far more if they did not tarry! For all his pock-marked face, he was greedy for his women, and they for him.

'Hush, my sweet Bethan—I ask only a brief moment.' He reached into his doublet. 'See, I have a small gift for you.' He saw her face soften at the bribe. Opening her hand, he pressed a parcel wrapped in velvet into her palm.

Bethan looked into his face and saw the nervous excitement there, and then her fingers cautiously pulled the exquisite material apart. The ring was three strands of gold, locked and interlaced with garnets, but its own singular beauty was dwarfed by an ornately carved amulet in the shape of a gilded fish. Each scale was a delicately worked flake of gold, each fin gold lace, each eye a brilliant ruby set in more gold. He pressed on a tiny clasp and opened the belly of the fish. On a tiny cushion of red satin sat a sliver of bone.

Edward looked at her wide eyes and saw the questioning stare. 'It is a gift from St Francis—part of his holy bones.'

For a moment she seemed unable to speak, and then her words came low, filled with awe. 'Edward, I cannot take such a gift! It must have cost a king's ransom. I am not worthy.'

Gratified, he took both her hands. 'My dearest Bethan, you are my future wife, and if it take a king's ransom to please you, I would give it. These gifts are a further token of the deep and eternal love I bear for you.' He saw the velvet lids of her eyes flutter, saw the heavy rise and fall of her delightful breasts as she held the golden offerings up to the candlelight. Dear God, how he wanted her! He picked out the ring from its nest of purple velvet and placed it on her finger. 'You are almost mine, my sweet. This ring symbolises my especial love for you, and the sacred amulet...' He took it carefully in his fingers. 'This amulet symbolises the Lord God's blessing on our future union.' He pressed the gold charm against her warm skin, feeling the thud of her racing heart. 'My sweet dove, my love, my Bethan...' He brought his lips down to plunder her waiting ones, crushing her against him so that he could feel every curve, every part of her, and then stealthily he brought his hungry mouth to her ear. 'I have besought my father to bring the marriage forward, my Bethan. You have only to agree, and we can be married in a matter of weeks.'

The pleading urgency of his whisper seemed to stir Bethan at last. She felt somehow that she dreamed, that this was not real. She still felt the ice cold of his hand and the burning gold of the amulet as he held it against her breast, felt the urging of his loins as he moved against her. God in heaven—she felt nothing! The whispering ceased, as if he had said all there was to say, as if he had achieved all he had set out to do. His lips returned to her parted ones, and she tasted the warm flesh of his tongue as he invaded her mouth. For a moment she tried to accept his lust, return the craving, but tasted only the stale wine waiting on his breath, felt only the harsh demand of his fingers as they dug into her flesh. She closed her eyes tightly as if by doing so she could shut out the torturing moment, but Edward was determined and greedy, and she felt his ruthless purpose. It frightened her, and she pulled away.

'Edward, not here—it is not seemly!' She turned her face away so that he would not see the distaste she could not hide.

He took a deep breath as he attempted to control the wave of desire within him. She would drive him mad!

But he saw the deep glow of red in her cheeks and mistook it for shame at her acceptance of his advances. Almost satisfied, he kissed her lightly, pressing the amulet back into her shaking hand. At least she had not denied him, at least the wedding could now be brought forward.

Hugh saw the gleam in the eye of Sir Victor's son as the two returned to the dining hall, and the smug look on his face. When his eyes turned to Bethan, her face was expressionless if a little pale. An unexpected stab of jealousy, like anger, flared within him; it was so plain what that young popinjay had been up to! He reached for his goblet, letting his hands slowly circle its ornate stem as if he would crush it. He brought the rich heady wine to his lips, filling the hollow of his mouth and letting it slide like cold fire into his belly. Angrily he chided himself. She was nothing to him, and never would be, so why should they not taste the fruits of love when they were able. Had he not done so often enough himself? He cast his envy aside, for it was nothing more, merely the need of a woman. Indeed it had been too long, far too long. He thought of Kate then and the warm embrace of her plump thighs, but it gave him no comfort.

When the evening drew to a close, Bethan left the men to their talk and saw herself to her bedchamber. She closed the door and walked slowly to the small stool set so invitingly by the roaring fire. Sir Victor had missed nothing in his hospitality. She looked down on the ring, which glowed and sparkled on her trembling finger, and then opened her hand to see the gold amulet lying like a brand-mark in her palm. Why did she seem to be full of a curious sorrow? Why did Edward's caresses no longer move her—if they ever had? A few weeks, even a few days ago, had she not longed for him? She remembered how the wedding had seemed so far off, and now the very thought of it filled her with strange dread. She stood up and placed the amulet on the carved mantelshelf; it needed a chain, she recalled absently. Edward had said he would have one especially made, to go about her 'bewitching neck'. Then she thought of Hugh D'Savoury, of the abbey, and all that had passed over the last few days. Yes, she realised suddenly, it had all started with the arrival of the fair-haired King's man. Pray God he would leave soon and give her some peace! Then, of course, Friar Dominic's sweet visage came to her. He would have known what to do; he would have comforted her with his wisdom and kindness. But Friar Dominic was dead. Bethan struggled with unbidden tears, and then allowed a small hope to glow within her— perhaps they had not found his body; perhaps he had not been in the chapel, after all. She knew that she hoped in vain, knew that he could have been nowhere else—it was the wine playing with her tired spirits. Hugh would know of that, she was sure, and would they not be discussing such a matter in the dining hall, now that the delicate ears of the ladies were, so they thought, no longer close? She turned to the door, and resolutely took the garnet ring from her finger, placing it next to the amulet. They would not know she was there in the shadows, would not know that she listened.

Even before she reached the bottom of the great staircase, she heard the low murmur of their voices. Padding softly down the passage, she stopped outside the dark frame of the doorway. She could hear almost every word.

'. . . You seem so sure, sir, that this was a local crime, and that therefore I may know, albeit unwittingly, the perpetrator?' It was Sir Victor's voice.

'It makes sense, does it not, Sir Victor? The drowned man was in the pay of the abbot and worked the abbey gardens for a few pence, and he was still wearing the colours of the King when we found him,' Hugh D'Savoury continued, in a voice that would not be brooked. 'What is more, his tunic, so cunningly made, was stained with blood—another's blood, sir—his fingernails filled with torn skin, as if from a terrible brawl, as though he had fought for his very life.'

Bethan's trembling hand flew to her mouth to stifle the sharp gasp of shock which hovered on her lips.

'You are therefore saying that this man was in the employ of this local man? A man of means, we must assume, and someone who would benefit from the burning of the abbey?' Sir Victor paused for a moment. 'There are a number of such men in these parts—indeed, even myself—and one must not forget those who spend their lives at court but who could still have arranged this monstrous deed from the safety of St James's. You have a difficult and perhaps delicate task on your hands, sir.'

'There is one more thing, and possibly of more significance,' Hugh said then. 'Only one body was found in the abbey ruins, that of one Friar Dominic.'

Bethan bit her fist to stop the cry of grief that rose into her throat.

'Bethan's dear friend,' Edward remarked.

'So I believe. But he was not overcome merely by smoke,' Hugh continued. 'A knife still lay fixed between his ribs when his blackened remains were recovered.'

'He was murdered? But, God in heaven, why?' It was Edward's voice.

Murder! The word slipped softly, blindly, from Bethan's mouth like a trickle of blood.

'That is exactly what I wish to find out.' The voice of the King's man seemed full of foreboding.

'You know, of course, that if I can be of service, you have only to ask.' Sir Victor's voice was filled with concern.

'I thank you, Sir Victor, and shall let you know if that will be necessary.'

Bethan heard their goblets play against the fine wood of the table and then the scrape of a chair as someone stood up.

'Now I shall bid you goodnight—it has been a long day.' It was Sir Victor.

Bethan moved further back into the shadows.

'I shall come too, Father. My eyelids feel weighted with lead.' She heard the two men move closer to the door.

'Please feel free to stay downstairs as long as you wish.' Sir Victor's words floated out into the passage as he opened the door.

Bethan felt her heart begin to pound, sure that they would see her crouching in the semi-darkness outside. But they did not. It was surprising how quickly their voices came close and then distant as they moved away from the dining hall. She would have to wait a few moments until they were safely in their rooms before she would go back to her own.

She leaned her head back against the old wood and thought frantically on what she had heard—on the murder of dear Friar Dominic. Why? She thought of Hugh's words, that it must be a close neighbour and very likely someone they knew. Who? The very idea! Surely none of their acquaintance, their friends, would be capable of such a thing? And the abbey gardener— blood on his clothes, flesh in his fingernails. What could it mean? Suddenly she was glad that Hugh was here, glad that he would stay until the culprits were caught. Sighing heavily, she bowed her head—how tired she was!

'Are you quite well, Mistress Bethan, or do you walk in your sleep?' The mocking voice made her nerves scream in fright.

Collecting herself, she said, 'Why, sir, you merely startle me.' He must be able to see the fear held in her eyes!

'One always startles those who would listen at keyholes.' Hugh moved more closely to her so that the light from nearby candles was shut out and the lovely face became tantalisingly invisible in the darkness.

'Sir, I do not listen at keyholes,' she protested weakly. 'I came to speak with Edward.' She knew he knew that she lied.

'Ah, Edward.' His words seemed to lie heavy in the air. 'He has gone to his bed, madam, as you will have seen.'

He moved his powerful shoulders slightly, and Bethan was able to see his face at last by a sliver of candlelight. His eyes seemed almost black, and his lips slightly parted so that she could see the fine whiteness of his teeth.

Hugh stared intently into her face, able now to take in all the perfection of her features. Eyes you could drown in, great grey pools of temptation; the warm velvet of her skin, which seemed to invite his touch; and the mouth—such a mouth!

She knew he would kiss her, and she knew she would not protest. It was beyond her power to stop him. His lips came to hers, gentle at first, searching, and she felt her mouth respond as if of its own volition, in answer. Her whole being seemed to cry out at his touch, as his arms encircled her and pulled her so hard into his body. She could feel his hands, so powerful, entwine themselves in her hair, pulling her neck back so that its cool whiteness was exposed to his lips. He followed the line of her neck, seeking the creamy hollows, tracing the pulsing veins. Unable now to hold back, he drank the sweetness of her skin until he found the full swellings of her breasts. Lifting her gently, he pinned her against the wall so that he could find her more easily. Expertly he exposed the two firm mounds of exquisite flesh, felt her rapture as his lips pulled and played at the erect nipples, heard a soft, delicious cry escape her lips and the sudden, sweet quivering of her limbs. Great heaven! The taste of her was like no woman he could re-

member—and she was his, because he could feel no re-
sistance and she had no defence against his greater
knowledge. He knew that he could have her now, on the
cold stone floor of the passage, and she would not deny
him—what innocence! Even as his conscience screamed
at him he could feel his hands loosen her girdle, lift the
heavy folds of her gown, searching hungrily for the warm
private mound that would be his.

Bethan wanted to cry out, to stop him. Dear God, this
was sinful, so sinful, and yet his touch, his hands, seemed
part of her, his warmth seeping into her, becoming hers,
as if she had waited all her life for this moment, for him!

No.

The word echoed in his head like a bad dream. No.

Slowly, so slowly, he halted and released her with a
long agonised sigh, letting her feet touch the sudden chill
reality of the flagstones.

'No, Bethan,' he said softly. Bringing his hands to her
breasts once more, he covered them again with the now
crushed whiteness of her gown. He saw that her mouth
quivered wet and bruised from the force of his kisses,
that her eyes round and wide stared up at him in
confusion.

'Go to your room.' It was a command.

She did not, could not, understand.

'Do I need to repeat my words, or are you now deaf
as well as foolhardy?' His voice was harsh, as he had
intended, and he took her arm roughly, pushing her in
the direction of the stairs. 'You are a child, Bethan,

playing at women's games. Get to your bed where you belong!'

For a brief moment she looked back at him, and he could see both bewilderment and hurt in her eyes. It reminded him of a young fallow deer he had once seen and wounded mortally. It made his heart sick.

Bethan ran all the way to her room, almost stumbling, half-sobbing as she reached the summit of the stairs. When she had closed the door safely behind her she threw herself across the bed, sure that she would die of humiliation. What had she done? How could she have allowed herself to behave like a harlot? What must he think of her? Her mind seemed to reel, and she knew it was not for the safety of her soul; it reeled from *him*! Her body had craved him, still craved him, still burned blindly from his touch, and yet she should hate him—hate him for dismissing her like a reckless foolish child. He had had his fill of her and then sent her to her bedchamber! No doubt the women he usually consorted with were worldly-wise, skilled in the arts of love, dazzling in their courtly grandeur, whereas she was only a country maid, boring and without any sophistication; he had made that quite clear! She willed anger to replace passion because that was something she could reason with—not this hunger, this yearning for a man she hardly knew! It was madness! She closed her eyes in desperation, trying to shut him out, but Hugh D'Savoury's face seemed to come out of the darkness, effortlessly—mocking and supremely arrogant. She gritted her teeth and clenched her fists trying to banish his unbidden image, but instinctively she touched her breasts, almost in wonder; they still ached for him. Even in her angry misery she knew that, no matter how much she tried to deny herself the thought of him, it would be in vain. It was as if he had stirred her very soul—and she had gone to him gratefully, like a willing sacrifice. She hated herself for it.

CHAPTER FOUR

THE FIRST bird testing its voice in the early morning stillness awoke her easily, for Bethan had slept fitfully, the night full of shadows and wretched dreams. Her heart was heavy, and she turned under the covers and saw a shaft of winter sun pour through to lie like a tremulous pool of gold on the black oak floor. Her eyes protested at the sudden glare and she closed them again, and his face, unbidden, slipped once more into her mind. Bethan cursed softly, hating herself—and Hugh D'Savoury. She pushed back the coverlets, at the same time casting him, or so she hoped, from her. It had been the wine, the wine. Oh, dear God, please let it have been the wine! How beautiful the day was! Courtney House sat on a slight rise, and its immediate grounds sloped down to a glittering ribbon of water—'the Meet', as everyone called it. Beyond lay the first fields, now covered in a dusting of frost, and further back a rich dark sweep of woodland rising and falling over the gentle hills of Somerset.

She touched her head against stone warmed by the sun, and as she did so, she saw some riders break from the trees and then stop, as if they waited. They were too far away to be identified, and then they backed into the shadows again. A sound in the courtyard made her look down, and she saw Sir Victor and Edward leading their horses out into the grounds. So early! Quite soon they disappeared behind one side of the great house. Looking back to the woodland, it seemed that the other riders had gone, too—perhaps they were out for some sport, but somehow she knew that was not the case. Her smooth brow creased in puzzlement, but then she shrugged her shoulders. She was too tired to concern herself with the business of others. Then she smiled—how she would tease Edward! He hated rising early, but something had driven him from his bed. She must remember to ask him.

Edward. Bethan turned her face to the mantelshelf and saw the golden glimmer of the gifts he had given her. How could she accept them? How could she marry him now? And then the question that had been skulking in her heart rose relentlessly to greet her: how could she find his caresses so distasteful, and those of Hugh D'Savoury so irresistible? Nothing was as it should be. Confusion washed over her, but there was one thing she knew she must do—return the gifts. She certainly could not marry Edward until this malady she suffered had left her. Bethan refused to look deeper into her soul, at the possibility that it might not ever leave her.

A soft knock on the door of her room broke into her thoughts, and she turned as a young serving-girl walked in to light the fire and fill the large bowl on her dresser with fresh water. The wood crackled and snapped as the flames took hold, sending flurries of sparks into the chimney. Bethan waited patiently until the girl had finished and left the room before she began to prepare herself for the day, glad to occupy herself with real things, glad to turn her mind to simple tasks that would not gnaw at her heart.

The house was quiet as she moved along the passage to the top of the stairs with only the rustle of her gown to keep her company. Aunt Matilda was already busy with a heel of new-baked bread and some cheese when she entered the dining hall. Thank God, she was alone. 'We are to eat breakfast alone, Aunt?' she said, seating herself.

Matilda nodded awkwardly as she chewed the stubborn crust, and fleetingly thought with longing of the teeth she had lost as she struggled to answer.

'Yes, my dear,' she said at last. 'Sir Victor and Edward apparently rode out early this morning, and Hugh D'Savoury left only minutes before you arrived—and in a great hurry. I bade goodbye to him from us both.'

'Thank you, Aunt,' Bethan replied curtly, and reached for a jug of milk.

Noting the dark circles beneath her niece's eyes and the soft frown on her face, Matilda stared long and hard at her. 'What's amiss?' she asked gently.

Bethan sighed with exasperation. She did not wish to be questioned! Why could the world not leave her alone?

'Nothing, Aunt—nothing.' Her tone was harsher than she had intended, and immediately she felt ashamed. 'Forgive me. I did not sleep well, and it has made me irritable.'

'So I see.' Aunt Matilda was not satisfied with Bethan's explanation, but knew with old insight that this was not the time to pursue the matter. She watched her toy listlessly with a piece of bread, her face turned to the window.

'Sir Victor has asked us to stay over for another evening,' Matilda said slowly, and saw how Bethan sharply shifted her gaze and stared angrily into her face.

'Why, Aunt? This was not planned! I am not sure I wish to stay another night...' Her voice trailed off weakly as she felt her aunt's searching eyes.

'But surely you would like to spend some more time with Edward? Have you forgotten that you are to be married in May time—don't you think they will wonder why you do not wish to stay? Indeed, I am certain that Sir Victor wants to discuss the wedding—and your dowry, of course.' Matilda reached for the jug of milk, a distinct feeling of unease creeping into her bones. 'He mentioned, Bethan, that Edward would like to bring the marriage forward.'

Bethan lowered her eyes guiltily, then looked up to the window again and the sky lying so pure and free beyond. To be a bird, to fly away from all these questions—from decisions. From Edward? She blinked her eyes shut for a moment. Hugh! It was his fault, his doing. Everything had been well until he came into her life.

'Well, child?' Her aunt's soft but firm voice snapped her out of her reverie.

'I feel a little unwell...' she mumbled.

'What is it, Bethan? Why haven't you mentioned this before?'

She heard the alarm in her aunt's voice and the scrape of the chair on the flagstones as she stood up. 'Dear Aunt, it is only a headache. But it does not seem to want to leave me.' Anything to avoid Edward!

Already Matilda was at her side, her gentle hand cupped over Bethan's forehead.

'You *are* a little warm.' There came the sharp intake of breath. 'God in heaven, don't let it be a fever!' Matilda felt her old heart begin to race in panic. Please God, not the sweating sickness, or the smallpox. Not my sweet Bethan!

'Dear Aunt, it is only a headache—truly. I drank too much wine, and did not sleep well, as I have said.'

Bethan saw the waxen face of her aunt and regretted, so much regretted, that such a small lie could suddenly grow so large so quickly. It had been like this for as long as she could remember. As a child, all she had had to do was prick her finger on a bramble or get a little wet in the rain, and she would see tell-tale fear in her aunt's face. After all, she had seen her own husband, brother and sister die of the smallpox—before her very eyes! Little wonder she was afraid that her niece would be taken, too. If it were God's will. God's will!

Bethan looked up into her aunt's stricken face, and kissed it gently. 'I feel better already, Aunt.' She saw doubt flee across the beloved features, and once again silently berated herself for her selfishness. Curse Hugh D'Savoury! He seemed to plague her, whether he were near her or not!

'Truthfully, Bethan? If you are unwell, I will put you back in your bed, for you cannot ride home in this chill.' Matilda let her hand stray to her niece's luxurious hair. So beautiful, so very dear.

'No, Aunt, I am getting better by the moment.' As if to prove it, she leaned across the table to cut herself a slice of cold meat, and set it determinedly next to the piece of bread waiting so forlornly on her platter. 'You see, my appetite has returned,' she lied, and was rewarded by a huge sigh of relief.

'Are you quite sure, child?'

'Very sure.' Bethan smiled broadly. More proof! 'Now please sit down and finish your breakfast.'

Gratefully Matilda did as her niece had suggested, and then returned her smile. 'I shall be glad when you are married! It is no life for a young girl to be saddled with a worrisome old woman. And Edward is so eager, so in love with you. Perhaps we should heed his desire to bring the wedding forward?' Her faded blue eyes glanced to the table, one crinkled hand playing anxiously with a beech-knot in the wood. 'Although I would not be telling the truth if I did not say that I shall miss you greatly.'

'But, Aunt, we shall be only a little distance away...' Bethan felt tears forming in her eyes. 'Indeed, I am sure Edward and Sir Victor would have you here—we all get on so well.'

Round and up came Aunt Matilda's eyes. 'No, child! I have my own home, which will one day be yours, and I will not live on Sir Victor's charity.' Her voice was harsh, and immediately she regretted her words. 'No— you must allow me a little melancholy, Bethan. Old women are given to such things!' She attempted to smile, but with little success.

'You are not old, Aunt!' Bethan said defiantly, not wanting to believe.

'Not young either,' she replied wryly, her humour beginning to return. 'Now, come—let us forget this un-

fortunate conversation and look forward to the day.'
Matilda pushed her platter to one side of the table and
began to peel a wrinkled apple. 'I understand that Sir
Victor is going to entertain us with some music this
evening.'

Bethan feigned interest. 'Is he a local man?' she asked.

'I think not.' Matilda's forehead creased into familiar
lines. 'I believe Edward said that his father had brought
him up from Bridgwater specifically for our pleasure.'

'We are honoured indeed,' Bethan said with some
curiosity, hardly able to credit the usually thrifty Sir
Victor with bringing a musician all the way from Bridgwater. Was he really so anxious to secure his son's all
but settled marriage arrangements with such extravagance? But she cast the thought aside and switched to
the subject that mattered most to her, and which lurked
furtively in the back of her mind. Hugh. She wondered
where he was, where he had gone. When she raised her
eyes to the window, she saw a sparrowhawk circling the
neighbouring meadow, sure and stealthy as it moved in
for the kill. For fleeting a moment she watched its sleek
deadly beauty, and then closed her eyes abruptly as it
dived earthwards to its prey. There was no sound, no
shriek of death. And she thought of Friar Dominic and
the hand that had stilled his old wise heart. Bethan
shivered; it would be a long day.

They had all eaten well—even Bethan, despite her mis-
givings about the evening, for Sir Victor had once again
set a superb table. Edward was particularly attentive
without being overly demanding, and his father

charming, the perfect host. Of course there were only four of them this evening, as Hugh was elsewhere, no doubt about the King's business. Bethan felt a curious mixture of relief and disappointment, but then the remembered anger and humiliation made her flush with indignation. How naïve, how gullible, she was becoming! Would not such a man be wenching in the local tavern—after all, nights were made for loving, not for the King's business! What a child she must seem to him! The snap of Sir Victor's hands broke her reverie, and she was glad for the respite from her uneasy thoughts.

Through the double doors at the end of the room she saw a minstrel walk haughtily towards them, his lute cradled in his arms. He seemed very young, indeed not much more than a boy, Bethan thought, but then changed her mind as he drew closer. It was simply that he was short and of a rather slender, boyish build, and some of his fine blond hair was even tinged with strands of silver. A bright red felt hat sat rakishly at an angle above his pert face, matching his crimson hose. His jerkin was of dark green embroidery, and the much-darned silk shirt white as a dove's wing. He introduced himself as Newt, 'minstrel and lute-player to all the mighty in the land'. Quite suddenly she wanted to giggle, but suppressed her mirth as he burst into song. Newt had a pure, lilting voice, and she found her senses lulled, her eyes pulled to the bright dance of the flames in the great hearth. Inevitably she thought of Hugh—and hated herself for it, but even as his face slid into her consciousness, she felt the pressure of Edward's hand on her own and wondered at this madness that had taken over her heart. She reached for the waiting goblet of wine and let the rich liquid slide warmly into her belly. Out of the corner of her eye she could see her aunt smiling and tapping her old fingers. Sir Victor was clasping his tankard and swinging it in time with the music, the shadows for once blotting out the ugly scars on his face. And Edward...Edward, so vigilant and generous, sitting beside her. Would she not be a fool to give this up, to deny him—all because of a girlish whim for the fleeting attentions of a handsome officer of the King? She sighed impatiently at her own confusion and then looked up abruptly as Newt stopped to moisten his throat with a sup of ale. He did not pause for long, knowing that his audience waited, knowing that his purse would be the plumper if he kept them entertained. He continued with a soft coaxing ballad that made Bethan's heart lurch. But had Hugh not made it quite clear that she held no interest for him? So why was she mooning over him? Had he not sent her to bed like a foolish girl, like something merely to be tasted and then forgotten? Automatically her hand returned Edward's pressure. She would make no rash decisions tonight, for she could return Edward's gifts at any time. There was no need for any haste yet.

The sun had gone, and the sabbath sky was white and heavy in the pearl-pale morning. Bethan stared at her tremulous reflection in the burnished silver of the mirror and noted with dismay the grey smudges just discernible beneath her eyes. Sleep had eluded her, and she had been glad to rise and pull the heavy draperies back even though the dawn was still only a pallid streak of yellow. But now, at least, her head seemed more clear and the cold water in which she had forced herself to wash had left her skin tingling and refreshed. She smoothed the folds of her gown, and felt ready now to make her way to the tiny chapel at the rear of Courtenay Manor for the customary service.

As her hand reached for the latch of the door, she halted in puzzlement. This was so unlike Sir Victor! For all his thinly veiled dislike of the Bullen girl, and the King's slow emergence as self-proclaimed head of the Church, he still bore no love for the old order, for Rome, or perhaps even for God, any god. And to hold a service, even for his guests, seemed strangely out of character. Yet, as she pulled the door open, Bethan sighed and wondered why she of all people should think anything strange or out of character of late—for was she not the worst culprit of them all?

Aunt Matilda was already waiting patiently at the balustrade that led down into the entrance hall, and she greeted her niece with a smile as she drew close to her. Linking arms, they made their way down the staircase to be met by a great fire burning in the hearth, and Matilda murmured appreciation as she warmed the joints of her swollen fingers against the dancing flames.

'I am so glad that Sir Victor seems to be getting his household in order at last. There is nothing worse than cold and damp—and a house that harbours it like perpetual winter, as Courtenay Manor has done for so long.' She rubbed her old hands together and clenched and unclenched her fists until some of the stiffness had gone.

'I think perhaps he is making ready for his son's new wife...' She lifted her head up slowly so that her eyes met those of her niece, but Bethan looked away, a shadow momentarily dimming their brightness.

'Let us go, Aunt,' she said quickly. 'We are already late, I fear.' Gently she led her aunt away from the fire and her musings. It was better not to talk of it—not of her coming wedding and wifely duties. There was still time enough to examine and quieten her confused emotions, but Courtenay Manor was not the place to do it.

As they walked quietly through the semi-lit passages, Bethan felt the sweet smell of incense touch her nostrils, and knew that they were nearing the chapel, and Edward. He was standing just inside the stone arch of the doorway, his straight, fine back now trimmed with black velvet and silver. He was handsome and kind, she reminded herself once again, and so generous! And did he not love her? How could she even contemplate casting him aside for the vagaries of a man such as Hugh D'Savoury? The dark brooding face slid effortlessly into her mind again, and she saw him as she had seen him in the half-glow of candlelight, felt excited fear give way to a slow delight that burned its way through every nerve and fibre of her being. She closed her eyes sharply, shocked once more at the heady feelings he conjured within her with such ease. He was like the very devil, and she would not let him usurp her soul and heart as he had doubtless done to so many others!

Edward drew her to his side as she approached, and she felt the sure spectre of guilt make her cheeks grow red. But surely she was safe from wayward thoughts by his side, and in a house of God? His hand searched for hers, and she took it gratefully and with relief—as though it were a charm that would keep her safe. But suddenly her thoughts were stilled by the soft chant of Latin; the age-old words seemed to lift her heart, soothing and calming her troubled spirits as they rose gently to fill the sweet air of the chapel. Bethan lifted her eyes to the sombre figure who stood before the altar, and automatically, as she should have known, the dear face of Friar Dominic slid into her mind. It could have been him standing there, so kind, so wise, so good! Tears pricked her eyelids as the figure turned towards the small congregation, and her eyes came to rest on the face half-hidden beneath the lip and shadow of a heavy cowl. She saw a mouth—tiny, like a false rosebud, almost feminine. And eyes narrow, like slivers of black glass. There was something familiar about him, in his voice, in his stance, as if she should know him. But no name rose to her lips, and she found her eyes following him with growing unease. Why should she feel concern; why should his name, or lack of it, gnaw at her memory thus? And, in any event, why should it matter? She gazed at the golden crucifix hanging in solitary splendour behind the altar and tried to concentrate on her devotions, but the voice, softly insistent, seemed to call her. She sighed inwardly with irritation. There seemed to be little peace anywhere. The words of the Kyrie began to fill the air, and she heard her aunt's sweet quavering voice: *'Kyrie eleison... Christe eleison...'* Bethan closed her eyes as she began to recite the familiar words, and relief began to filter slowly into her heart. She was jumping at shadows, at dreams and imaginings. What, in heaven's name, was there to imagine?

The crisp air stung her face as she followed her aunt out at last into the courtyard. The sky had cleared, and as the morning grew late, a winter sun was endeavouring to shine through banks of grey-white clouds. Edward helped her on to a mounting-stool, and as she sat safely in Tallow's saddle for the journey home, Bethan felt thankful. Sir Victor did not see them off. He had lingered in the chapel with the friar, and when Bethan had turned to bid him goodbye he had not even noticed, and once again she was touched by curiosity. No doubt he was discussing the abbey, and she shook her head gently as if to shrug off such thoughts. The morning was too beautiful to dwell on that unhappy episode. As Tallow began to move away from the house, she turned back to wave at Edward. He blew her a kiss, but somehow she could not return it, and only waved more enthusiastically as if this would make up for her lack. She asked herself with exasperation: Was a kiss blown on the wind so much to give? With no answer, she spurred Tallow on, determined to rid herself of the nonsense that seemed to be whirling in her head.

The day seemed to be growing more glorious by the hour. A heavy dew during the night had turned to frost, and as the sun gathered strength, every leaf and twig and blade of grass seemed hung with diamonds. The ground was as hard as iron, so their headway was good without the usual lurking danger of glutinous mud to impede their progress. But as they neared the fork which led in one direction to Astwood House, the other to the

village, Bethan slowed her horse, and her aunt turned
and stopped with a look of puzzlement.

'I think I shall go to the village while we have the
benefit of this good day,' she said in response to her
aunt's expression, and Matilda's face puckered into a
frown.

'I do not like you to go alone, child; you know that!'
Matilda wondered silently why she bothered to protest
at all. Bethan would have her own way, and that, she
knew, did not include taking either of their escort with
her.

'Good heavens, Aunt, it is only a short distance, and
I shan't be very long, I promise.' She flung her braids
back in a gesture that brooked no argument. 'It has been
an age since I called on old Jenna.' She paused for a
moment, and then added, 'Neither have I been able to
visit my parents' grave, and my conscience troubles me.'

Matilda made no reply. It was true, and she had no
argument, no words, that would stay her niece. So she
watched helplessly as the girl slowly disappeared among
the twisting turnings of the bridle path. For a moment
she stared at the empty track, at the fading foggy
whiteness that lingered where horse and rider had
breathed, and wondered at the depth of loss and loyalty
her dear Bethan felt she should accord to the parents
she had never known. She shook her head gently and
then turned her horse back in the direction of her home.
It was a beautiful day, but the sky seemed hard and
sharp, somehow, cold and brittle as though it would
break at her touch. She shivered slightly, and thought
of the fire that would be burning in her bedchamber in

readiness for her return. For all Sir Victor's time and
trouble in affording his guests such unaccustomed lavish
warmth and comfort, Courtenay Manor with all its
grandeur was still a cold place, and Matilda was glad
with all her heart that the kind walls of Astwood House
would soon be looming up to greet her.

Bethan drove Tallow steadily down the narrow path,
guiding her away from the ruts and potholes that could
appear suddenly and without warning to the unwary
rider. The branches of trees stooped low, and she kept
her head down so that their black skeletal arms and
fingers would not clutch at her as they passed. But the
wood was quiet with only the sound of bird calls to break
the stillness. She breathed deeply, luxuriating in her
sudden freedom, and bade Tallow go faster so that she
heard and felt the whistling rush of the cold, unbridled
wind against her cheeks, felt it tear at her hair so that
the loose heavy braids separated and hung free, whipped
back like a mass of jet behind her.

As she cleared the edge of the trees, her eyes caught
the first familiar outbuildings of the village, uneven walls
of clay and timber—the smithy—and she heard the distinct comforting sound of hammer on anvil as she approached. John never stopped working, even on the
sabbath, and his great arms and shoulders were proof
of it. But that was the way it had always been, and she
supposed that nothing would ever change that, except
old age or the soft sleep of death. She greeted him
warmly, and was rewarded with a shy crooked smile as
he looked up briefly, but then his enormous bull-neck

bent over again to continue working the molten metal that glowed ferociously between clamps of unyielding iron.

She urged Tallow on into the village. A few dogs roamed listlessly, scavenging between the spaces of cottages and outhouses, but there were few people to be seen and these were only the old or enfeebled, and even for the sabbath, this was unusual. But as the path began to widen into the central core of the village, the first murmur of voices, like the echo of thunder, pierced that peaceful morning. They grew louder, pitting the stillness with their clamour—raucous, shrill, mocking.

There was blood on the young man's face where a stone had been thrown; rotting vegetables spattered his cheeks and shoulders and poured down his tear-stained face. Bethan winced. Even as a child, the stocks had always repelled her, making bile rise into her throat. She closed her eyes for a fleeting moment, hoping that by some strange magic the pathetic figure would have been spirited away by the time she reopened them. But that was not the way of things, as she well knew, and she gritted her teeth in readiness to turn her horse away, and it was then that she saw him—and he, her. The blazing red of the King's colours stung her eyes, and she gazed instead at his face. She felt the white heat of a blush seep into her cheeks, and her fingers shook as they clutched the reins of Tallow's bridle as if she might fall. She could not go now, could not run, unless he were to think that she was running from him—and that she would not do.

*   *   *

Hugh checked his horse, and moved slowly round the crude semicircle of jeering people until he drew close to her. For a moment, his mind played tricks on him and he was back in the dark teasing shadows of Courtenay Manor, touching that exquisite flesh, feeling that sweet yielding which had been his for the taking. But he had not taken.

'What is the meaning of this barbarous display, sir?' Bethan's words, harsh and guilt-ridden, broke into his musing.

He drew in a sharp breath, and swallowed in the depths of his throat. 'The boy is a thief, Lady Bethan.'

'I thought thieves were usually given fair trial, sir.' She paused, past shame and anger making her voice shake. 'And my name is Lady *Elizabeth*! "Bethan" is a pet-name reserved for my family and certain friends.' His face remained irritatingly impassive at her rebuke, and her eyes held his and rested there, until she pulled them sharply away as memory recalled her searing humiliation.

Hugh sat quietly for a few dangerous moments, watching the profile he had unwittingly come to know so well, saw the eyes brilliant with anger—and shame! Oh, yes, he knew her shame, as if it had been his own, except that he had cast aside such a luxury years ago, until now. Until now.

'Forgive me, I meant no offence, my lady.'

Bethan had turned her head abruptly away so that once again she was faced with the image of the unfortunate still held captive by the wooden embrace of the stocks. Some of the slime and filth had slipped from his half-bowed head, and she felt a tremor of shock as for a moment the head lifted and she saw the anguished face of Walter, her stable-boy, staring up at her.

'Walter...' Her voice trailed off into nothingness. 'It cannot be!'

'You know him?'

'He cares for our horses. He is a good boy, kind and thoughtful. There must be a mistake!'

'No mistake. He was caught trying to hide his haul.' Hugh stopped then, weighing his words carefully. 'I believe some of the items, if not all, were part of the treasures stolen from the abbey.'

Round and up came her eyes in disbelief. 'No, not Walter!'

He looked away from her as he spoke, his face veiled, brooding, as his sharp eyes flickered over the victim in the stocks.

'He says he found them.' Hugh's voice was soft with contempt.

'Perhaps he did! Surely that is possible?' she pleaded.

A mocking smile began to tip the edges of his mouth. Such an innocent, it was almost not to be believed! He shrugged. 'Do you think I permit this spectacle with ease, without thought or evidence?' His words were suddenly impatient. 'Think, Lady Elizabeth—why was he hiding them? Why has he not been seen for three days? How does he now come to have a horse, when before the sacking of the abbey young Walter had barely the rags on his back to call his own?'

He threw the questions at her harshly, and she heard the same voice that had called her a child, that had com-

manded her to go to her room. How dared he talk to
her in such a way! Not again—never again!

'You forget yourself, sir,' she said brusquely.

His eyes glinted suddenly with surprise as he looked
into the lovely oval face flushed with anger, the wide
mouth beautiful and trembling. He felt an underlying
unease, and his mind slipped into dangerous shoals of
thought. Abruptly he withdrew something from the
breast pocket of his leather jerkin. The chain seemed to
wink in his fingers like fine gold sand. 'There are other
such things, but this interests me.'

He held it out to Bethan, and she saw the tiny rubies
glistening like drops of blood among the gold. Her eyes
fell to the large gold loop hanging empty and loose.

'Obviously the locket or amulet that hung there has
been lost, or is lying in some other scoundrel's pocket.'
He took it back into his palm. 'Is that enough proof for
you, Lady Elizabeth?' He deliberately stressed each syllable of her name as if he mocked her. Her eyes widened
in contempt and loathing as she stared unblinking into
his face, but there was fear, too, and he saw it even as
she tried to hide it beneath her outrage and indignation.

'It may be proof of *someone's* guilt, sir, but not of
Walter's. You are wrong, and before God I shall make
you eat your words!'

He raised one cynical eyebrow. 'I think not, my lady.
If he is innocent, why does he not say so? Why does he
refuse to answer my questions?' He drew in a sharp
breath as if he were growing weary of their conversation. 'Sometimes life is not pretty—it does not always
come up to our expectations, my lady,' he finished

patiently, and she felt he spoke to her as if she were a child to be chased away with soft words as if she were having some bad dream.

How she longed to slap the self-satisfied face, longed to push him from his horse so that his smug expression would be wiped away by the damp bracken growing carelessly at their feet! 'Do you think I am not aware of that? Do you think I have spent all my life behind the coddled walls of Astwood House?'

'You put it very well,' he said, letting a half-smile settle on his lips.

'You go too far, sir, with your thinly veiled insults! You, who only ever bring misery and bad tidings into good folks' homes!' She felt anger swell in her breast as she faced him at last in open hostility. 'I do not envy you your free and easy ways under the King—and your lack of warmth and humanity which accompanies it, like a lost, wild, rootless rogue, drunk with shallow power...' Bethan stopped, feeling her heart hammering like a mad thing against her ribs. She had said too much; rage and fear had loosened her ever-wilful, stubborn tongue.

'More like drunk with wine, Lady Elizabeth!' There was no escaping the mockery, the condescension.

'And wine makes fools of us all, sir!' Bethan turned abruptly away, whipping Tallow into a gallop.

Hugh watched her go, his eyes narrowing. She was afraid, and not just for the foolish young whelp in the stocks. For herself? He felt exasperated, but his eyes did not leave the fast disappearing figure as it bolted into the arms of the forest.

Once she was sure he could no longer see her, Bethan slowed Tallow to a canter, stopping beneath the shadows of a great elm, but her heart still raced. Oh, yes—she had been angry—he was insufferable! But the chain, the chain! And she thought of her future husband, of a piece of rich purple velvet—and a golden fish with ruby eyes.

CHAPTER FIVE

BETHAN'S HEART seemed weighty, enormous, in her breast. Surely there could be no connection between that sliver of gold which had run so ominously through Hugh D'Savoury's fingers and the amulet Edward had given her? He had said that it had needed a chain... but not that one. Never! There must be many such chains. Bethan bowed her head in weariness. And now there was Walter somehow embroiled in this terrible mess. Sweet Walter, who would never harm a hair on any living soul's head. It was not possible that he was involved, there must be a mistake. Her head came up angrily as she recalled the smug face of the King's man—so sure, so complacent in his impatience to punish someone, anyone, for a crime which was beginning to prove too hard to solve for his pleasure-loving head! Impatiently she pressed Tallow on towards home. Her aunt might know something; perhaps she could throw a merciful light on all that was happening.

As Bethan drew away from the village, she looked sadly over her shoulder. The purpose of her visit had gone, swallowed up by the repercussions of this wretched abbey fire. She turned back to the path, promising herself that she would return as soon as she had secured Walter's release, and that would be no easy task.

* * *

'I know nothing, child,' Matilda said as she saw the distress in her niece's face. 'He was taken this morning, in the midst of burying some of the items stolen from the abbey.' She sat down with a heavy sigh. What next, in heaven's name? A member of her own household involved in this wicked business! But even as the thought crept into her head, she doubted. Her heart told her that Walter would never have done such a blasphemous thing. Why, she had known him since he was a babe!

Bethan paced restlessly across the room, all her instincts telling her that there was something very wrong in all this, something that did not fit in with the facts that the King's man had gleaned. She felt sure that she overlooked something, something she could not grasp, which lay tantalisingly just beyond her reach.

'Sit down, Bethan—you make me weary walking to and fro like that!' Her aunt patted the space on the bench beside her. 'Come, have some of this warm ale, and we shall think together about what best should be done to help poor young Walter.'

Bethan obeyed, simply because she had no better idea. She took the pewter mug between her cold hands and warmed her fingers against the metal. For a few long minutes both stared absently into the fire, almost as if all their thoughts had suddenly fled.

'I shall go and see old Jenna,' Bethan said at last. 'I was on my way to her, when... She may know something.'

'Oh, child—are you sure? Perhaps it would be better to leave this matter to the King's men,' Matilda said anxiously.

'If Walter's arrest is an example of their conduct, I would rather trust to my own enquiries.' Bethan stood up and then turned round to look down on her aunt. 'But please don't worry, I shall take great care. What harm can a few questions possibly do?'

A few minutes later as Matilda watched her ride slowly through the courtyard, she could not help but wonder if Bethan were right. Questions, no matter how innocent they seemed, had a way of planting seeds in people's minds, seeds that had a tendency to grow, and grow.

Old Jenna lived beyond the village a small way into the forest that bordered Astwood land. As Bethan guided Tallow through the web of undergrowth, she wondered whether anyone ever found the old woman except from the familiar thin landmark of black smoke, and the sure smell of some strange brew cooking in her hearth. Jenna was not a witch (although some thought otherwise) but a wise soul who had a remedy for many ills. Bethan had often taken her good advice as she sat watching the embers spark and fly into the chimney of the tumble-down ruin that old Jenna chose to call both apothe-cary's parlour and cottage. Her husband Jonathan was enfeebled, or 'simple' as some folk preferred to describe him. A bad fall had left his brain 'wounded' and he had no movement down one side, but he managed to get about quite easily and still managed to find some of the rarest plants and herbs for his wife's special brews. But as Bethan rode up, Jenna was sitting alone outside the cottage, a thin clay pipe balanced at the side of her mouth.

'I thought you would come,' she said, pushing a sparse piece of her white hair up into a much-darned coif. Her rheumy old eyes lifted up to settle on the young girl's puzzled face. 'It's young Walter, isn't it?'

Bethan nodded in response and jumped gently from Tallow's back.

'What can we do, Jenna? I am sure that he had nothing to do with the sacking of the abbey or its treasures.' She crouched next to the old woman, following her gaze which seemed to penetrate the shadowy recesses of the forest. Once, years before, Bethan had slipped out from her aunt and the big house, intent on some game, but very quickly had found herself lost amongst the labyrinth of these same trees, and Jenna had found her. Like Friar Dominic, Jenna had always been there.

'He came to me a few nights ago,' the old woman said quietly, her words empty of expression, and Bethan looked with curiosity into the leathery seams of her face. 'He was confused,' she continued, 'and afraid. He said he had been given a sacred duty, and must not break his word.'

'His word?' Bethan caught her breath. 'His word on what?'

Jenna turned to the young woman she knew so well, a wry smile making her thin lips lift at the corners. 'Do *you* break your word so easily, child?'

Bethan lowered her eyes guiltily, and fell silent.

'It seems he came upon some of the rogues connected with the sacking of the abbey, although he prefers to call them otherwise. He let a few remarks pass that told me much, and he did not realise the significance of what he had said.' She sighed heavily. 'I believe the precious hoard he carried was perhaps a cruel trick to make him believe he was saving some of the treasures in some way. Walter would be so easy to deceive, to tell such a story to—like a child.'

'But what can we do?' Bethan pleaded.

'Well, I have told what I know to that officer of the King—the fair-headed one.' She stopped as she heard the sharp, impatient drawing-in of Bethan's breath. 'What is it, child? Does he trouble you?'

'Not at all. I find him insufferable!' But she could not hide the crimson which crept so stealthily into her face.

'Ah, so that is the way of it,' Jenna said, smiling.

'There is no "way of it"!' Bethan retorted angrily.

'Well, if you would believe otherwise...but I know what I see.' There was quiet for a moment and then Jenna told her, 'He is a good man, child, with a difficult task— and a difficult master.'

'I came to talk of Walter, Jenna.' Her eyes glittered with indignation and shame, as if she had suddenly been found out at some childish prank. 'In any event, if the officer were such a good man, why would he allow an obvious innocent like Walter to be put into the stocks?'

'What choice does he have if the boy will not speak? I think he is hoping that fear will prise open Walter's lips, because there is no doubting that he knows something—and, Bethan, he *must* speak, or he will get much worse than the stocks before long.' Jenna shook her head in angry impatience. 'He is being used, and does not know it. I shall try to speak to him again and talk some sense into that thick skull of his.'

They talked a while longer of other things, but Bethan grew restless and was anxious to be gone before dusk. As she waved goodbye to the old woman, she wondered if anything she could say would help the boy. Surely old Jenna, if anyone, could do that? At least there seemed a thread of hope. Her eyes lifted to the late afternoon sky now touched with fists of grey cloud. Perhaps it would rain; it would suit her mood.

The cold deepened that evening, and Bethan and her aunt ate supper alone, huddled round the hearth. Light and shadow fled across their faces as the fire rose and fell and sparks crackled and soared into the black mouth of the chimney. There had been a time when her aunt had told her stories round that same hearth, when the dark hours were cosy and filled with the charm and magic of fairies, sorcerers, and kings and queens of old. Now she was no longer a child, and there were no sweet stories to believe in and to take away the harsh edge from life. Both of them were touched with melancholy as they sat in silence. It was not to be wondered at, not with all that had happened. Finally, Matilda rose stiffly from her seat to make her way to her bedchamber. Bethan stood up to follow her, and as she did so, she looked through a window only half-covered by a thick curtain of heavy brocade. Snow was falling. She moved quickly over to stare out.

'I dare not think how my old bones will feel tomorrow!' Aunt Matilda sighed, peeping over her niece's shoulder.

Bethan smiled at her aunt's remark, but her eyes remained on the tiny specks of white that swirled and danced so magically in the night sky. Already a thick cushion of snow sat on the broad sill, and even the feeble shaft of light from the window told her that the courtyard had disappeared beneath an icy white blanket.

'Perhaps it will stop during the night. I pray so, because many of the sheep will not have the sense to find shelter.' Matilda shook her head slowly. 'More work, more hands needed to force a path through the courtyard and beyond, and to break open frozen ponds for the animals to drink.' She sighed again. 'Perhaps God will be merciful and we shall find that the snow comes for only a short visit.'

Bethan let the curtain fall back into place and then slipped her arm through her aunt's, guiding her to the door.

'Well, dear Aunt, we must sleep, and it is already growing late.' But as they walked together through the door, a shadow of sadness settled on Bethan's face. Walter. He would still be pinned in the stocks—freezing, hungry, alone. But then with relief she thought of old Jenna. She would never allow him to suffer through this long night. God in heaven—if only he would talk! Her aunt's voice calling her from the bottom of the staircase snapped her out of her reverie and she turned back, closing the door behind her.

By morning, the cold brittle sunshine of the previous day had disappeared, frozen overnight into the glistening white stiffness of winter snow. Bethan knew even without leaving her bed that the fall had been heavy. A thick, velvety silence seemed to have wrapped itself about the world. She could hear no birdsong, no animal cry—none of the familiar sounds of the morning. Quickly she got up, briefly freshening herself in the stinging cold of the water, and then dressed, but as she moved to the door, she noticed the purple knot of cloth that held the precious gifts Edward had given her. She closed her eyes for a moment and then determinedly opened them. Today. She would return the gifts to him today. And no matter how much he would try to persuade her, she would not change her mind. She needed time, time to order her troubled heart, but that was not all—she needed to find out where he had purchased them. The dreadful seed Hugh D'Savoury had unwittingly sown had to be destroyed if she were ever to trust Edward again. Her suspicions were, of course, ridiculous! It was not possible that Edward could have had anything to do with the burning of the abbey. Ridiculous! But she had to find out.

The cold white glare of the snow momentarily hurt her eyes, but the path was not as difficult as she thought it would be, since she and Tallow had gone this way so many times before. Bethan had firmly put aside her aunt's protestations, promising to stay overnight if the day grew too late to return safely. But she had no intention of staying long, and certainly no desire to spend the night at Courtenay Manor. Nevertheless she found that she enjoyed the ride and did not feel the cold, so warmly was her woollen mantle wrapped about her. The familiar countryside was transformed and, for a while, her thoughts were pleasant, uncomplicated ones as her eyes took in the strange beauty of the fairytale woods. She smiled to herself as her mind played pretty tricks with this new white world—as if some quiet magic hovered just out of sight.

Men were busy clearing the huge drive of Courtenay Manor when she at last saw the great house through the thinning trees. Her early optimism about the ease of the journey had gradually dissipated as rider and horse ploughed doggedly through banks of virgin snow. Now both she and Tallow were exhausted, and she knew, even for the mare's sake, that she would have to stay longer than she had wished.

The warmth of the house struck her like a wave as she moved into the hall, and as she followed the manservant down the passage to the large parlour at the rear, she heard his voice, firm, low, persistent. Hugh D'Savoury stood a little beyond the doorway as she walked into the room. Sir Victor was in front of the fireplace, his hands locked behind his back, and he turned to her with surprise as she appeared.

'My dear—such a surprise! But I'm afraid your journey is a wasted one, Edward is not at home.'

Bethan could not look into his deeply scarred features, and was forced to avert her eyes. Had he seen her distaste? She shuddered, and then collected herself before meeting his eyes once again.

'I see. May I wait until he returns?' She felt a nervous smile touch her lips.

'I fear he may be a while yet, as he is searching for that young rogue who had a hand in stealing the abbey treasures.'

'Do you mean Walter? Has he escaped from the stocks?' Bethan felt her hand rise automatically to her throat. Surely this was the worst thing he could have done!

'Someone set him free, my lady.' Hugh's voice cut across the room.

Bethan turned her head slowly towards him.

'How?' Even as the word dropped softly from her mouth, she saw the blatant suspicion in his eyes. *He thinks it was I!*

'Some well-wisher, perhaps...? Someone who thinks he knows better than the King's justice?' His eyes were almost black, unblinking, as he scoured her face.

'I am sure no one could be so foolish as to think that, sir.' Her chin tilted proudly in response to his veiled accusation.

'Well, it will do him no good. Indeed, it can only make him appear more guilty—and all his foolish talk of sacred duties is merely lies to save his stupid hide!'

'Walter is innocent, I know. There is not a drop of bad blood in him!'

'Why did he run then, my lady? Why would he not tell us where he got the treasures he was so carefully burying? Use your wits, madam!' His voice cracked like a whip, and she felt the nerves dance wildly in her stomach as his gaze beat her down.

'Perhaps you should attempt to use yours, sir!' she replied, raising her chin proudly. 'Perhaps you should look elsewhere—to the person who so obligingly gave abbey treasures to a simple stable-boy who could know no better!' *He would not bully her again; not this time!*

'What do you mean, my dear?' Sir Victor broke into their angry words, and she was forced to turn to him.

Bethan took a deep breath, fighting for control, and to contain the tide of bitter tears that waited just behind her lids.

'He told old Jenna that someone had given him the jewels to bury—as a holy task, to save them—and he believed it...' Her voice trailed away as she saw the glint of a patronising smile tip the edges of Sir Victor's mouth.

'And you believed him?' The ghost of a smile broadened into a grin, mocking, as Sir Victor let disbelief tinge his words, as though she were a child, not be taken seriously. 'Come, my dear, you can do better than that! The young rogue thought he could make his fortune with his haul. Even one of those precious baubles would be worth a king's ransom.' He turned his face from her in a gesture of dismissal, and addressed Hugh. 'The sooner you catch this blasphemous scoundrel, the happier I shall be. You know, of course, that if I can be of service in any way...'

'That will not be necessary, Sir Victor,' Hugh interrupted, 'I have men enough to find a young runaway, no doubt weakened by hunger and frozen half to death in this cold.'

Bethan straightened her half-bowed head as she realised that their talk was coming to a close. There were no qualms now, no doubts about returning the golden gifts lying so heavily in the small leather pouch of her skirt.

'I would like to return home now, Sir Victor,' she said, as both men turned to her once again. 'Perhaps you would be good enough to give this to Edward on his return.' She left the pouch on the polished table and did not glance at either of the men as she moved towards the door.

'But you cannot go now, Bethan. It grows late, and the sky is filled with more snow!' She heard the conciliatory note in Sir Victor's voice, but it was too late for that. She would not stay, not even if she were promised all of England!

'I promised my aunt that I would return immediately...' (it was not so much of a lie) 'and in any event I shall no doubt be better off on my well-fed mare with my warm mantle wrapped about me than others I could mention!'

Sir Victor crossed the room and took both her hands.

'Please, my dear, let us part as friends, if we must part at all. You are such a headstrong girl, and I did not mean to doubt your sincerity or your good intent in championing young Walter, but let those who are older and wiser than you be the judge of such things.'

Although his voice was soft and coaxing, she would not relent, not while fury and humiliation still burned like a hard knot in her throat.

'I understand, Sir Victor,' she said, lifting her eyes to his face at last, 'but I still intend to return home. It is better that I go now before the light begins to dim.' She heard him sigh with exasperation, but then Hugh's voice snapped into her thoughts.

'I shall gladly escort you, my lady. I am just leaving myself.' His words were almost soft, as though he too regretted his harsh tone.

'I am quite capable of conducting myself home, sir,' she persisted, determined not to ease his guilt.

'I am sure your aunt would never forgive me if I did not insist that you allow an officer of the King to escort you home in such weather, Bethan.' Sir Victor sounded quite convinced.

Her breath came in deep, angry bursts as she realised she had been outwitted. 'It seems that I have no choice.' Bowing her head curtly to him, she swept out of the room.

For some time they rode in silence with Bethan leading, her head held high despite the keen wind that blew spitefully into her face. She was aware of Hugh's presence behind her, of his eyes seeming to bore into her back as if they saw into her soul, saw her unease at his closeness. So she spurred Tallow on, in order to widen the distance between herself and the man who was her escort.

'It is foolish to go too quickly in this snow, my lady.' His voice followed her like a taunt, and instead of listening, she hastened her pace so that for a moment Hugh lost sight of them behind a spit of snow-clad trees.

'Damn her! One of these days she will try my patience too much!' Even as his words were lost in the chill air, Bethan's horse stumbled, unable to see or sense the pothole filled with snow. Tallow's front legs immediately buckled and she fell awkwardly, sending her rider over her head into the frozen ditch. Bethan's feet crashed through the thin ice and her body slid swiftly into the freezing water. She felt her hands and fingers grasping uselessly at slush and snow, felt the growing numbness creep so quickly up her calves and into her thighs.

'I should leave you there, my lady. It would be a kindness, as you seem so hell bent on killing yourself!' But already Hugh was leaning towards her, reaching down to pull her free.

For once Bethan ignored his words, only grateful for the strength and security of his arms as he pulled her with such ease from the water. She did not listen to his cynicism and the mockery in his voice, too aware of the ferocious chill seeping into her bones.

Hugh stared anxiously into her face, now so white that her cheeks looked almost blue. She was unsteady on her feet as she leaned against him, and he held her in his arms so that she could gain some warmth from his body. Her eyelids had closed and he allowed his eyes the luxury of sweeping over the lovely child-woman face; the rich velvet rim of lashes and the pale pink of her parted lips. He wondered why she continued to haunt him, and why he had not allowed himself to take her as he should have done—then perhaps this madness would have left him. Even through the damp of her cloak and the layers of clothing beneath he could feel the lush roundness of her, and there was even a sweet smell, a woman-smell tinged with roses. God, he was thinking like a fool! But her eyes flickered open, sea-grey rimmed with black in a pool of pure white like melted jewels, and he could not look away. He felt himself harden even as his lips came down to hers, felt again that dizzying, lovely mouth, and knew that, once again, she was his.

Bethan lay utterly still as though afraid to move, only her body seeming to respond to his exquisite caresses as her breath quickened. But slowly, so slowly, he withdrew his lips, only to gaze at her silently, his eyes glittering and fierce.

'We must get you home before you die of cold, my lady.'

He did not wait for her reply as he lifted her on his horse and led Tallow back over to their little group and tied her big neck loosely to his saddle. Carefully he mounted beside Bethan and gently spurred his horse on, taking her into the curve of one arm. She did not move for the rest of the journey, strangely content to stay safe against the sure warm beating of his heart, but aware of a blurry sense of anger that she had succumbed to him once again, but too cold and weary to care.

Bethan blinked open her eyes only when she heard the changed sound of the horses' hooves on the blanket of snow that covered the courtyard of her home. But she would not look up, staying shivering in the cloak of his arm.

'You are cold, my lady. Well, you are almost home now,' he said, but he did not let his eyes fall to the face which caused such conflicts in his soul.

'Will you come in to warm and refresh yourself, sir?'

'No, I have work. That young rascal is skulking in these woods somewhere.' His voice rose perceptibly, a note of authority creeping into his tone. He was glad, for his duty gave him an anchor, putting the rest of his actions into perspective, into order. The kiss had been foolish—a weakness. Bethan Astwood was, after all, only a woman.

'He has probably frozen to death by now.' Her face wrinkled into a frown. 'Have you no pity?' She heard the pleading tone in her voice and hated herself for it, except that it was for Walter.

'It was his choice to run. In any event, the boy is a thief until proved otherwise—and a traitorous thief at that! Why do you persist in this unwise attitude towards him?'

'Because I *know* him.' She sighed impatiently, tired of his obstinacy, the magic of his kiss now like a pretty dream. 'Have you never listened to the quiet voice in your heart—to your instincts—which can tell you so much more than base logic?'

His mouth hardened, clamping into an unyielding line. He had shut that door to his heart many years ago, had closed his ears to softness and love and all the trappings that inevitably went with that word; it spelt only disillusionment and gullibility. But Bethan Astwood came too close, too close. Sweet Jesus, why did the King not recall him, not take him away from this backwater and all that went with it? My Lady Bethan had a way of touching his soul that no woman had done for a long, long time, and Hugh did not like it. He did not like it at all.

'It is time you changed out of those wet clothes before you catch cold, my lady.' Still he would not look directly at her, choosing to ignore both her question and the puzzlement in her face.

Bethan felt her temper begin to rise. What a charlatan he was! What an infuriating, bumptious, philanderer! One moment he kissed with so much passion it was as if the very earth seemed to move, the next he treated her like an idiot child! Was this what King Henry's court taught one? Was this the courtly veneer she had heard so much about? What a great jest it all was, like a foolish game! Without further ado, she slipped from his arms and his horse, thankful to feel firm ground beneath her feet again.

'Good day, sir. I thank you for your patience and tender care.' Her words were laced with sarcasm. 'I trust your hunting goes well and that your prey proves worthy of your undoubted skills!' She pulled her mantle round her, suddenly feeling the biting chill through her wet clothing, and abruptly turned from him. She hoped dear Walter had found a warm and dry hole to hide in. She also hoped that Hugh would fall neck-deep into a bank of snow for his pains! But even as her cheeks burned with irritation, she thought of his kiss—how he had taken her so easily into his arms as if she were his, as if she belonged there. Damn him! Oh, damn him!

Her aunt fussed over her like an anxious mother hen with her chick, insisting that Bethan go to her bed to keep warm—'and to fend off any evil humours that might be lurking in the air'. She sighed heavily in resignation, but did as Aunt Matilda requested, knowing that it would make her feel easier.

The house slept early that night, each member of the household glad to go to their beds to hide from the cold that crept relentlessly through the thick stone walls. Fires were kept burning as long as possible and tapestries and draperies tied tightly against windows and walls to shut out the vicious winter wind. Bethan lay awake for a long time, unable to sleep, watching the dying fire in her room send light and shadow dancing across the ceiling. Inevitably she thought of Hugh, and wondered guiltily what it would be like to have him lying next to her, to feel that deep searching kiss take her again. Then she closed her eyes to shut out the vision. Surely it was sinful, surely there must be something very badly wrong if she had such wicked imaginings when she was betrothed to another man! Edward. She had hardly thought of him all day, and immediately her mind turned to the gifts she had left at Courtenay Manor. Did he realise the silent message they brought him? Impatiently she pushed back the covers and padded softly across the room. Perhaps a cup of sweetened milk would help her to sleep, would help to quieten her thoughts.

A few candles still burned along the corridors and in the darkened cellar that was the hall; they swayed sharply, indignantly, as Bethan passed, almost as if she disturbed them as they slept. The great kitchen was at the back and to the side of Astwood House, down four shallow steps. As she neared the door, she saw a dim light just visible, slipping from underneath the heavy wood. Gently she pushed the door open and saw a large figure bending over a plate piled with food. Each hand grasped a fistful of meat or bread or cheese, and painfully brought it up to the anxious mouth.

'Walter!'

The young boy looked up, his face pulled into a mask of fear—eyes wide, food dripping from his trembling lips. In the half-light, Bethan could see his hands still blue with cold, and his boyish cheeks tinged with a dark growth of soft young stubble, like down. For a moment it seemed that he would bolt like a deer out into the cruel white night, but then his features fell into a terrible parody of sadness, hopelessness, as though he could go no further. With a great whimpering sigh he sat down, his head bowed—cowed and lost.

'Oh, Walter! Poor Walter, you have no need to be afraid of me!' Tears of rage stung her eyelids as her gaze settled on this 'blasphemous scoundrel . . . this traitorous thief'. Never had she seen such an unlikely candidate, so sad, so pathetic. She moved closer to the hunched figure.

'You need help, Walter, and you must allow me to give it. I know what trouble you have unwittingly got yourself into, but there is a way out.' Hesitantly she placed a hand on his shoulder, and he slowly lifted his open face so that she could see that he was crying. Her kind words seemed to have opened a dam, and his weeping came in short and ugly bursts, as though there were an animal inside that was shaking him, torturing him, trying to get out.

For long moments she listened to his anguish until, with some pride, he gulped the pain away and looked expectantly into his mistress's face. 'You must tell me everything, Walter. No matter what you have promised others, you must tell me everything.'

Up came his eyes, black with fear. 'No, mistress, no!'
Immediately he hung his head, shamefaced at his outburst as she stepped back in alarm. 'I cannot... I
cannot!' He shook his head in resignation. 'I gave my
word, an oath.'

'But to whom, Walter? Just tell me that much—
otherwise how can I help you?'

He looked longingly into her face, and for a moment
she thought that he would speak, but his eyes darted
guiltily away and she knew she had lost.

'I shall find a way, mistress,' he said at last, and stood
up, his great limbs stiff with weariness and cold, but she
could see no hope in his eyes, for all his brave words.

'Then take this, if you must go out into the cold.'
Bethan slipped her woollen mantle from her shoulders.

'No, mistress, it isn't right!' A flicker of pride fled
across his face.

'I shall get no sleep if I lie awake thinking of you
freezing to death.' She held out the heavy cloak, and
with reluctance he accepted it. As a last gesture, she
bundled the remnants of his hasty meal into a piece of
cloth and handed it to him. Before he moved to the door,
he stopped, and she saw that his face was filled with a
curiously peaceful sorrow, but he said nothing more. Her
hand seemed to rise up automatically as if she would
still somehow stop him, but the night swallowed Walter
as though he had never been.

The snow was relentless, and by morning a new layer
blanketed the soft rolling hills that were Somerset. It
was the worst snowfall in living memory. Livestock froze

quietly to death in their graves of white ice; birds fell stiff with cold and hunger from trees and hedgerows; wolves, deer, boars, foxes all slunk into hiding from the ferocious bite of the wind and ventured out only when driven by starvation.

Bethan stared through her window, staggered at the extent of the snowfall. The landscape she knew so well had disappeared, replaced by one that held no landmark she could recognise, but it was beautiful—austerely, chillingly beautiful. Her thoughts turned to Walter, who would die. No living thing could survive in such fearful cold. She was suddenly sure of what she must do. There had been too much talk, too many theories—too much blame placed in the wrong quarter. Men seemed to spend their lives debating on such things, whereas women turned to their hearts, their instincts—and listened. Men never listened. She wondered fleetingly if King Henry were wondering whether he should have listened to his conscience before he cast old Queen Catherine aside and took the Bullen girl who now seemed to disappoint him so much—and had given him only a daughter. Bethan could have no idea that the King was already making arrangements to rid himself of yet another Queen.

A great wall of cold struck her as she shut the side entrance of Astwood House close behind her. She had ensured that Aunt Matilda still slept; on no account would her aunt allow her to go out on such a day. It was much wiser to slip out before the household awoke. The stable door creaked only a little as she opened it and was greeted by Tallow's sweet whinny as she moved over to her stall. The mare was covered in a heavy blanket, as were the other horses, and the silken back trembled beneath Bethan's fingers as she removed it.

'You will not be cold for long, my pet! I shall soon have the blood pumping hard and fast through your strong legs once we are out of earshot of the house.' She led her quietly from the stable, careful to follow the path of ashes scattered on the snow the previous day; it was hardly visible, but at least it was better than nothing.

The sun was still faintly crimson from the dawn and in some shadowy corners the snow was rosy pink, even violet, beneath the spellbound skeletons of trees and shrubs. Walter could not have gone far, and perhaps, with luck, he might have left a discernible trail that would lead her to the one who had tied his tongue in such unholy and sacred oaths. Whoever had made him swear on his soul must have a great deal at stake, in which case Walter must be a terrible risk, for who could say when his tongue might be loosened? If only he had spoken. Life seemed to be full of 'ifs'. Bethan turned Tallow in the direction of Courtenay land, where there were many lairs, many deep hedgerows that could hide a man. A long hour seemed to pass before she reached the fork that led to 'the Meet', and her eyes ached from the glare of the snow. The ribbon of water she knew so well was frozen into a sheet of glittering glass, but as she paused before the narrow bridge which would take her on to the great drive of Courtenay Manor, she saw that the ice had been broken, smashed into a drinkable hole. She lifted her head to scan the nearby trees. It could only have been Walter, and her eyes scoured the trees and snow for any sign of life. Suddenly the silence seemed thick, heavy; the biting wind had dropped, and hardly a branch or stalk moved as she wove between the trees. She was careful now as she remembered the previous day's foolish accident . . . and Hugh. He would think her foolish again, no doubt. Was he, too, out this early, searching for the same prey? How simple things had seemed before he entered her life, before the sacking of the abbey. Now there was only unease and mistrust, and he had awakened something within her she had never known existed. Bethan rebelled at the way her stomach leapt with wild, childish hope as his face slid into her mind, at the way her cheeks burned as she relived his hand grazing her breast.

The sound shuddered through the stillness, obliterating her thoughts. Tallow drew back in fright, and Bethan felt icy fingers wrap themselves about her heart. It was a shocking noise—primitive, like an animal in terrible anguish or pain, except that she knew it was no animal. It was a man's cry. She caught her breath in fear, but still urged Tallow forward. Suddenly she thought of the traps, mantraps, that littered the fat, game-rich, lands of the Courtenays. How many times had she told Edward what evil things they were, but he never listened. And she wondered if such a terrible death was worth the life of a pheasant or a wild pig when you were starving? Sometimes she never understood him. As she visualised Walter lying in such a trap, she made Tallow go faster, careless of her own safety, panic making her heart pound in her ears.

But Walter was not lying wounded or dying between the greedy jaws of a mantrap; he was already dead by the time Bethan reached him. His body lay half covered by her own woollen mantle, now stained a crude red with his blood. There was no wind, no movement of bird's wing or branch as her eyes stared unbelieving at his strangely quiet form. Nothing in her seemed to be functioning, not limbs, mind or heart. A tight knot, like a sob, gathered in her throat as tears welled into her wide grey eyes, making Walter's body move and dance obscenely against the snow. Even as the first salty tracks made their way down her cheeks, her face contorted in fear and puzzlement as Sir Victor's tall figure moved away from the shelter of a tree. He knelt carefully beside the body, his hands searching the sad, ragged clothes. There was no pity, no mercy, in his hands, and she knew instinctively that he had not seen her. But even as the thought took shape in her mind, he looked up. She drew back as if she had been stung, and almost immediately wondered why. This was, after all, her father-in-law to be, a man she had known all her life as neighbour and friend. As he saw her, the cool, pitiless expression was replaced so quickly by the easy tolerance she knew so well that for a moment Bethan felt that she must have dreamt that look of stealth—of guilt?

'He attacked me, Bethan!' His eyes flickered back to the body. 'He was wearing your cloak—I thought he had murdered you.'

She shook her head in disbelief as she dismounted, stunned into silence, unable to look into his face, unable to believe what he had done. Slowly she knelt down and stared into the now curiously peaceful face.

'He was not much more than a boy,' she whispered almost to herself.

'But he did a great wrong, Bethan. You must not forget that.' She felt Sir Victor draw close to her, heard his attempt at placating her. She gritted her teeth to prevent the scream that hovered just behind her lips.

'It was never proved, Sir Victor—you knew that,' she said fiercely.

'Am I not supposed to defend myself, then? Am I supposed simply to let him kill me?' His voice snapped at the silence, aggrieved and guilt-ridden.

'I do not believe it! I shall never believe it!' Her voice rose trembling into the air, on the edge of hysteria, as the shock of what Sir Victor had done suddenly tore at her heart. It did not seem possible that Walter would never walk or talk, breathe again—why, he had hardly lived! And she could think only of her own guilt and how she had not tried hard enough to prevent him leaving the safety of Astwood House. 'How could he attack you?' she cried in her anguish. 'He had no weapon—he was cold, over-weary!' But even as she spoke, she saw Sir Victor's eyes darken with suppressed rage.

'You take too much upon yourself, Bethan. Would you still take his part against me? Still you go your own wilful, foolhardy way, and I begin to wonder whether you would indeed make such a suitable wife for my son.' He drew so close that the anger in his words almost stung her cheeks. 'You lack both obedience and respect, which can be only as a result of the absence of the strong hand of a father.' He saw her stiffen, knowing he had wounded her. 'Your own would never have stood for this disgusting outburst—that I know.' He moved away, his eyes shifting suddenly to the trees behind her.

'So you have done my duty for me, Sir Victor...' Hugh's voice checked Bethan's anger, somehow triggering more tears as she heard his horse come closer into the narrow glade.

'I had little choice. He leapt at me from the bushes, pushing me from my horse.'

'I am surprised you were out so early,' Hugh replied coolly, but Bethan heard the strange edge in his words.

'I would settle this abbey affair as quickly as you, sir!' Sir Victor's indignant face turned to him. 'He also wore my future daughter-in-law's cloak—I thought he had murdered her!'

'Not only was poor Walter a traitorous and blasphemous thief, but a murderer as well! I am amazed that you allowed such a viper to nestle in your bosom for so long, Sir Victor.'

'Do not bandy words with me, sir—I have had enough foolish talk already this morning,' Sir Victor said sharply, his eyes darting angrily at Bethan. 'Perhaps you would be good enough to take care of the body. I intend to return home, and trust that I shall hear no more of this regrettable affair.'

'I only wish that were possible, sir...' But Hugh's words were lost to the air as Sir Victor turned abruptly on his heel to walk to his waiting horse.

Bethan watched him ride away until his figure disappeared among the trees, still unable to believe what she had witnessed. Then her eyes were pulled to Walter's body lying so pathetically still in the snow, and she bowed her head.

Hugh walked over to the dead boy and covered his quiet face with the edge of Bethan's mantle. 'He is at peace now, my lady,' he said softly, and she was surprised at the gentleness she heard in his voice. 'My men are close by. I shall ask them to carry the body back to the village, if you would wait for me here until I return.'

But she did not watch as he mounted his horse and rode in the direction of his men; her limbs were numb with shock and she was suddenly very cold. It seemed difficult to lead Tallow away from the glade and through the troughs of deep snow back to the path. She would not wait for the King's man, for she could not bear him to see her tears; he had a way of making everything worse, somehow.

Much later, she could not remember the journey home, only her relief at seeing the outbuildings of Astwood House through the thinning trees. She led Tallow into the stables, heedless of her gown which trailed through the snow, catching at damp straw, clinging to her heels. Neither was she aware of the horse that had followed her, and the footsteps that had trodden so softly behind her through the snow.

'Why did you not wait?'

His voice, sharp yet warm, roused her, and she turned to face him, startled out of her misery. Her eyes were unguarded, and he saw all her pain, all her longing.

'Bethan, why did you not wait...?' But she had no answer as his words trailed into a whisper, as his hands fell to her waist to draw her to him.

Hugh kissed her lips, careless of honour or safety, lips no longer tense with terror, but suddenly warm, eager and sweet beyond belief. His mouth touched, caressed, played with her lips again and again until at last the soft pinkness parted and he tasted the delightful moist flesh of her inner mouth with his tongue.

It had been her tears, like molten diamonds, that had been his undoing. He had been stung, wounded, as her pain touched him, but then she had not waited as he had told her, and it was as if he had been inextricably drawn to this place, to her, and the tears that he would kiss away. But as his hands glided over her back, down to the exquisite roundness of her buttocks, his strange mood of softness, of protection—of love?—began to slide away and he felt only the sudden compulsive surge of desire that made his hands suddenly greedy, searching as she pressed so innocently against him. Hugh could not wait—not this time. She had a way of making all other women seem like shadows, breaths of thin, flimsy air—leaving him with a gnawing feeling of dissatisfaction each time he finished making love to them.

Bethan felt so warm, so unexpectedly comforted in his arms; there seemed so much all at once. She gasped softly, astonished that his mouth, his hands, the closeness of his body could give her such pleasure. But then his kisses and his hands became suddenly, terrifyingly, demanding. This was not the candle-lit passage of Courtenay Manor when she had been made pliant by wine and the discovery of her own passion, neither was she quite the innocent she had been then—after all, was Hugh D'Savoury not a connoisseur of women, tasting each one as he would a good glass of wine? But even as warning thoughts crept into her mind, she closed her eyes to appreciate better the giddy sensations aroused by his mouth, his tongue and the sudden new hunger that rose up in eagerness within her. She shivered as his fingers touched her naked skin, as his head bent to her waiting breasts. She wanted to cry out at the terrible joy and the terrible disquiet which all at once began to filter through the waves of pleasure. He made her feel like a butterfly pinned to a board, pulsating to escape and yet not wanting to. Then the image of Walter's pitiful body slipped into her mind and the fact that once, not so long ago, he had lived and worked in this very stable. A wave of deep shame swept through her.

'No! Please, Hugh, no!' She tried without success to push him gently from her.

'Not here—not like this!' she pleaded.

But his only response was to cover her words with his mouth so that he would not hear her denial, and once again she was nearly overcome by her own desire which seemed to obliterate all common sense and the sure anchor of reality with such ease.

'*NO!*' In desperation she tore herself from him, bringing both her hands up to his chest so that she held him away. 'I must not—I cannot!'

'Isn't it what you truly want, Bethan? Why do you deny what you so obviously wish to give?' His words sounded so sweet, so softly coaxing—so practised!

Suddenly she felt the saving grace of anger. She was only another woman, another body to be plundered and used! For a moment, for a beautiful, fleeting moment, she had thought he really cared. How artful he was—a true product of his master!

'I said no, sir.' Bethan lifted her eyes to his and saw how black was his fury and desire, and she felt a twinge of fear. But Hugh stepped back, releasing her.

'You learn quickly, my lady.' His voice was laced with contempt and mockery.

'I have had a good teacher, sir!' Once again her anger surfaced, but her heart knocked frantically, giving the lie to her words.

He smiled then, but it was a false smile, full of derision and, somehow, regret. For a long, weighted moment he watched her, and then turned away. And he was gone, his footsteps swallowed up in the soft snowfall.

Bethan remained quite still, her eyes lingering where his figure had stood. She wondered how such beautiful feelings could turn sour, so quickly. But they had, and it was all her own fault for being such a fool—such a country bumpkin! Hugh D'Savoury was merely an arrogant womaniser. But as she endeavoured to cover the naked breasts that only a short time ago he had so lovingly caressed, she knew that that was not all—because she still wanted him. Even now—even now!

CHAPTER SIX

'WHERE HAVE you been, Bethan?' Aunt Matilda faced her across the room. 'I give you much freedom, perhaps too much, so that you take advantage of my good nature! Have you any idea how worried I was to find that you had already risen—even before the servants?' She stopped to catch her breath, surprising herself at her anger, and then waved Bethan impatiently away as she saw that her niece was about to speak. 'I have not yet finished—and, for once, you will allow me to do so!' She was rewarded with the lowering of Bethan's eyes as she fell silent beneath her damning gaze. 'The weather has made only the most essential journeys worth risking, and I cannot believe that you had any such essential journey in mind when you stole out of the house and took Tallow into the dangers of such a deep snowfall. If you had no care for yourself, you should have had care for the horse you say you love so well! You of all people know how easy it is for poor beasts to break a leg in such conditions. Then what would have happened? You would have frozen to death in the snow, and I would have been left here, not even knowing where I should begin to look for you.' Matilda stopped, all her anxious fury suddenly vanishing as she saw the contritely bowed head of her niece. She sat down, still trembling from the unaccustomed outburst and the worry that had eaten into her heart ever since she had discovered Bethan missing.

Bethan was overwhelmed by regret as she saw her aunt's white face staring helplessly into the fire. She moved softly across the room and crouched close to her, so that her head leaned against her knee. She felt crushed by guilt and remorse. Not once throughout the whole morning had she given her aunt a single thought.

'Forgive me,' Bethan faltered for a moment, trying to order her thoughts and the words that must follow.

'Walter was here, during the night. I found him half-starved in the great kitchen.' She met her aunt's eyes as Matilda turned her face back. 'I begged him to remain here so that we could help him, but he was too afraid and insisted on leaving.' She paused, her face suddenly pulled into lines of sorrow. 'I did not beg hard enough.' She shook her head in remembrance as the words came out alone and disjointed. 'But I gave him my mantle for extra warmth, and then could only watch him leave because I could do nothing.' She was pleading for understanding, and was rewarded by a beloved hand softly stroking her hair. 'I hardly slept. I kept seeing him trying to hide in all that terrible cold with no one to help or guide him. By dawn I felt almost compelled to find him and bring him back here, and I had hoped to do that before you were up and about.'

'But things did not happen the way you planned them, my dear,' Matilda said gently.

'No, they did not.' Bethan's eyes returned to the pull of the flames. 'Sir Victor found him before I . . . and ran him through!' It was as though she did not hear the sharp intake of her aunt's breath. 'He said that Walter had attacked him, that he had had no choice, that because he was wearing my mantle he must have done me some harm...' Her words poured out in a tumbling rush, trailing off into nothingness, and then her aunt was holding her, crooning to her as though she was a babe. But she had not told her all! How much she wanted to pour out her heart—to tell her of her confusion, of her terrible doubts—and of Hugh D'Savoury; but she could not, not now, perhaps not ever.

Sir Victor arrived as Bethan was half-heartedly making lists of her aunt's preserves carefully stored in the cellar; it was the last thing she felt like doing, but she did not want to sit idle, letting wandering, dangerous shoals of thought disturb her even further. She heard his distinctive voice from the bottom of the dimly-lit steps, and froze; she did not want to see him, and surely it would not matter if she stayed where she was, away from prying eyes and prying questions. But then there was another voice, and with a sinking heart she realised that it was Edward. There would be no escape now. Sure enough, she heard his familiar footsteps, and they drew closer. No doubt her aunt had told him where she was. Bethan sighed with resignation; now she would have to face him, to tell him why she had returned the gifts that had seemed to fill her heart with such irrational fear.

'Are you there, Bethan?' She saw his shadow fall across the door.

'Yes, I am here, Edward.'

Slowly he came down the steps and she watched each footstep, each one, come closer and closer until he drew level with her.

'Why did you return my gifts?' She saw humiliation and hurt written plainly on his face, but it was no more than she had expected.

'I did not think it was right for me to keep them.' She lowered her eyes, not able to meet the ones that stared so relentlessly into her own.

'You are my future wife; that should be right enough!' Indignation began to creep into his voice.

'Everything is so confusing, so upsetting, at the moment, Edward. I need time to think.' Even to her own ears her excuses sounded feeble and unconvincing.

'To think on what?' He drew in a sharp, impatient breath. 'Whether you love me—whether you even wish to be my wife, perhaps? Is that it? Well, Bethan, I am waiting for your answer.'

She felt cornered, trapped by both his words and the cellar. He even blocked the way out, and now, like a coward, she wanted to run from him.

'I just need time to think, Edward, that is all,' she repeated lamely, still not meeting his eyes.

'That is not good enough. I must say that I find your behaviour of late most disappointing—even my father has noticed it.'

She lifted her head up at last, resentment beginning to seep into her soul. 'I am sorry for that, Edward, but it is not something I seem to have control over—as your father had little control over the slaying of poor young Walter.'

'What do you mean by that? More foolish, womanly notions! You really are losing your sense of what is right and fitting, my dear Bethan!' he sneered. '*Poor young Walter*, indeed!' He emphasised every word, every syllable, as if he would wound her with each one. 'Can you no longer tell the difference between a rogue and a gentleman? Can you no longer accept gifts that are given in love, either?' His voice began to rise, haughty in his rejection.

'Where did you get the gifts, Edward?' The question she longed to ask slipped stealthily from her mouth like a thief, and she felt her heart begin to beat faster, harder.

'What do you mean—and why should you ask?' Edward's mouth dropped open for a moment.

'I merely ask, Edward. They are such unusual objects and of such value. I am only curious.' She watched his face carefully, but could see no attempt at guile, no shadow of deceit in his face.

'My father, Bethan—my family, if you choose. They are old family jewels, handed down from generation to generation.' All at once his face became contorted with contempt as he realised the implication in Bethan's question. 'No, my sweet Bethan—they are not abbey relics, abbey treasures! How could you dare to think that I would have a hand in such a thing!' He stepped back as though he had been stung. 'And I thought you loved me, Bethan. I realise now how mistaken I was!' He turned from her as if to go back up the steps.

'No, Edward, please wait! I did not mean to offend you,' she said, her voice filled with remorse. 'Everything has been so terrible, so confusing, of late—and you can have no idea of the stories that are rumoured!' she pleaded, reaching out to touch his arm.

'No doubt from that loud-mouthed braggart of the King! He would say and do anything to turn you against me!' For a moment Edward's expression seemed to be torn between indignation and hurt. 'Don't you see that he wants you for himself?' He seized her hand in exasperation. 'And you are taken in by him! Is there nothing left for me, Bethan?'

Confusion and guilt swept over her. Was he right? Had she changed so much that she had allowed a virtual stranger to turn her against Edward?

He seemed to sense the chaos of her thoughts and took it as a reprieve, moving close and pulling her into his arms. 'Come, come, my sweet, we can solve all this disorder. Am I not the Edward you have always known, the man you have loved for so long?' As if to prove his words, he tilted her chin up towards him and brought his lips down to her trembling ones. It had been so long— so tantalisingly long. He had left her too much on her own, so that she grew afraid of shadows. Edward sighed silently with satisfaction as he crushed her against him. This was how it should be! Bethan was always at her sweetest when she was repentant and compliant, almost as if he could mould her to his will. She was wilful and stubborn, two characteristics that would have to be broken and tamed once they were married. It would be so different then: she would have no choice, no free will and no right to deny him.

His hands and mouth were asking far more than she was normally prepared to give, but Bethan found herself

allowing him favours she had never done before, as
though it were some form of penance for her harshness.
But she hated herself for it and her head went back in
silent agony as she felt him fumble clumsily at the folds
in her gown and his tongue force her lips apart and
invade her mouth. There was no rush of passion now,
no glimmer of the ecstasy that seemed so sure when she
had been in the arms of another man. She gritted her
teeth as Edward's words slipped distastefully into her
ear.

'See, my love, my sweeting—flesh against flesh can
be a wondrous thing, a beautiful thing...'

'Bethan, Bethan?' Aunt Matilda's voice cut across the
muffled silence of the cellar. 'Edward, are you there too?'
Immediately Bethan started, overwhelmed with tremen-
dous relief. She had endured Edward long enough, long
enough to tell her that whatever he may have said about
the King's man, it was not magic, imagined insults or
slights that had turned her from the man she thought
she had loved. As she ran thankfully up the steps towards her waiting aunt, she knew that she no longer loved
Edward Courtenay.

Bethan followed Matilda warily into the parlour; she
did not relish another encounter with Sir Victor. No
doubt he was here to express his regret that she had been
witness to the sordid business of Walter's apparently
necessary death, and no doubt to let her aunt know how
rude and ungracious her niece had been that morning.
She wondered how she would endure it, but she was mistaken on both counts.

'My dear Bethan, I have news!' Sir Victor's usually sombre countenance was aglow. 'News that will drive all our present troubles and evil humours away!' So unexpected was this greeting that she could only stare at him. 'The Earl of Somerset is coming!'

He paced restlessly across the room and reached for a large jug of ale. 'Hugh D'Savoury was able to inform me a few hours ago—a special messenger was sent. It seems that the King would like his grace to lend his wisdom and diplomacy to our difficulties—and he will stay at Courtenay Manor!' Sir Victor shook his head in a gesture of happy disbelief. For nine years he had festered out of favour in this forgotten backwater; a few careless words, and he had slowly and insidiously been expelled from court. *She* had been his undoing, the Bullen whore. How could he have known that the King intended to marry her—that she was much more than just another of his mistresses? But he should have seen! Had she not always had ideas above her, and even her father's station? It was not good enough to be a mere mistress of a king, she had to be his wife and *queen*. Those great flashing eyes had bewitched the King, and her absurdly affected French ways had impressed a bitterly disappointed husband who had only an ageing, over-pious Spanish wife who could give him no sons. But unlike all the others, Anne Bullen had been both clever and patient. Sir Victor paused in front of a window, a small smile tipping the edges of his mouth. But she had not been clever enough; even she could not produce a son if God would not will it! Arrogant bitch! And now she was, at last, finally out of favour and *he* was being given some recognition—they remembered he existed. And then, who knows? It was a start, at least. For a moment glorious images of his reinstatement at court passed through his mind. Perhaps it was not too late, after all . . .

'When is he coming, Father?' His son's voice brought him back to the present.

'He has already left Somerset, apparently, so we can estimate three, perhaps four, days.'

'No doubt he will be bringing a large retinue, which we shall have to house and feed and generally keep entertained. It will mean a lot of work and expense, Father!' Edward's face fell into a frown.

'Nothing will be too much for my Earl of Somerset! In any event, he may well be delayed by the weather, so we shall probably have more time than we imagine for our preparations.'

'If you should need any assistance with planning, or extra utensils and bedware, please let me know, Sir Victor.' Aunt Matilda felt sure he would need her help, for it had been years since her neighbour had entertained on such a scale.

'No, thank you,' he replied impatiently. 'Anything I need can be brought direct from Bridgwater or Exeter if there is time. Indeed, recently I sent in a large order for new fittings for my household, and they may, even now, be on their way here.'

'I see,' Matilda replied evenly, feeling a little rebuffed.

'But, please—you must be my honoured guests during the time the Earl and his company are here,' he said, all conciliation now as though to compensate for his

TEMPTATION

YES PLEASE!

... send me my 4 FREE Temptations together with my FREE GIFTS. Please also reserve a special Reader Service Subscription for me. If I decide to subscribe, I shall receive 4 superb new titles every month for just £5 post and packing free. If I decide not to subscribe, I shall write to you within 10 days. The free books and gifts will be mine to keep in any case. I understand that I am under no obligation whatsoever - I can cancel or suspend my subscription at any time simply by writing to you. I am over 18 years of age.

8A8T

(BLOCK CAPITALS PLEASE)

Name _____

Address _____

_____

_____

Postcode _____

Yours Free! when you return this card.

**Reader Service
FREEPOST
P.O. Box 236
Croydon
Surrey CR9 9EL**

SEND NO MONEY NOW

NO STAMP NEEDED

sharpness. Already it seemed that Sir Victor was elevating himself to greater rank; there was a new pomposity in his voice, and even in the way he held himself. But suddenly he turned back to the small group.

'We must be going, my lady. There is, of course, a great deal to be done, and I have already wasted much time.' He turned his gaze to Edward. 'Come, my son, we still have the snow to contend with before we reach home safely.'

Mechanically Bethan bid them goodbye, suffering Edward's lingering kiss on her cheek. The horses were brought, and Sir Victor mounted and rode quickly ahead of his son, waving to the two women with one flick of his hand. Was this the same man she had seen that morning? Had he forgotten so quickly that a young boy had died, and by his own hand? Did life mean so little to him? Or was it because she was a woman, and women—as she had been told so often—were weak, emotional creatures who allowed their sensitivity to get in the way of manly decisions and wisdom. But she cast that thought stubbornly aside, refusing to accept it. It was simply that Sir Victor was suddenly filled with false pride and too busy to think or remember a mere peasant's death—and a criminal at that. Except that she knew, somehow, that Walter was not a criminal, only a scapegoat, and she had every intention of proving it to Edward's father, whether she married his son or not.

As if to grant Sir Victor's wish, no snow fell during the rest of the day, and before Bethan climbed into bed that night she looked out at a sky that was intensely black, pitted with bright, brittle stars and she wondered, sighing softly, what the new day would bring. As she closed her eyes, her lids seemed to be weighted with lead, but when sleep crept over her there was no respite from her uneasy thoughts; they came instead as dreams, chaotic and disquieting, full of foreboding.

By morning, the whiteness was frozen in sheaths of ice, and the very air seemed frosted with cold. The severe weather froze activity too, so that little work around the estate could be done, except to ensure that the livestock were fed and watered. Bethan found that she could not settle to any task because her thoughts always seemed elsewhere—if it was not the death of poor Walter, it was Friar Dominic, or Edward and her coming marriage...or Hugh—always Hugh. She let memory seize her in its gentle, but unrelenting, grasp. She had not wanted him to stop, not wanted his hands to leave touching her body. How could such a man fill her with such astonishing delight? It was as if he could sweep away all doubt, all reason, stripping away any denials, so that she was left with a raw, all-engulfing passion that seemed to burn its way through every nerve and fibre of her being. Yet she had denied him, and God in heaven it had been so hard—so hard!

As the hours ticked slowly away, she found that she was drawn to the window and the world beyond, but she dared not go out. She had worried her aunt enough, and there would be little purpose in any journey. When she thought on past days, it seemed that each time she had ventured beyond the safe walls of Astwood House, the whole world had turned upside-down. She was roused from her musings by the sound of her aunt coming along the corridor. The door opened almost tentatively, as if Matilda were afraid to disturb her mood.

'What is it, Aunt?' Bethan asked a little reluctantly, as she pulled her eyes away from the window.

Matilda drew in a deep breath, as she ordered the words she must say. 'I have just heard through Dickon that young Walter's funeral service is to take place tomorrow morning.'

Bethan stared into her aunt's pale face and wondered at the way she had said 'young Walter', almost as though the boy still lived. 'Will you come with me?' she said at last.

Her aunt shook her head slowly. 'I cannot—and do not press me, child. You must represent our household, because I am too old and too weary of spirit to see such waste put into the earth.'

Bethan nodded in response and watched sadly as her aunt gave her a careful smile and then closed the door softly behind her.

The sky was suitably grey, suitably sombre, for Walter's burial. Bethan lifted her eyes to the roof of bruised clouds as she moved away from Astwood House. More snow. She had left her aunt in bed, her trembling fingers playing at a crochet weave. Bethan guided Tallow along the icy path. Since the burning of the abbey and Hugh D'Savoury's untimely arrival into her life, she had been aware only of her own feelings; her aunt's had hardly entered into her mind. For the first time she realised that Matilda was almost an old woman, and that all the recent distressing events had seemed suddenly to have taken their toll on her body and soul. She shivered, trying to dispel the lurking spectre of a life without her aunt. It did not seem possible.

Most of the villagers had come to pay their last respects to the boy they had known since his birth in the lean-to cottage at the end of the village. They were all pinched and almost blue with the appalling cold, their ragged grey-brown figures hunched around a grave that was shallower than usual because the ground was too hard to dig any deeper. The service had been short and almost abrupt; Parson Nollys persuaded to perform it only because his flock, the villagers, left him with little choice. But, as far as he was concerned, the boy was a rogue, and a blasphemous one at that. He shook his head absently as he placed a black ribbon marker in the leather-bound prayer book in his hand, but it had not ultimately been proved, so he had excused himself before God on those grounds. He raised his head to survey the shabby group lingering at the graveside, noting, with disapproval, the presence of Lady Matilda Astwood's niece. Such a headstrong, wilful girl! Aligning herself with the local peasantry must lead to unease—and trouble, he had no doubt of that. But he cast the thought aside as his mind turned to the subject that mattered most to him—home, and the fire that would be burning so delightfully in the hearth tended with such loving care by his housekeeper, Lettice. The prayer book closed with impatient finality, and he nodded his head curtly to the congregation with practised ease. He should have plenty of time to reach the parsonage with ease if he took reasonable care—and if, God willing, the accursed snow held off. He sighed heavily and then turned briefly to look over his shoulder, and sighed again. The Astwood girl was still standing at the graveside. His lips pursed in irritation, as a vague feeling of guilt touched him. Foolish girl! Perhaps he should speak to her aunt. Then he closed his eyes, for it was really none of his business, just as it was none of his business if Friar Anselm wished to observe the service from a small window of the church. Why, he had no idea, and he let his thoughts go no further. There would be time enough for such things later, at the parsonage.

Bethan stood woodenly, her limbs cold and stiff in the chill air, remembering the words of the parson, bleak and soulless as they dropped into the grave. Her eyes scanned the group of people. Had she not hoped to see Hugh—for all her fine words and protestations? Even through her grief for the young stable-boy, she longed for the man who had so suddenly and irrevocably forced his way into her life. She closed her eyes for a moment and tried to pray fervently and with true meaning, but felt only shame when his face, Hugh's face, slid into her consciousness and with it sudden and painful desire. When she looked up reluctantly in a bid to rid his image from her mind, she found herself staring into the face of Edward. Her disappointment must have been plainly visible, for his features tautened in anger and his fists clenched in a gesture that railed against a truth he already knew in his heart. His outraged gaze beat her down, and she wished, God forgive her—and Walter, too—that she were anywhere else in all of England but here.

'I thought you might be here, Bethan,' he said in a dry tone.

'Is that why you came, Edward?' she said.

He saw the accusation in her stare, and faltered, 'Not only that, of course. I came to see that the boy's funeral went as it should. My father wished it.'

She turned her gaze back to the coffin, which was now being sprinkled with handfuls of the frozen soil. There was an air of tension between them now, cutting them off from the ragged group of people and the words of Parson Nollys. Edward was unsure of her now, not liking the weighted silence that had slipped furtively between them, and she felt his uncertainty, his doubt, like a growing thing.

'I also came to return...' He reached into his jerkin and brought out the golden baubles he had given her before.

Her heart sank as he opened his palm to reveal the golden fish, its ruby eyes glistening like two drops of blood against the whiteness of his skin. She wanted to fling it away, so that it would sink without trace amongst the snow. But instead she heard her own words, controlled and surprisingly soft, refusing him once again. 'No, Edward. They do not belong to me.'

'They belong to no one else,' he persisted. 'Only to my future wife.' She heard that familiar coaxing lilt to his voice, and wondered why she had never really noticed it before.

'I do not think I can be your future wife, Edward.' She could not look at him, not now!

'I will not listen to such foolish talk, Bethan! We are meant for each other; we have always been meant for each other.' He lifted her chin up and let the golden fish on its new golden chain fall gently over her head, and then took her rigid hand as though to put the ring of garnets on her finger, but she drew swiftly back, as if he had stung her.

'No, Edward, I do not want it. It is too late.'

'Why too late? Why?' The extent of his fury startled her, his pale blue eyes turning black with rage as he took a step towards her.

'Just too late, Edward! God help me, I did not want it this way!'

'*You* did not want it this way! How amusing you are, my sweet Bethan—and so obvious! Do you think I have not seen you make great wide eyes at that King's man! Do you think I am blind?' His face contorted with contempt, but there was resentment too at all he had lost.

'He means nothing to me, Edward—nothing!' But even as the words spilled from her lips, she knew that she lied—to him, to God, to all that would hear.

'Liar! Lying harlot!' His outrage at her rejection spilled out in a rush of obscenities from his mouth. 'You dare to refuse *me*—to humiliate *me*!' Terrible, furious tears stood in his eyes and for a moment she thought he would strike her, but instead he turned away so that she would not see his shame, and then ran to his horse.

She watched him go. Nothing in her seemed to be functioning, not legs, or mind, or heart. If he had struck her it would have been easier somehow, given her an outlet for all the remorse that hung about her shoulders like an ugly weight.

Once the sound of his horse had died away, the sudden quiet seemed to wrap itself about Bethan like a cloak and she turned back slowly to the open grave. All had gone, and she was left utterly alone. Her eyes fell to the pathetic wooden box sprinkled with soil, and she knelt and added her own to the small, sad pile. She caught a trembling breath and turned away from Walter's grave, still shaking from her confrontation with Edward. Automatically her feet seemed to take her to the icy path cleaving the church ground and on to the other stretch of ground that arched behind it. Her parents' graves lay behind the church, beneath the overhang of a weeping willow her aunt had had especially planted in their memory. Her feet seemed to drag before she reached the familiar headstones, and for long moments she stood beside them—'Elenor, beloved wife of Richard...' She lifted her eyes to the sky, which was lightening, and tried to shrug off her mood of weariness and desolation. Moving into the shadows of the willow, she let its long naked branches cascade round her as she leaned against it.

The figure had not seen her, had not been aware that she had moved behind the church as the villagers trudged back to their homes. But she had caught the flicker of movement, and her forehead creased in sudden, wary curiosity as she noticed his cowl and the garb of a friar, but then her heart began to pound as the swift, dark shadow crouched down by the far wall. She realised that he must have been watching the service and the burial, that much was clear. It was also clear that he did not want to be seen. For a while she stayed still, straining her eyes in an effort to recognise the friar. But then he broke away from the wall, his face half-turning towards her, and she caught a glimpse of narrow black eyes and a tiny pink mouth. He had said the service at Courtenay Manor; he had been the one who had taunted her memory! Quietly he moved away into the woods, and she felt a tiny shrinking of her soul as he looked back and seemed to stare directly at her, but then he was gone, and she thanked God for the curtain of fronds the willow had provided. She became aware of the strange fear that made her heart hammer—then she remembered.

It seemed so long ago, as the memory prompted her. He was the brother she had spoken with on the morning the abbey was burnt down, the one who had blamed the King's men for its sacking. She had not recognised the now clean white face that had once been covered with blackened smoke and smears of blood. After he disappeared into the woodland, her feet began to move after him. Even as she found his tracks in the snow, she knew it was foolhardy, but it was quite obvious that he must be connected with the abbey fire. She trod softly, her breath held in her throat like a sure tight knot. Where could he be going? Common sense told her that he would surely be meeting someone to tell them that the funeral had gone as planned—that there had been no scenes, no recriminations, no accusations or fingers pointed in other, less obvious, directions. If only Hugh were there, if only she could tell him her fears. But he never seemed to be there when she needed him, and she wondered wistfully whether their destinies were never meant to cross, never meant to intertwine.

The clamour of some crows leaving the shelter of the trees broke into her thoughts and she chided herself for her lack of attention—Hugh had a way of haunting her that she was sure would cost her dear! She took a deep breath and paused for a moment behind a bank of tall frozen shrubs, realising that she could no longer see the man she followed: it was as though he had vanished into the chill winter air. She shivered suddenly, aware all at once that she had ventured quite unprepared into the wood; her feet were wet through, and the hem of her gown sodden with snow. For a fleeting moment she wondered about the wisdom of going any further, but her feet could not get any wetter, or her body colder, and perhaps, just perhaps, the friar might take her to the centre of this mystery—and the murderer of Walter. For, surely, whoever had allowed him to die like that had killed him deliberately, knowing that he had never betrayed them. She raised her skirts a little so that she could walk more easily through the snow, and she wondered where on earth he had vanished to. Even he, for all his stealth, would leave tell-tale footprints. But as she neared the spot where she had last caught a glimpse of him, another quiver of fear assailed her: was she not being rash—foolish, even? She thought of her aunt safe at home, and then of Hugh, but the vision of his handsome face only served to gird her with more determination. He had condemned Walter out of hand; not once had he allowed himself the thought that the boy might have been innocent—but now, with luck, she would prove him wrong.

The footprints had almost disappeared, but when she did find them, they seemed to point at an angle well away from the spot where she thought the friar had been. She stood quietly for a few moments, but heard nothing that could help her. Suddenly a bird rose, frightened, from a tangled spray of white bushes some distance away, and she lifted her eyes, knowing that he was there. His footsteps were clearer now as the snow deepened, and his path easy to follow. For a time she forgot the cold and the wet, intent only on the man who moved with such swift stealth through the labyrinth of trees. A great tree lay across her path, its roots brutally exposed to the freezing air, and it gave her a brief opportunity to catch her breath as she leaned against its slowly rotting trunk, totally shielded from the eyes of the friar ahead. She was sure he had not seen her, did not know that she followed so closely in his footsteps, but as she made her way carefully round the black, paralysed roots, she realised that she could see no more footprints. He could not simply have vanished! She looked about her again, sure that she would see some sign, some small detail, that he had overlooked. It seemed that she stood there a long time— just looking, waiting—only to see no movement. It was then that she looked behind and her heart began to knock frantically, pounding in her ears, as her eyes fell on her own footprints—and those of another, who had obviously followed her. He had known all the time! And now he had outwitted her. She drew in a sharp, fearful breath.

'Show yourself, friar! I know you are watching me from your hiding-place!'

The sound of her voice seemed to crack the stillness in two, echoing through the black and white wood. But no voice answered, and she swallowed slowly, nervously, realising how easily the roles of hunter and hunted had been reversed. What an idiot she was! Was this man not schooled in stealth—and she only an ignoramus when it came to such things! How Hugh would laugh if he could see her now, but Hugh was not here, and she became more afraid. There was still nothing to be seen, and she felt that that was somehow worse: knowing that the friar watched her like an invisible, faceless thing. For a fleeting moment memory stung her, forcing her back to her childhood when she had been lost in these same woods, terrified and alone—when all the spectres, witches and evil spirits of her nightmares seemed to hide behind every tree, bush and shadow. Trying to cast her fear aside, she moved sideways round the bowl of the fallen tree and over to another that stood on a small rise. It gave her a better view, and it was so huge that she could survey everything without anyone coming upon her from behind. But still the friar would not show himself, and a sliver of proud anger began to pierce her fear. What a coward he must be—he who called himself a man of God! Even as the thought slid into her mind, she thought of Friar Dominic. Hugh had said that he had been murdered—a knife buried deep between his ribs. What if the man who lurked so skilfully amongst the trees had held that knife, had used it against the old man? It made terrifying sense.

She caught a trembling breath, realising the danger she had so thoughtlessly placed herself in. She had no knife, no weapon, with which to defend herself. Bethan closed her eyes briefly in an effort to ward off the knot of panic growing in her stomach. Surely she could not be so far from Courtenay lands? If she ran, and she had always run well, at least she would stand a good chance of reaching a safe road before him. A pretty thought came to her then: that he might not bother to come after her at all, but go on his way. But she laughed silently, knowing that a pretty thought was all it was. She took a deep, long breath, and then bolted, pulling her skirts up about her knees. There was no time to be cautious, no time to look carefully and avoid small ditches and dead wood concealed so well beneath the pall of snow. She stumbled, but did not fall, and as she gained her balance again she looked behind and saw him at last. His cowl had fallen back and she caught a fleeting glimpse of his thin, white face before turning her face back to run again. She felt it was not just he who chased her, but fear itself that snapped at her heels. The little remaining breath seemed to make her lungs want to burst as if it would choke the life from her. She fell, but picked herself up quickly, half-tripping on her sodden gown. She did not need to look behind her to know that he was drawing closer. How much longer could she run? Already her legs screamed from the unaccustomed exertion, and he was fast, unexpectedly fast. A sob caught in her throat as she stumbled again, dragging herself up and forward once more, only to find no sign of the road she had been so sure was within her reach. A frightened cry rose into her mouth as the sound of his laboured breathing seemed to touch her and a bank of brambles blocked her path, but she side-stepped so that the branches pulled and tore at her hair and she thought it was his fingers, his hands, reaching out for her at last.

The scream she had held in her mouth trembled, and finally broke free, the sound raking the silence like a wild, shrieking wind. But then, like a lifeline, she saw the road, and scrambled up the icy bank towards it, only to slip back. Her fingers clawed hopelessly at the snow, and she knew that the chase was nearly up because his shadow fell black against the whiteness and she crumpled to her knees, knowing that he had won. Even as she did so, there came the sound of bracken smashing as a horse forced a path towards them. The noise was like a re-prieve, and she felt faint with relief as she recognised the face of Sir Victor.

'Well, well—so it is Bethan...' A strange, patronising smile rested on his lips as he looked down at her from his horse. 'For a moment there I thought it was a wild cat caught in a snare, but it is only you, my dear.' Then his glance turned from her white face to that of the man who stood hesitantly behind her.

'And you, Friar Anselm, do you walk in the snow for your health?' There was mockery in his voice, and she thought he almost laughed.

'Please, Sir Victor, I would be glad if you would escort me home...' Her words quavered as she tried to rise to her feet.

'Home? Why home? Do you not want to have a sup of sweet wine with the good father and myself?'

Bethan felt as though she were taking part in a charade that was going badly wrong—that she moved in a private trance of her own, like a vile, distorted dream.

'But he was...' Her voice trailed away uncertainly, weakening as she realised with a sudden, searing clarity that her plan had indeed worked and that Friar Anselm had led her to the source of the troubles that had plagued the county—the burning of the abbey, the murder of Friar Dominic and then finally Walter's death.

This new knowledge wrapped icy fingers around her heart as she stared with disbelief into Sir Victor's eyes—eyes that suddenly seemed lighter, clearer, more empty and expressionless. Pieces of the past seemed to float tantalisingly before her—the morning she had seen him so early with Edward, the way he had begun to refurbish Courtenay, his closeness to the friar at the chapel, and ultimately the way he had so neatly slain poor Walter. All the memories came rushing back to taunt her with new clarity.

As Sir Victor returned her stare, he saw the fear in her face blossom into terror. 'So clever, so obstinate! You do not listen to your elders and betters, do you, my sweet Bethan? You, who never learn.'

He leaned down towards the pale cameo of her up-turned face and in one swift movement wrenched the golden fish from her neck. She heard a small, terrified sound, which must have come from her own throat.

'This belongs to me.' He let the chain with its precious load fall extravagantly through his fingers. 'At times, I doubt my son's wits! Did he think to win your heart by giving you stolen treasure? If he had had half your

brains, my dear, I would have a little more confidence
in the future. Instead, I was forced to make my own
future...'

'By burning the abbey, stealing and murder?' There
was strength at last in Bethan's voice as she thought of
all he had instigated and done in the name of fortune
and greed.

'No one need have died if everything had gone to plan.
But no, your wondrous Friar Dominic had to get in the
way of Friar Anselm's knife, and that pretty fool Walter
come upon me as I was gathering my hoard. And you,
Bethan, never content to keep that lovely nose out of
the business of others!'

Suddenly she felt cold, a raw, unforgiving cold. But
he had not finished.

'Always so clever, my dear.' He smiled then, a small
thin smile. 'Your defence of that boy was quite right: it
was *I*, I was the one to whom he had sworn by the living
God, and on his parents' graves, so that he would not
burn in hellfire for all eternity. Such a simple lad! It was
so easy making him believe that he was protecting the
holy gold...' He paused then, letting memory prompt
him. 'He could not be allowed to live then, of course;
I knew that sooner or later he would tell. And it was I
who arranged to set him free from the stocks, knowing
that he would seek me out and beg me to speak on his
behalf.' He shook his head in a gesture of disbelief. 'You
know, my dear, he still did not realise, even then, that
I had planned it all, that his death would be the only
way I could rest easy.'

An icy mist was ghosting up from the snow, and Bethan seemed to hear the sough of the wind from somewhere far away, but then she spoke, her words filled with sorrow and regret. 'But he was only a boy—he did not understand. How could you!' Then she thought of Friar Dominic, and tears stung her eyes.

'How could I?' His words cracked the heavy silence, the pale eyes icing up momentarily, and she felt the nerves jangle wildly in her stomach. 'Did you think I was going to spend the rest of my life humiliated, a wasted failure, with what was left of my fortune dwindling daily before my eyes?'

Then she remembered how in recent years he had sold off parcels of his land and that Aunt Matilda had pointed out the lack of comfort in his home. It had all been so clear; why had none of them seen it? Why had *she* not seen it until now? His face was cool and pitiless and his gaze beat her down, contemptuous and scathing. He would kill her now, because he had no choice.

'Yes, sweet Bethan, that is how it must be.' He had seen the knowledge written plainly on her face. 'But it will be a sad accident; none of Anselm's crudeness for you.'

Again a wave of disbelief struck her, and she felt a tiny shrinking of her soul.

'But you have a little time yet,' he continued. 'As you know, I have much to prepare for my Earl of Somerset's visit, and you had not figured in my plans... No shadow of unpleasantness must fall anywhere; there has been too much of that already.' He looked beyond her to the forest and the gentle hills in the distance. 'Nothing must ruin this last chance that God has given me to redeem myself.'

'You talk of God?' Bethan's eyes blazed with sudden anger and outrage at his blasphemy.

'Yes, God, sweet Bethan.'

'You are mad!' The words slipped from her tongue to wound, to sting, but his face remained strangely impassive as his eyes returned to rest on hers—as if *she* were the one who did not understand, as if she were the one who was mad.

'Perhaps.'

'Listen!' The dry, nasal voice of Friar Anselm was raised at last, breaking into their talk. 'Horses.'

'Get back well into the trees. Quickly, quickly!' Sir Victor demanded, his words regaining their usual timbre of authority.

Bethan felt her arms being forced behind her back and gripped firmly, and she thought vaguely how the slight build of the friar belied the strength within. He pushed her before him and then behind a stout tree, pressing her against its trunk so that she could not see. But she heard the thunder of the horses and the music of men's voices come closer. How she wanted to cry out, to break free and run to the sweet safety of that sound! But Anselm's thin hands covered her mouth so that she could hardly breathe, and she recollected the knife he had used so easily to still the life of Friar Dominic. No, she would not struggle. Not now.

The riders slowed and stopped. She could even hear the lusty white breaths of the horses—so close, so close! But then Sir Victor's voice snapped easily into the air, making a greeting as though all were well with the world. And then she heard *his* voice and her heart leapt wildly with longing as she realised, all at once, how much it meant to her. How strange that the last time she should hear Hugh's voice she was unable to answer him, to touch him—or he to touch her. She closed her eyes in helpless, beseeching agony. The newcomers stayed but a few moments, and as they rode away she thought her heart would die from the pain of it, a pain which turned slowly to gentle grief, expending itself into emptiness and the chill air that was once again pitted with specks of brittle snow.

CHAPTER SEVEN

EVEN THOUGH Anselm had blindfolded her, Bethan was sure they were going in the direction of Courtenay Manor. But they walked slowly, through a path strewn with closely-packed trees and dormant undergrowth. At one point on the nightmarish journey Sir Victor went off, and she was left terrifyingly alone with the friar, who was obviously concentrating on reaching their destination without discovery. She thought the journey would never end; her legs ached with exhaustion and strain and her feet seemed to have frozen solid in the soft leather boots. He stopped only once, to gag her, and she sensed that they must be nearing habitation or at least the sight or sound of some people, and she felt tenuous hope rise in her breast. But she heard nothing, only the monotonous crunch of their feet until they touched stone sheathed in ice and she was pushed roughly through a doorway. A faint essence touched her nostrils and she frowned, trying to identify it and where she had smelt it before.

Incense! It could be nowhere else but the chapel. It was hardly ever used, and lay at the back of the house well away from the day-to-day activities of the household, she realised that Sir Victor would certainly ensure that no one had an excuse to visit it—not even to say their prayers. Anselm guided her to the left, and then abruptly they came to a halt. A door creaked as he pulled it open, and the insidious smell of freezing damp and stale air made her wrinkle her nose in disgust. They walked a few steps on, to another door that cried out for moisture as it was opened with the greatest difficulty, and then she was pushed inside and the door closed sharply behind her and bolted with deliberation. She did not need to remove her blindfold to know that she stood in total darkness, and as her trembling hands reached up to undo the small tight knot and the ragged cloth fell from her face, she was still shocked by the unrelieved blackness, like utter pitch. She swallowed hard, slowly, kneading her hands together in an effort to control the shivering that stroked her body. Gradually her eyes grew used to the dark, and she realised that she stood only inches from a set of moss-covered steps that seemed to lead down to a cellar of some sort. Tentatively she moved forward, taking each step with great caution, her hands sliding down the saturated icy walls until she reached the bottom. Immediately she saw a faint light at the end, and once more hope took root in her breast only to be dashed again as she became aware that it was merely a tiny grille set in the wall. Logic told her that Sir Victor would have made sure that there was no way out, no window or aperture from which she could either escape or call for help. The air was ferociously cold and seemed to eat through to her bones, but she was comforted a little by the small light and the way her eyes were so quickly becoming accustomed to the remaining blackness.

Along one wall shapes began to emerge, and even in the shadowy dimness she could see that they were great blocks of marble. She moved closer, nervously, as their purpose became clear. One had an effigy of a woman carved on its surface, the other was pathetically small and plain. This was the crypt, and the dead woman was obviously Sir Victor's wife, Anne. The other must be the sickly child she had died in giving birth to. A shiver ran through her, and for a moment all the ghostly spectres of her childhood fancies began to take hold again. But, taking a deep breath, she chided herself, knowing that, even in death, these two would not harm her. For a moment she allowed her eyes to rest on the two sleeping forms, and she wondered sadly if things would have been different if Sir Victor's wife had lived, and she was almost moved to feel sorry for him, except that his deeds were too monstrous for any pity. She must try to pull her weary thoughts together. Her aunt would have begun to worry by now, and would no doubt have sent someone to look for her once they found her rider-less horse, but even if they found her footsteps leading from the church into the forest, they would never dream of looking for her here. In any event, Friar Anselm had taken great pains to cover their tracks as much as poss-ible, taking the most difficult and uncomfortable route, and the scratches and bruises on her legs were proof of it. And then there was the snow that had begun to fall again . . . by now there would hardly be any footsteps left to follow. She thought of Edward, then. Surely he would not allow her to rot in this dreadful place for long— surely he would not allow his father to do as he proposed? But she would not allow herself to believe it, she was not even sure how much Edward knew, or rather how much he was allowed to know. Finally her thoughts turned with strange relief to Hugh. He was skilled in such matters as these, but nothing he had said or done had laid blame for the abbey events at Sir Victor's door. Yet there must be something, anything, that would make him look twice at all the factors and lead him here. She shook her head in exasperation—why should there be, simply because she wished it? Everything seemed so obvious now and she wondered how she could have been so blind, so stupid, about it all. She raised her eyes to the gleam of fragile light held in the wall, and then bowed her head in sudden and painful anguish. Hugh must find her. He must!

'In God's name, what could have happened to her? She would never leave her horse like that, never walk into the woods alone!' Aunt Matilda wrung her hands in fear.

'Your niece has a tendency to be wilful, my lady. She may still turn up with a perfectly reasonable explanation.' Hugh hoped his words sounded more confident than he felt. What little light there was was fading fast, blurred by the fast falling snow.

'Perhaps, perhaps. Yet, no matter how wilful she might be, she is a good girl. She would not worry me knowingly, like this. Why, only the other day she promised she would be more cautious in future.' She sighed heavily. 'There is something wrong, I know—I feel it.'

'Is it likely that she called on Edward Courtenay? After all, they are to be married shortly.' The words seemed to stick in his throat as he spoke of their forthcoming marriage, and he wondered why her loss to the Courtenay boy would mean so much to him.

'That does not explain her leaving her horse, sir. It would be madness to walk from the church to the manor in such weather!' Matilda said abruptly, surprised at his careless remark.

'But I understand that Edward arrived at the funeral towards the end, and she might have ridden back with him. I agree that it doesn't explain the horse's being left, but your niece's actions are not always logical, my lady.' Hugh realised he had said too much, and that his explanation was a poor one, but it was clear that the old lady would make herself ill with worry if he did not give her some hopeful tale to cling to.

'Bethan is no saint, sir—as none of us is—but she has many virtues of which I am proud!' Arrogance and pride flashed in the rheumy old eyes, and even Hugh was beaten down by her gaze.

'You have every reason to be proud, Lady Matilda, and I meant no offence. I am, in my clumsy way, trying to ease your fears.' He wanted to smile at the way she had prickled so suddenly at his veiled criticism, but knew she would not appreciate his gentle mockery.

'I shall do what I can before the light is finished, and then shall start afresh in the morning if she has not turned up by then,' he continued, his face suddenly serious.

'Good, good. That is all I ask.' She looked away to the fire with a soft sigh. 'Please find her for me,' she murmured, all fight gone now from her words.

'If I have to move every tree and overturn every stone in all of Somerset, my lady.'

The churchyard was deserted when Hugh reached it, and the snow was busy covering the tracks left by the mourners. He would have liked to have talked with Parson Nollys, but he had left long since to return to his other parish a few leagues beyond Astwood land. Hugh moved cautiously between headstones worn away with age until he came to the path that crossed ground, where he saw the rough outline of footprints. It did not take him long to find the graves of Bethan's parents and further faint tracks that were obviously hers. He stood there a moment, knowing that he stood where she had stood, knowing that she must have been in need of comfort to come here. But when he shifted his gaze to the woods and the stretch of ground leading to the edge of the trees, he could just discern more footprints as they skirted the headstones and disappeared through the church gate, which now swung open. When he reached the wall and the spit of snow that reached out to the first trees, he saw another set of prints, and his eyes narrowed. Edward's footprints? But he had been seen riding away from the church. He walked further into the wood, where her track was easy to follow because the ground was sheltered by the outstretched trees. Now he had the dusk to contend with, and he cursed himself for not having come properly prepared, with more men and lighted torches, and he made himself work the harder until he knew it was pointless to go further. Standing upright at last, he groaned with the ache in his back and the cold which made all his limbs numb like blocks of ice. The snow had ceased at least, but now there was a freezing chill lying possessively over everything, and he hoped to God that she were safe somewhere. Nothing could survive without shelter in such conditions. He stood and called her name, knowing it was useless, yet unable to resist the sweet sound as it echoed, lost and unanswered, through the darkening trees.

A mat of white-grey cloud lay across the sky, the horizon still tinged pale yellow by the retreat of the dawn. Hugh had risen before the first cockcrow and had once more found Bethan's track, and that of the other. He knew he was working towards the road skirting the forest and the border of Courtenay lands, and wondered, yet again, why she had allowed herself to be drawn into danger. He could not help feeling a wary admiration at her bravery. Two people she cared about had died through the burning of the abbey, and she had been like a constant thorn in his side because of it. But he had also tasted the rose that grew beside that thorn, and the memory of it was dizzingly sweet, lingering like the aftermath of rich, heady wine. He remembered how the touch of her naked flesh had almost made him abandon all caution, and knew at once, with reluctant, searing clarity, that he could not rest until that flesh became his completely and unconditionally, whatever the cost.

When he came to the dirt road, there the tracks joined, but nothing was clear, as so much had been smeared and spoiled. His eyes scoured the ground for any hint, any clue, to her whereabouts. At the line of trees, he could trace the rim of the bank and saw the first hoof-mark shadowed beneath the overhang of a shrivelled hawthorn. He had come this way himself yesterday with his men, and had met only two travellers—Parson Nollys and Sir Victor. His forehead creased into a thoughtful frown and then he spurred his horse on, up the bank and towards Courtenay Manor. Perhaps, after all, Bethan might be safe and well with the man she was betrothed to, but he knew instinctively that there was something he could not grasp, which slid furtively beneath the surface of his thoughts.

He let his mind wander back to Walter's arrest and Bethan's stubborn defence of him, feeling somehow somewhere that there was a link. He had never admitted to the girl his own doubts about the boy's guilt, but he had been left with little choice but to arrest him, and by the time they had caught up with him after his escape from the stocks it had been too late: he was dead, slain by Sir Victor's impatient hand. Hugh looked briefly over his shoulder at the spot where he had seen the owner of Courtenay Manor, and once again felt touched by unease. He would be glad when the Earl of Somerset arrived. He had known Sir Victor in his time at court—which could prove useful—and had compiled a document on his known assets and fortune, just as other documents had been compiled on other prominent men in the area. What the documents might hold could prove everything—or nothing at all.

Bethan had torn her heavy woollen petticoat into strips in order to bind her freezing feet for extra warmth, and now the ruined leather boots lay discarded on the stone floor. She shivered with fear and cold, and the hunger that gnawed at her grumbling stomach. No one had come with so much as a cup of water, but there was some comfort in the fact that she would not die of thirst, because the walls of the crypt were deeply cracked, and from each crack protruded ice that she was able to prise free and eat, each frozen droplet making her teeth chatter in protest. The night, inevitably, had been the worst, so quiet that the silence seemed weighted with lead and broken only once by a lone wolf's searing cry. She had tried to crouch on the floor to sleep, but soon found the cold unbearable. In the end she had had to resort to lying on the tomb of the dead child, praying to God and to its dead mother to forgive her. But daylight brought renewed hope, and the distant comfort of familiar morning sounds that managed to filter down to her cell. Yet no one came, and as the day wore on she wondered if this was the 'accident' Sir Victor planned for her—to be left alone to die of cold and starvation... She rebelled against the idea: no one could be so cruel! But as hour followed weary hour, the idea took root in her heart and the first seeds of despair began to grow.

'How long has she been missing?' Sir Victor was all concern as he turned from warming his hands at the fire.

'Since yesterday morning, sir.' Hugh looked directly into the older man's face. 'I followed some tracks in the snow, which led from the church into the wood and eventually up to the road bordering your lands.'

'The road we met on...' Sir Victor shook his head in feigned bewilderment, 'it must have been about the time she disappeared?'

'I wondered if you might have seen anything, or anyone, while you were riding?'

'Why nothing, nothing at all.' He turned his face to his son, who stood unusually quietly by the window. 'Did you see anything, Edward?'

'Nothing either, Father.'

'You seem strangely calm, considering that the girl you are soon to marry is missing—perhaps lying somewhere hurt or distressed!' Hugh's eyes glittered in anger as he looked at the young man who seemed so reticent.

'What I do and what I say are none of your business, sir!' Edward's pale face grew red with indignation.

'My son is understandably upset, sir,' Sir Victor intervened gently. 'Perhaps you do know that the lovers quarrelled shortly before Bethan's disappearance, and Edward is now blaming himself.'

'Why did you quarrel?' There was no mistaking the purpose in Hugh's question.

'I do not have to discuss my personal affairs with you!'

'Be assured, sir, that you do,' Hugh persisted.

'Tell him, Edward,' his father said, his words edged with warning.

Edward glared defiantly into the eyes of the man he had come to despise so much, and knew he had no choice. 'She is no longer certain about our future attachment...' He turned his head abruptly away as if he could not bear them to be aware of his shame and humiliation.

'You mean that she no longer wishes to marry you?' Hugh almost wanted to laugh at this boy-man, but no laugh rose to his lips. Then he recalled the small, significant, pouch she had delivered to Courtenay Manor, which she had instructed be returned to Edward.

'Did she return a betrothal gift to you?' He was not even sure why he asked, except that something urged him, as he remembered Bethan's ashen pallor when he had let the gold and ruby chain run like fine sand through his fingers.

Edward's mouth trembled visibly as he turned reluctantly to stare into Hugh's face. 'Why do you ask?'

'I ask, sir, that is all. Now please answer me.'

Edward stole a glance at his father, then his eyes fell to the floor. 'Yes... Yes, she did,' he replied at last.

'What was it?'

'A ring. Just a ring,' he said, turning again to the window.

'There was more than a ring in the pouch Bethan returned to you, sir,' Hugh said stubbornly, remembering the plumpness of the leather purse.

'Has this any relevance to Bethan's disappearance? I think not,' Sir Victor interjected.

'Perhaps. Perhaps not. I like to follow all avenues, sir.'

'Surely you would do better to arrange a thorough search for Bethan, as Edward plans to do, than worry about what betrothal gifts he thought fit to give his absent bride?'

'A search is already in motion, Sir Victor.' Hugh's dark eyes flicked over the scarred face and saw only the same impassive stare. 'And you can be assured that I never do or ask anything without relevance.' He turned once more to Edward, who now sat toying sullenly with the stem of a goblet. 'My men are scouring the woods. Perhaps you would like to join them?'

'Yes, of course he will—but first there are a few matters I must discuss with him,' Sir Victor interrupted again. 'I shall send him down immediately we have finished.'

Hugh let his eyes rest on first one and then the other of them, and then bowed his head curtly before leaving the room. But as he closed the door, he made a silent vow to see the betrothal gifts that Edward Courtenay seemed so reluctant to discuss.

'What an utter fool you are, boy! Did you think to impress my Lady Bethan with abbey relics stolen from beneath her beloved Friar Dominic's murdered nose?' Sir Victor had waited with barely concealed impatience until the sound of the King's man had died away, nurturing his anger until it could wait no longer.

'I did not think that anyone would realise...' Edward replied weakly.

'You did not think! You *never* think, except of your own desires, your own lust, and the quickest way to assuage them!' Sir Victor turned his back on his son, unable to bear the sight of him any longer. 'It did not occur to you to think that the King's man might have an inventory of what was believed stolen? What if your sweet Bethan had appeared, wearing that accursed golden fish, at the banquet I am preparing with such loving care for my Earl of Somerset!' Even the image of such a disaster made him feel sick with panic as he thought of the inevitable charge of treason that would follow and its grisly, agonising punishment. 'You will go to your mother's jewel-case now, and take out the only thing left of any value—a small silver clasp set with beryls. A stone is missing, but that can't be helped, and if you are asked again for your precious betrothal gifts, show the damned man that and the gold ring from your little finger!'

Cowed by his father's fury, Edward was unable to speak. It had always been this way, ever since he could remember. He seemed to possess an unfortunate knack of incurring his father's wrath. But Bethan had been his prize, the one thing he thought he had done right; her undoubted beauty alone would almost have been enough, but the Astwood lands as well would have doubled the Courtenay estate. Yet he had lost her—and to a loud-mouthed bully from the glittering arena of Henry's court!

'What of Bethan?' he ventured at last.

'You will cease thinking of that foolish girl. It is a pity, but she has sealed her own fate,' he replied, turning finally back to his son.

'What do you mean, Father? I thought you meant only to scare her?' But as the question slipped from his mouth, he sensed its futility.

'Are you really such a simpleton, Edward? Scare my Lady Elizabeth Astwood into silence? You know and I know that she does not know the meaning of the word!'

'But you can't mean to...?' He stopped, not wanting to say anything further, knowing exactly what his father intended to do, yet not wanting to believe.

'Everything I do has meaning, my son—and you should learn from me!' The pale blue eyes grew dark with excitement. 'She is not the only pretty maid in Somerset, and by the time I have finished with my Earl of Somerset, you can no doubt have the pick of the ladies in London!' Sir Victor moved to the window, his eyes looking out and beyond at the lands that seemed to stretch and roll as far as the eye could see. 'I need heirs, Edward—lusty heirs to follow in my footsteps,' he said dreamily. For a few long moments the room was strangely quiet, expectant, until his voice once more broke the silence. 'Now leave me. I am weary of talking— and that King's puppet is waiting for you to join his precious search.' He smiled then, a smug, self-satisfied smile. 'I would accompany you, of course, except that I hate to know the answer to a riddle before it has even begun...'

'But what if we should find her? I know he will leave no stone unturned until she is safe,' Edward said in response, not at all pleased at the thought of riding with the man he despised and of whom, although he would never admit it, he was afraid.

'Think, my dear, simple son! Think where he would not look, would not *dare* to look...'

Edward's face seemed to drain of blood as he stared with disbelief at his father's arrogant expression.

'Here? Not *here*, Father?'

'I told you I was weary of talking.' A secretive smile hovered on his mouth, but then he waved a hand impatiently to ward off the inevitable question waiting on his son's lips. 'Now go.'

The first of the Earl of Somerset's retinue arrived the following morning, the tired forward guard of a group numbering nearly fifty members. They arrived throughout the day, in a never-ending stream of dribs and drabs, cold, hungry and exhausted. The Earl arrived as discomfited as the rest, and insisted on retiring to his room immediately. The others were left to Sir Victor to entertain, and he moved among them gladly, nodding his head at their every request or whim, even filling their tankards and goblets himself, almost as though his cellars were filled with a tireless flood of liquid gold, priceless and without end.

Bethan had watched the day very slowly losing its colour, had heard through the tiny grille the intermittent sounds of horses approaching the house, and hope had once again made her heart beat a little faster, but then the damning silence came again. Early in the morning she had heard a vague noise tantalisingly close to her cell and had cried out, her voice rising shrilly, close to hysteria. After a moment, the sound had drawn closer and she had held her breath, a wordless prayer issuing from her trembling lips. But it had only been a dog, wild and hungry, scavenging around the perimeter of the manor, and her whimpering cry of disappointment had made him run, as disappointed as she. For the first time, she had wept, abandoning herself to all her ghostly fears. No one had come, and so her hunger had become a gnawing insistent pain in her belly, but it was the stinging cruelty of the ferocious cold that was worse than the hunger. She refused to think of the other lurking spectre that threatened to send her running agonisingly to the door to beg with each blow from her fists that she should not be left to rot, forgotten and alone. It was only the thought of her dearest aunt that made her gather strength, and the brooding handsome face of Hugh D'Savoury would slip into her mind, somehow giving her renewed hope. No longer did she allow herself to question her feelings, her desires, or her need of him, because the time for pretending, for games, was over.

'Bethan! Bethan!'

The voice seemed to come out of some sweet dream. She lay curled up on the tomb of Sir Victor's dead child, and was afraid to believe that someone had actually called her—perhaps saved her—only to have her hopes destroyed again.

'It is Edward, Bethan! Get up, get up—are you ill?' He crouched in front of the narrow grille so that any fragile light was prevented from entering her cell. It was the sudden, painful blackness as it fell across her face that made her believe, and she almost stumbled in her excitement to reach the grille, her heart hammering with relief.

'Edward! Oh, Edward, please let me out! Help me to get home!' Her voice seemed to run dry suddenly, and she felt a sob catch in her throat as she thought with longing of the place where she would be safe and loved.

'Soon, Bethan, soon.' He hesitated uneasily. 'But you must promise not to speak of this, not to implicate myself or my father in the events at the abbey.' His fingers ran nervously along the slender iron bars.

She stared up with a sense of disbelief at the face she thought she knew so well; it was almost invisible, for the sudden darkness had painted the grille and his hidden features black.

'If you wish, Edward.' Anything, anything to release her from this terrible place! Once she returned home, it would be different, but now—now she must use her wits.

'There is something else, Bethan...' His eyes swept over the dishevelled figure, still so beautiful, even now, and he was shocked by the surge of desire which rose within him, driving any qualms or hesitations aside. He did not wait for her reply, intent only on the thing that mattered to him most.

'You will be mine, Bethan—mine alone.'

The quiet that descended between them was glacial, seeming to weigh on her shoulders, leaden and almost unendurable. But she made her mouth move, made it make the right sounds, shape the right answer. 'Yes, Edward.'

'Now you must swear—make a pledge, an oath, if you like—so that what we have said is binding and sacred before God.' He pressed his face closer to the grille as though by doing so he could bring himself closer to her.

'Swear on the Lord God's holy wounds, Bethan—
swear on your aunt, Lady Matilda's, life.'

His words seemed to drop into the air like weighted
things and she felt her whole body stiffen. Nothing in
her seemed to be functioning, not legs, or mind, or heart,
and she thought she would die from the pain. She could
not say those words, not now, not on such an oath. Tears
poured angrily into her eyes as she realised how he had
trapped her, how her hopes had once again been dashed.

'Well, Bethan, speak. Just a few words, and you will
be free.'

She could hear his excited breathing, almost feel the
warmth of it touch her cheek. 'I can never say those
things, Edward. Surely you, who have known me all my
life, must know that?'

'Is it so much to say, my Bethan?' His voice was still
coaxing, almost as if he had already won the game.

'You ask me to commit sacrilege, and then say "Is it
so much"?' Round and up came her eyes—outraged with
disbelief. 'Then, no doubt, I could go to hell with you
and your father!' She took a deep, strangely satisfying,
breath. 'Oh no, Edward! I would rather rot in this black
hole than burn in hellfire with the murderers of innocent
old men and boys!'

He did not speak for a moment, as though he were
unable to comprehend that she had refused his offer; he
had been so sure that in her vulnerable position she would
yield to him. He had even allowed himself the thought
of her body, and how she would give him all he had
craved for in exchange for her freedom—and her life.

'You are a fool, Bethan! An over-pious, misguided fool!' he hissed.

'No, Edward, it is not I who am the misguided fool, but you! Do you really think you will get away with your crimes? Already there are too many clues only waiting to be put together to make a very pretty picture!' She hoped it was true!

'What do you mean?' She heard the fear at last in his voice.

'Do you think I would tell *you*!' she taunted.

'I could make you tell me, Bethan.' What had his father overlooked? Did she bluff?

'There are others who know far more than I,' she persisted.

'That great puppet of a King's man? He knows nothing! That dullard can hardly see beyond the end of his nose!' But panic began to crawl softly in his stomach as he remembered the interview he had had with Hugh that morning.

'He is hardly likely to tell *you*, Edward!' She closed her eyes, fighting a wave of dizziness. 'And if any harm should befall me, your crimes would be terrible before God and the King!'

'But I did nothing!' he protested weakly. 'I knew that my father was involved only when it was too late. I killed no one and stole nothing!' His voice quavered with fear.

'Do you really think anyone will believe you?' Her heart was knocking frantically. Now, now! 'It would go far better for you if you were to tell all you know, and then it is likely you will be pardoned.' She sighed heavily, shaking her head in desperation. 'Oh, Edward, try before it is too late!' Please God, please God!

He fell silent, and the silence seemed to send chains around her heart. Choking.

'No!' He shrank from her. 'You are using me, trying to frighten me, so that I will release you, but you will not frighten me so easily.' A shaft of the exiled light cut across his face, and she saw that a smile tipped the edges of his mouth. 'In any event, I could not release you even if I wanted to—my father has the key.'

There had been no clue beyond the fading footprints leading to the road. Hugh had directed his men to another area although, as he watched them leave, he knew their errand was useless. He turned his horse away in the direction of Courtenay Manor; the Earl of Somerset would expect his presence, and he had little choice but to obey. His eyes lifted to the oppressive skies, and in the far distance he thought a pale sun was endeavouring to penetrate the heavy cloud. Although the snow had stopped, he felt the tremulous beginnings of a cutting wind blowing from the north, and knew that by nightfall any trace of Bethan's path would be covered by a freezing pall of whiteness. He thought of the last time he had seen her, touched her. The memory crowded in on him as he relived that last sweet, dizzying kiss. And yet she had denied him. Her damned sacred pride! He closed his eyes, as a vision of her slid effortlessly into his mind and a longing, like hunger, made his blood seem to burn. Sweet Jesus, he would find her, because he knew he would never have any peace if he did not! A bitter smile rose to his lips as he urged his horse on beneath the naked, sprawling branches of a tree—black skeletal arms and fingers. Like bones.

CHAPTER EIGHT

COURTENAY MANOR was lavishly aglow. Every window, every aperture blazed with the light from a hundred torches and candles. Hugh had not yet reached the final stretch of path up to the great oak doors, but already he could hear the soft thunder of voices and laughter. He thought of the man he had come to see, a shrewd and powerful extension of his master, the King. But Somerset would not talk until he was ready, and that would mean a long evening. The Earl would feast and drink well first, and demand to be entertained. He hoped for Sir Victor's sake that he had prepared himself sufficiently or there would be hell to pay, but from what he had seen of Sir Victor's purse lately, it was ever full. He thought of the careful information the Earl had had prepared and documented and a sudden itch of curiosity made him impatient for the end of the evening.

Sir Victor's steward looked both anxious and bewildered as he escorted Hugh to the great hall. Already several drunkards sprawled in the embrace of two vast wooden benches, their goblets carelessly discarded and the rich red juice they had held spattered like blood across the flagstones. The doors stood open, and Hugh thought he could hear music somewhere among the cacophony of sound. Sure enough, at the end of the hall the Earl of Somerset was being wooed by a minstrel, and Hugh realised that it was the lute-player Sir Victor had brought from Bridgwater on a previous occasion. Further down the room was a group of jugglers and the Earl's jester close by spraying them and the audience with a filthy fountain of wine from his mouth. Hugh cursed silently. It was worse than he had anticipated, and a flick of his eye over the Earl told him that there would be little talk tonight; the older man's lean aristocratic face already glowed with the effects of too much wine, and a plump, laughing girl sat in his lap, her bodice so awry that most of her generous breasts spilled over into his waiting hands. Somerset seemed to toy with her with practised indifference, his attention, so it seemed, totally absorbed. But, in that, Hugh was mistaken. As though the Earl had sensed the newcomer's appraisal, his eyes caught the look of resignation in the gaze of the King's man.

'Why is it, sir, that a sober man always looks upon those who are less sober with thinly-veiled contempt, almost as if a drop of ale had never passed his pursed, pious lips?' The Earl's eyes had narrowed as he stared, unblinking, into Hugh's face.

'Envy, my lord,' Hugh replied carefully. 'And, in the case of this sober man, too much time spent in the saddle and not enough time spent in toasting the King's good health ...'

They were but a few feet apart, the air between them suddenly tense, cutting them off from the bawdy laughter and talk. But all at once the Earl smiled, and the moment was gone.

'You redeem your miserable hide yet again, Hugh. I congratulate you on your quick wit!' He raised his goblet to him, and then bade the officer who sat next to him to move so that Hugh could sit down.

'You are anxious to talk; but there is time enough for that.'

It was not a request that he should relax and drink, but a command, and a jug brimming with wine flooded an empty goblet before Hugh could say another word. But he did as he was told, glad to relinquish his responsibilities for a while. The wine tasted warm and heavy on his tongue, sliding easily into his belly, and he suddenly realised how hungry he was. An ox was roasting in one of the great hearths and several whole lambs garnished with herbs were laid out on the tables. He leaned over to the nearest carcass, severing a joint and tearing at the soft, tender meat. It was sweet and succulent, tinged with rosemary and basil, and for a few moments he allowed himself the luxury of tasting, of savouring, of abandoning himself to the pure need of his body. But even as he did so, his eyes with long habit scoured the room for the two he sought.

Sir Victor was propped against a fireplace, half hidden by a fawning woman. Hugh noted the new doublet he wore, brown velvet trimmed with gold and fox fur. Edward lolled in a chair not far from his father, two young girls and a pretty boy sitting at his feet. Hugh felt the food harden like a knot in his throat. Bethan. It was as though she had never existed for them, and his anger, like a wave, rose. His hand itched for his sword and the outlet such a surge of physical rage would give him, but then he wanted to laugh at his own impulsiveness—as if he were a hot-headed youth and the wine had flooded his brain. His head went back in silent frustration; he had no proof.

'As you will see, I have been very thorough.' The Earl sank into one of the soft chairs by the fire. He and Hugh had eventually retired to his room, but he had no intention of talking at length, deeming it enough that Hugh should have access to the papers he had prepared so that they could meet in the morning. 'I am weary,' he said firmly, 'and in any event you are far more likely to be able to make sense of my estimates than I am at this stage.' He lifted his half-closed eyes from the flames to look into Hugh's face. 'The sooner we find an answer, the sooner I can leave this Godforsaken place.'

'And the sooner I can, my lord,' Hugh replied, looking into his thin, deeply-lined face. He had a reputation for ruthlessness, but that was usually tempered with justice. Yet he could be cruel, even vicious, with those who crossed him.

'I am glad our minds run along the same lines.' A small smile tipped the edges of his mouth as he turned his face back to the fire. 'Now leave me. I need to rest.'

Hugh read until his eyes grew sore, until the black of the night sky had begun to fade into pale purples and blues as dawn approached. Finally he put all the papers down and moved wearily across the room to kindle the dying fire. He crouched close to the shrunken flames, watching the embers spark and fly, and he wondered for the hundredth time where she could be. Her aunt would be waiting for some word, but he had no word to give her; he knew that the longer she was missing, the less chance they would have of finding her alive. The fire was ablaze now, and he stretched to a standing position. There was enough evidence in the report the Earl had documented to make Sir Victor's sudden displays of wealth a cause for suspicion. True, he had sold off several parcels of land in recent times, but everything pointed to this revenue having been used to pay off outstanding debts, not to refurbish himself and his great house so lavishly, and also to provide huge quantities of food and entertainment for an entourage of over fifty people.

Bethan must have stumbled upon something it would have been better for her not to know—that was clear, but would anyone dare to harm her? And where could they hide her in safety and without discovery—if she still lived? But he knew she still lived; a gnawing certainty told him that there was no doubt. He splashed freezing water over his face and returned his thoughts to Courtenay. The house was huge, riven with a labyrinth of corridors and little-used passages. Such houses always had storehouses and privy chambers filled with nothing more than old, stale air, and maybe the odd ghost or two. An easy place to hide, or to hide someone... He smiled at his fancies, almost ready to cast them aside. Yet they made strange, irrational sense. His eyes narrowed slowly as his mind went through the possibilities. So easy, so simple, so perfect!

By sunrise, the ferocious cold seemed slightly muted at last so that people wondered if the freezing spell were drawing to a close. The sky was almost pure, except for a few stray tufts of cloud drifting lazily against the blue.

The Earl's retinue emerged slowly from their drunken slumbers to take breakfast, most of their heads aching from the previous night's feasting. They were anxious to take up Sir Victor's suggestion of a ride across his estate to cast any remaining cobwebs to the wind. Hugh had hoped to speak with the Earl before they left, but he could tell from the older man's sullen countenance that he was in no mood to speak with anyone. Impatiently he left the dining hall, frustrated at yet another delay. His eyes flickered across the cavernous hall and down the dark fingers of passages, but his brooding thoughts were abruptly interrupted by Sir Victor's anxious steward.

'Lady Matilda Astwood has just arrived, sir, and wishes to speak with you.'

Hugh sighed. He had no news, nothing that could allay her fears, and as the gentle sound of a rustling gown approached, he wondered what to say to her.

'I know you have not found her, sir, but I could not sit alone waiting, waiting, a moment longer...' Matilda stood uncertainly in the doorway, and her voice shook as she tried to retain her composure.

'I am sure we shall have news soon, my lady.' God in heaven, he hoped so!

'But where can my girl be? She cannot have vanished into thin air!' She lifted her eyes from the moving knot of her hands to his face, and he saw the anguished tears waiting to fall.

'Please, my lady, you should sit down, and I shall get you some warm wine.' It was small comfort, he knew, but he had nothing more to give.

'What is this, sir?' The Earl of Somerset's voice came sharply from the bottom of the staircase.

With relief Hugh turned to the man who now held such power over this whole business. 'Lady Matilda Astwood, my lord. Her niece Bethan is the girl who is missing.'

Immediately the Earl's face softened, and he moved over to the woman, who was endeavouring to stand. 'No, please stay seated,' he said gently. 'I think very soon we shall have some news of your niece, and I shall deliver it to you myself.' He paused. 'You have my word.' He turned back to the dining hall, where Sir Victor was hovering. 'You will ensure that this lady receives refreshment, and sufficient escort when she is ready to return home.'

'Of course, sir. The Lady Matilda is like my own.'

'I trust that goes for her niece, too, Sir Victor...' the Earl remarked and swept past his host. 'I understand that your son intends to marry the young lady in question, yet one could hardly say that he is very concerned at her mysterious and worrying absence—indeed, he seems to be enjoying himself greatly!'

For a moment Sir Victor's mouth hung open in surprise at the Earl's barbed comment, but then his eyes grew dark with anger at the slight, and the cause of it, and he moved over to his son, who still seemed half-dazed from the previous night's revelry as he languished in a chair. The wretched boy must not ride with them!

He would have to stay at Courtenay, well out of the way of the Earl's sharp eye!

The air whipped their faces red and their breaths came white as fog as the group lingered on a small hillock overlooking Sir Victor's lands.

'Rich soil, sir,' the Earl said as his eyes scanned the nearby meadows and gentle slopes. 'Such soil must yield much revenue for you,' he continued.

'In good years, very much, my lord,' Sir Victor replied proudly.

'You have sold a good deal of it in recent times—not a wise thing to do, I would have thought? But I have no head for such concerns.'

Hugh pressed down a smile at Somerset's apparently innocent remark, but he was not deceived—and neither was Sir Victor, if the sudden absence of colour in his cheeks was anything to go by.

'I have an impulsive streak, my lord, and indeed was foolish enough to grant the villagers some more land at my own expense when times were particularly hard...'

It was a sweet lie and almost true, except that he omitted to add that he had increased their rents almost twofold. Hugh laughed silently. Sir Victor could not know that everything had been written down, each tiny detail, and that the evidence was lying in one of his own guests' bedchambers.

Somerset did not respond, but stared at the land that stretched out before them, almost as though he were seeing a private vision. 'We must increase our efforts to find the missing girl,' he said at last, and turned his face back to Hugh, glancing briefly at Sir Victor. 'It is not enough that the forest, copses and deserted buildings have been searched. Now we must be truly thorough, and turn to less obvious places.'

'What do you mean, my lord?' Sir Victor asked. He felt uneasy, for something in the tone of the Earl's words made him wary. Surely there was no way he could know anything—there was no evidence, no finger to point at *him*.

'Perhaps the girl is shut in accidentally somewhere— or perhaps, more likely, the culprits are members of a nearby household. Most great houses have rooms that are never used, that have probably been locked and bolted for years.' He again stared out at the distant white horizon. 'When we return, Hugh, you will initially instruct your men to begin their searches at Astwood House and Courtenay Manor.' Before Sir Victor could respond with the expected outraged surprise, Somerset spoke again. 'I know you will bear with me in this fancy of mine, Sir Victor, as I am aware that you are as anxious as I to see an end to this tiresome business.'

'Of course, my lord.' There was only a moment's hesitation in his voice before he replied, because he knew he had no choice. Did they suspect? They must! He swallowed hard as though he would choke, and fear softly touched his spine.

The quiet that followed was broken only by the whistling rush of unbridled wind and the impatient, lusty breaths of the horses anxious to be gone. The party moved off down the slope towards a branch of the river, and Hugh remembered that a small distance from the far bank, only a few days ago, the boy Walter had been killed. He would never forget her face—white and stunned, her lovely features etched with pain as though she were the one who had been mortally wounded. He had tried to keep her memory at bay, but always effortlessly her face slid into his mind. The last time they had met she had pushed him away as though his touch burned her, and even now that memory still tormented him. But he had not learned, because he still wanted her.

Somerset led the ragged line of riders across a narrow stone bridge and on to a rough track bordering a deep expanse of trees. Hugh hung back, letting each horse pass him, noting that Sir Victor dawdled at the rear, talking intently with his young servant. He frowned as that same servant turned his horse back across the bridge to retrace the path along which they had come. Hugh moved further into the trees so that he could not be seen from the track and waited until Sir Victor rode past him, just as he knew he would, waited until the one-time courtier of the King had disappeared from sight.

It was easy to follow the young lad who had left the group so promptly at his master's bidding. The black snow-crushed holes he left in his wake would not matter in the least, as he was merely going to the Convent of St Agnes to give a message to Friar Anselm, one of the poor fathers who had been made homeless by the burning of the abbey. He assumed that the strangely worded message related to a service Sir Victor wished to have said for his guests, but he did not understand the urgency his master insisted upon.

Hugh was careful to keep within the shadows of the sharp, leafless woods. His heart pounded excitedly with anticipation, for he could almost smell the closing-in of the hunt—every instinct told him so. He had known that, sooner or later, something would prove him either right or wrong, and now let him be right, please God!

The Convent of St Agnes nestled in the curve of a hill, surrounded by carefully tended gardens and fruit and vegetable plots now paralysed by the cold. Hugh hung back, waiting patiently beneath the shelter of some trees as the boy tethered his horse and ran into the ancient building. His patience was rewarded when one of the abbey friars appeared, outlined in the black frame of the arch. But Hugh's eyes narrowed in puzzlement as the figure swiftly mounted the horse that the boy had obviously relinquished to him, yet he did not hesitate when the friar urged the horse away from the convent. He followed, but this time with even more care, because he was deeply disturbed by this unexpected turn of events. Had he judged wrong? Did Sir Victor plan to woo the Earl by a special service drawing attention to his pretended piety? He cast the thought aside as ridiculous. Then why the haste? None of it seemed to make sense, none of it seemed to fit into the pattern he had woven in his mind. But while he followed this 'good friar', he was surprised at the man's stealthy care and local knowledge as he moved with ease through lesser-known paths. A sure blade of suspicion began to slide into Hugh's soul, a chilling furtive fear that wrapped icy fingers round his heart. He thought again of Bethan,

and was suddenly and irrevocably afraid that he would
be too late.

The Earl of Somerset had grown weary and cold. Sir
Victor had insisted on them examining the whole of his
estate, but it seemed that several times he had taken a
wrong turning, losing at the same time some of their
group, and they were forced to double back until they
were reformed. Inevitably he began to wonder at his
host's overdone enthusiasm, wondered why he was so
anxious to keep them from returning to Courtenay too
soon. His face was red-blue with cold, his hands stiff
and uncomfortable as they held the reins of his tired
horse. There seemed to be only one explanation. Much
earlier he had noticed Hugh's absence but had deliberately not voiced his curiosity, and he had also noticed
Sir Victor's tense face once he, too, realised that the
King's man was no longer with them—he had said
nothing.

'We shall return home now, Sir Victor,' the Earl said
finally and firmly. He had had enough of the Courtenay
lands! 'We shall take the shortest route to the house . . . I
want no wrong turnings, or back-tracking.'

Sir Victor lowered his eyes, beaten down by the Earl's
gaze, but then they shifted in the direction of his home
and he was a little comforted: it would be a while before
they would see the house through the thinning trees, and
surely he had played for enough time, surely he had done
enough? He sighed silently, his heart pounding in anticipation of the future he had so carefully carved for
himself. Nothing could go wrong now! He had risked

too much, done too much, to go back. A sudden shrieking scattering of some crows broke into his uneasy thoughts, their harsh cries searing the air as they flew out into the darkening sky.

Hugh had lost him. The friar had disappeared as though the forest had swallowed him, and he wasted precious time going back the way he had come, taking unlikely paths in an effort to find the man he was following. Eventually he took the most obvious one, that led in the direction of Courtenay Manor. Sure enough, when he reached the perimeter of the trees, there were the recent prints of a horse. For a moment he paused, scouring the sudden sweeping white flatness, but the rider had come and gone. Hugh urged his horse into a gallop so that the snow ghosted up in tiny blizzards as they rode. He realised, as he neared Courtenay lands, that the approach was quite different from any he had taken before, that it would ultimately take him to the rear of the manor. A ribbon of half-frozen water wound raggedly before him, and he crossed in the shallows, praying that his horse would not slip or falter. Then he saw the house, starkly beautiful against the backdrop of trees, saw a riderless horse tied carefully behind the stables, its drooping head and glistening coat proof of the merciless ride it had endured.

Hugh approached warily, but still sure that the friar had no knowledge of his presence. The great iron padlock was rusty and warped with age, so that only the arched doorway into the chapel was within easy reach. Where else would a friar go? But the door was bolted from the inside. He rested his ear against the stout wood, but no sound broke the quiet that seemed to have fallen so ominously. He ran, then, instinctively, his feet sliding on the icy ground, his heart hammering painfully. And he saw her again, that sweet knowing look of bruised regret making a great choking gather in his throat.

His fists pounded on the great doors of the house, and when at last Sir Victor's steward opened up, he pushed him roughly aside so that he cried out in alarm, and the sound brought Edward running. At the sight of the boy who had constantly irritated him and who, he was sure, knew far more than he would say, Hugh's face pulled into a mask of frustrated anger, and Edward stepped back, suddenly terribly afraid.

'Where is she?' His hands reached out for the soft fur curling at the apex of Edward's doublet, and he drew it tight so that the squealing youth was lifted from the flagstones. 'You had better tell me, you young sop, or I swear to God that I shall kill you!'

'I don't know what you mean—I know nothing, nothing!' he pleaded.

'Nothing? Nothing?' Hugh spat out the words so that Edward felt each one was almost a blow, and he thought he would die from the trembling fear that coursed through him.

'Are you deaf, boy, or did you not hear that I shall kill you? Be sure that I do not jest!'

'Please, sir—please! I have done nothing!' Even as the words stammered from his mouth, he knew that he played for time. And he wanted to run, to hide, like a little boy.

'If you use that word once more, I shall throttle the breath from your lungs and find her myself, because I am sure she is here!' Hugh's lips drew into a thin, bitter smile. 'I followed your friar; I followed him all the way to the chapel. If you do not show me the way, I shall find it myself, and be assured that if one hair on her lovely head has been harmed, you will wish you had never been born!'

'She lives! She lives!' he screamed, as he felt Hugh's fingers bite deep into the shallow hollows of his neck, terror making his voice rise, unheeded, to rend the silence of the household.

Matilda suddenly appeared from the parlour, where she had been trying to rest until she returned home. 'Stop this, stop this! What do you do? Stop! Stop at once!' She was shocked, utterly shaken, and her hands rose to her cheeks in bewilderment and confusion.

'Tell him to take me to your niece, my lady.' Hugh's voice came low, full of warning.

'My niece—my Bethan?' Matilda's troubled face moved from the face of the King's man to the young man she had known since a babe. 'You know where my dear girl is?' Her voice was almost a whisper, and her tense features contorted in disbelief as realisation began to filter through her weary brain. She closed her eyes in an attempt to shut out the painful vision that now faced her. And it was true: the guilt was painted in chilling clarity on his young face. 'Take us to her, Edward. If you have ever cared for me at all, you will do this one last thing.'

Her desolate gaze beat him down, and tears sprang into his eyes as shame and guilt at last poured into his soul. 'Yes! Yes—of course.' His voice came meek and soft. Like a child's.

The outer door was closed, but unlocked, and the inner one swung open to waft freezing damp air from the crypt into their faces as they stood at the top of the moss-covered steps. The stairs coiled down into darkness, and Hugh pushed the reluctant boy ahead of him as he bade Matilda wait by the door. It was only as they neared the bottom steps that he heard the thin, sad whimpering, and for a moment he could not see, but a shaft of light pierced the gloom from high up in a far wall. The cold was ferocious, and Hugh felt a shiver run down his spine. But it was not only from the cold. The friar's gaunt, spectral figure was outlined by the fragile light as he stood over a crouching form in the furthest corner. Disgust, anger and a terrible desire for vengeance welled up in him as he realised what the man was about to do. Pushing Edward to one side, he reached for his sword almost automatically, and the chilling sound as it cut through the icy air made the cowled figure turn, his face nearly invisible in the shadow.

Friar Anselm's fingers tightened round the knife; only his stealth could save him now! For a strange, fleeting second it was like the abbey fire all over again as he recalled the old man, Dominic, who had seen the tell-tale torch in his hand, saw the guilt in his eyes. He had had no choice but to kill him, just as he had no choice but to kill the girl—and this man.

But Hugh was not an unsuspecting old man or a defenceless girl, and he saw the intent of the figure before him with ease, saw how a sliver of light from the grille settled on the blade of his knife as he brought it out from the recess of his sleeve. And, in response, his sword came up with deadly accuracy, burying itself deep in Anselm's heart. The body crumpled to the floor with hardly a protest, and for a moment Hugh could hear only the harsh, frantic sound of his own breathing as his eyes fell on her mute form.

Bethan was curled up against the saturated walls, and he did not know whether she was alive. He was afraid to move, afraid to touch the soft, lovely hand that might lie like a dead thing in his palm.

'Bethan...' His voice was gentle, almost pleading, as he took a step towards her. 'Bethan?' He knelt beside her then, his great arms lifting her away from the flagstones to lie, so still, against his chest. The feeble light from the tiny grille fell across her face and he saw the delicate velvet of her lashes tremble, saw the slightly parted lips shudder as though all hope had fled. 'We go home now, my sweet...' he whispered. 'Home—where no harm can come to you.' He brought his lips down to her own, full of warm, tender longing, as if to breathe strength into this Bethan, who was like a pale shadow of the lovely creature he had known.

Edward stood by the bottom of the stairs, his head bowed, cowed and frightened.

'Get out of my way! And it were better for you that *I* carry this maiden you said you loved so well! Otherwise, sir, my hands would be freed and I would beat your pitiful brains against the stones of the wall until they poured out on to the flagstones...'

Matilda had ventured down the steps, appalled and terrified at the sounds she had heard, and a sob caught in her throat as she saw the thin, ashen face of her niece. It seemed to her at that moment that her girl was hardly alive. Hugh saw her fear and shared her anguish, but chose his words carefully, knowing that she would need all her strength for the care of this girl who was all she had in the world.

'She is starved, madam, and frozen, but I do not think she is injured. With care, I am sure she will recover.' He hoped to God his words sounded more convincing to her than they did to him, and for a fleeting second he allowed his eyes to rest on the fragile form he held so lightly in his arms. Like a flimsy spring flower whose delicate life is all too short.

In their confusion and anxiety to save Bethan, no one was instructed to bind Edward, there was no staying hand to ensure that he did not evade his punishment. Instead, he ran, taking one of his father's sturdiest horses. He had no idea where he would go, except that he knew with a sinking heart that he would have to leave England. Nowhere could he hide while Hugh D'Savoury lived and while he himself could still be brought to trial as a traitor to his King. The grisly death of a traitor was something he dared not allow himself to think of, and he found it difficult to draw breath; he had seen some men executed for far less than he had done! Angry, resentful tears filled his eyes. But he had only been a pawn in the game! Even as his bitter thoughts stung him, he recalled the

Carthusian monks he had seen only last spring, who had suffered a traitor's death for incurring the King's wrath— their inhuman sufferings had not been checked by the hangman's hand, his work only finished when the bodies were slit open, their bowels drawn out and burned. Edward shuddered as he remembered how the ghoulish makers of charms and potions had crowded round the mutilated corpses, the blood not yet dried on the scaffold, to gather it into vessels for safe keeping. He closed his eyes to banish the ghastly visions. He would head for the Devon road—to Barnstaple, and a ship; he had a little money, and some jewels from his father's hoard. For a fleeting moment he was touched by shame, but then he cast it aside as he thought of his own safety. Suddenly the small leather pouch that lay in the pocket of his doublet seemed strangely heavy, weighted like a burden, and he thought of a golden chain and a gilded fish with ruby eyes, and longed to weep.

Bethan felt the unbelievable luxury of warmth and softness around her, heard the crooning, loving voice of her aunt as she stroked her brow. It was over, and yet she was almost afraid to open her eyes in case this wonderful dream suddenly turned into the nightmare she had endured for days too long and hideous to think of. But then warm, sweet wine touched her lips and slipped delightfully on to her tongue, and her eyelids slowly opened.

'Oh, child! Oh, my darling Bethan, I thought you were lost to me...' Matilda started to weep, pulling her niece softly against her.

It was truly over, and Bethan drowned in the blessed scent of the lavender her aunt always wore and which reminded her of all she thought she had lost. But gently and reluctantly Matilda released her, knowing that she should rest, and knowing also that the King's man waited patiently outside in order to question her. She sighed heavily, realising that the interview must be completed very soon, before the Earl's party and Sir Victor returned from overseeing the estate. Disbelief still lay heavy on her heart. *He* had planned to let her Bethan die, alone and afraid, but even that in the end had not proved enough, because she would have been found too soon. Therefore he had arranged for that unholy friar to murder her... Matilda pulled the silken coverlet up about her arms with trembling hands. So cruel! So wicked! And she thought she knew him—this man who had been both neighbour and friend for as long as she could remember. Shaking her head in sad bewilderment, she moved to the door and to the man who waited on the other side.

Bethan lay like a soft, waking dream; hair billowing across the milky white of the pillow—the face so pale, like the colour of a pearl-drop. Her fragile loveliness unmanned him, and he fell silent, his thoughts in turmoil as the past, the present and the future mingled to taunt him with their possibilities. But then her eyes opened gently and with an obvious effort, as though she had sensed his gaze.

'Hugh...' She smiled tiredly, as his name slipped so easily from her mouth.

She disarmed him; she was his weakness. And the realisation stung him, frightened him, that one person could mean so much—so many things. He tried to govern the chaotic, whirling emotions that made his heart hammer like a mad thing, as her pretty lips parted and he saw the fine whiteness of her teeth, the way she caught a breath so that her lovely young breast rose and fell. And he swallowed, painfully, in the depths of his throat.

'He would have killed me, Hugh...' The smile had gone, and there was only fear in her face as memory seized her. 'I know too much now...' Her voice seemed to die, and the desolate shadow that fled across her face made his heart lurch.

'Who, my Bethan, who?' But he already knew the answer.

The grey eyes grew dark, widening, in panic. 'Sir Victor. He will find another way to silence me. He has no choice, don't you see?' Her hands gripped the coverlet in slow, twisting pain.

'Never, never! Not now, my love,' he said, carefully choosing each word. 'We all know too much, and it is now *his* turn to be afraid.'

For a moment he wondered whether she had heard him, but then the white hands loosened their grip and her heavy lids fell with weary relief over her eyes. But when they flickered open again, quickly, to touch his own, he could not look away. Then she was in his arms, his hands coming to take her head between them so that his mouth could caress, drink, sup all that he had craved, but had denied himself. For long, timeless moments he thought he might drown, and gladly, in the heady rose-sweet perfume of her. His fingers wove themselves into her hair, coiling the rich, heavy locks about his hands so that he drew her head back to rain kisses on her slim neck. Her silky skin tormented him, but he felt the intrusion of bone, only thinly covered, that told its own story, and his touch suddenly became tender. She was not ready for him yet, not for all the hoarded passion he had for so long withheld, and he closed his eyes in frustration, begging for control. As he gently released her, he heard the soft thunder of horses and the muted voices of men carried by the wind. They were returning at last! He placed her head carefully back on the pillow, bringing the coverlet up to conceal all that only moments before he could so easily have taken.

Bethan felt his lips touch her forehead, exquisitely soft, as though she were some precious jewel, and she wondered how such tenderness could come out of one so hard and ruthless. She sighed wistfully and with longing as she watched him walk to the door and then close it softly behind him. All she could do was to stare at the space in the air where he had stood, to relive the searing touch of him, because he had made her body sing, and the song was wild and beautiful, yearning, like the trembling heart of a captive bird.

Hugh was impassive, expressionless, as he needlessly instructed Bethan's aunt to stay with her. In the end he had asked her no questions, for there was little that he did not know already. It had just been an excuse, a reason to assure the gnawing doubt within him that she would recover. He smiled then, a small derisive smile—and had he not wanted to touch her, to hold her against him once more? Well, he had had his wish, and now he felt trapped by an emotion that he thought he was no longer capable of feeling. With just one glance she seemed able to strip him of his cynical indifference, to awaken a softness in him that he had learned to submerge. He did not want to need her touch, did not want to hear that voice which stung him with such desire—did not want to love her! Hugh drew a sharp breath, biting his lip in exasperation, tasting blood. But then a door slammed far below, telling him that the others had returned, that he would face Sir Victor at last. The moment was gone.

All without exception had moved into the warmth and comfort of the dining hall, where yet another huge table had been set in readiness. By the time Hugh walked in, many were already seated. One of his men stood near the door, and immediately he was instructed to arrange a party to go after Edward; the boy had a head start, but his own men were better riders, and better hunters! After they had gone, he reached for a jug of ale and poured himself a long draught, draining the tankard in one thirst-quenching swallow. It gave him a moment's respite before making another move.

Somerset stood with Sir Victor next to the fire, his face a mask of irritability, but suddenly his gaze shifted and came to rest on Hugh. 'You deserted us, sir.' His eyes narrowed slightly. 'Perhaps you would like to tell us why?'

'I was bored, my lord, weary of the chase.' Sir Victor's eyes were on him. 'I thought my time would be better

spent in following that other member of our group, who
had left us with such haste.'

'Who was this?' the Earl said carefully, realising that
Hugh was not mouthing polite nothings.

'Why not ask our host, my lord? He has answers to
many things that we do not.'

Somerset turned slowly to the man who stood so
silently just behind him. 'Well, sir, who was this other
member, and why did he leave us?'

Two pinpoints of red stood out on Sir Victor's scarred
cheeks, but otherwise his face was white, ashen. 'A
servant, my lord. Merely a servant whom I sent on an
errand,' he replied evenly, but his heart began to race.

'Could it not have waited?' the Earl persisted.

'That did not occur to me at the time... As far as
your lordship's comfort and welfare are concerned while
you are in my home, nothing should wait, nothing should
be imperfect.'

Somerset stared and then smiled, but the smile was
humourless. How many times since his rise to power had
he heard such sweet, lilting words thinly disguising the
avarice and corruptness beneath. 'A pretty speech, sir,
but I am still waiting for the reason for this errand.'

'To the convent of St Agnes, my lord, to bring one
of the homeless friars to Courtenay. There was a special
service I wished to have said, and the arrangements
needed to be discussed.' He heard the slight tremor in
his own words... How much did that damned King's
man know?

Hugh sighed silently. So this would be his story, but
it was flimsy nonsense, as well he knew!

'Is this true, Hugh?' Somerset asked quietly.

'Oh—up to a point, my lord. Up to the point where I found the friar's horse standing exhausted at the rear of the house—up to the point where I caught that same friar about to murder the Lady Elizabeth Astwood...' Anger and disgust welled anew in his heart as he remembered again, as he saw the man before him stiffen and the wine in his cup shiver as his grip loosened, and he stepped back, away from the men whose eyes now gazed at him with open hostility and distaste.

'You lie, sir! This is some trick to put the blame for the burning of the abbey on me!'

'But I have not mentioned the burning of the abbey, Sir Victor.'

Betrayed out of his own mouth! Fool! Fool! Just as he had betrayed himself the first time over the Bullen whore. And he saw his sweet, glittering dream of reinstatement begin to fade and die.

'Why not ask your son?' The question broke in on his bitter reverie. 'He showed me where she was imprisoned. Except that no doubt he is many miles from here by now. However, my men at this very moment are in pursuit, so we only have a little time to wait.' Hugh paused for a moment, as if he expected Sir Victor to interrupt, but his host seemed beyond words. 'Or, of course, there is the Lady Elizabeth, who is anxious to tell my lord of Somerset all that she has told me.' Not quite true, but he could see from the man's stricken countenance that his arrow had struck home. 'It was only a matter of time before your little plan was revealed,' he continued. 'Eventually everything led back to Courtenay Manor and the vague hints that did not make much sense at first, but then your sudden arrogant displays of wealth, the impatient killing of that boy by your own hand—even the path of Bethan's disappearance led in this direction. Sweet Jesus, you must think us all fools!' His words were laced with contempt. 'And do you also think that, even in such a country backwater, the King's all-powerful, all-seeing hand does not reach?'

'Enough, Hugh.' Somerset touched his arm in an effort to cool his temper and bring some order to the uneasy gathering. 'Well, Sir Victor, have you anything to say in your defence?'

'Lies, all lies! He has never liked me, not from the first!' The words rushed and stammered from his mouth as he grasped at frail, empty straws. 'Jealous—jealous of my position and wealth! He had planned it all from the very beginning...' But he knew they knew that he lied, and he wondered why he was still endeavouring to fight.

'That is something the court will decide,' the Earl said finally.

'No—NO!' Sir Victor stumbled back, appalled. It was over; his so-carefully-laid plan was over, and the realisation was terrifyingly shocking. He felt his foot touch the curb of the hearth, and in one swift movement he grasped a burning log that protruded, and proceeded to brandish it in front of them so that none could get close.

'Do you think I shall let you take me—like a lamb to the slaughter? Do you think I would allow myself to suffer a traitor's death—because, let us not deceive ourselves any longer, you and I both know that would happen! There would be no mercy for one who tampers with the King's bounty, no mercy for one so uncivilly cast out from his service because of that stewed whore, Bullen! I pray God that the unholy bitch reaches the scaffold before me!'

The whole room had grown still, waiting. Sir Victor's shrill protest rose into the great vaulted ceiling as he swung the burning torch from side to side. Hugh made a wary step towards him, and was thrust back immediately.

'Oh no, sir—you do not reach me so easily...'

He was greatly outnumbered, alone, and in his panic his eyes darted in every direction and then longingly at the beckoning door, which now seemed so unreachable. There was nothing he could do, and he would not even be allowed to die fighting because they would ensure that he stayed alive long enough to face his accusers, long enough to endure the hangman's skilful hands. They were beginning to circle him. All at once he sighed heavily, wearily, and the small noise was like a sob. With an anguished, frantic cry he stepped back and let the torch touch a great tapestry that covered almost the whole length of one wall. The flames leapt from the burning wood and ran greedily up. The tapestry was old, stiff with the grime of ages, so that it burned with frightening ease, the blurred, once fine colours now given new life by the garish flames. Tongues of fire soared into the ceiling, licking at the ancient beams until they began to glow red and smoke. A woman screamed, and the scream was like a signal to the assembled company, who began to move in a great heaving mass to the open doors. Hugh stood his ground next to the Earl, sure that at any moment Sir Victor would run, but as precious seconds passed and the fire took irrevocable hold, they backed away from the ferocious breath of heat on their faces. Once they reached the doors Hugh paused, his eyes resting on the man now crouching in a far corner, the torch still held in his hand, his face blank and empty as though he did not see the flames, did not see the walls of his proud home begin to blister before his eyes. A beam cracked and groaned, sending sparks showering down upon the room, then the trestle tables caught, and several stools were alight. The flames danced wildly across the ceiling and down the heavy draperies against the windows. For a moment he could no longer see Sir Victor but only a wall of fire, then the wall crumpled before gathering strength again, and he thought he saw a figure of a man, like a grotesque dancing doll, burning, burning.

The doors of the once magnificent dining hall were closed in an effort to keep the fire confined, but most knew that it would serve only to give them more time to get themselves and their belongings to safety. Hugh groaned as he thought of Bethan lying so weak in the room above. She would have to be moved immediately, as they all would. He sighed at the waste of it all, re-alising that Courtenay Manor would burn well, that it would die as surely as its master had.

Matilda almost echoed his words, as she came running out of the room in which Bethan lay. 'It is such a waste—all such a waste! So needless...' She clutched his arm for reassurance as he came into the bedchamber. He lifted the drowsing girl into his arms and was relieved to see she was wrapped warmly in a rug. 'I have given her a sleeping-draught so that she will not, with luck, know any of this,' Matilda continued, pulling the heavy material around her niece's face. 'And, pray God, the snow will hold off until we get to new shelter.'

Hugh drew an anxious, impatient breath as he saw smoke already rising between the cracks in the floor-boards. Let them all reach the open air before they were overcome by smoke! By the time they found their way to the main doors, the upper floor was already alight, and most people had found their way out into the grounds. They gathered wearily on the gravelled path; furniture, paintings and any remnants from rooms and galleries piled haphazardly about, and for long moments they stood watching embers from the flames rise like black snowflakes into the sky, watching as beams screamed and crumpled and great tongues of fire leapt and clutched wildly at the chill, empty air.

'So needless,' Aunt Matilda repeated sadly as she stared at the dying building, but then she turned to Bethan, who had been placed carefully in an up-holstered cart. She turned to Hugh, whose horse stood impatiently beside them, her eyes filled with tears. 'He was not always a bad man, you know... Life had been unkind to him, and bitterness eaten into his soul.' She lowered her eyes, a thousand memories making her old heart ache.

Hugh smiled gently in understanding, knowing that Matilda would never believe that anyone could ever be truly evil: there must be a good reason somewhere, somehow, behind their wickedness! Then the thunderous roar of a great crash startled his horse; a huge crack had appeared down the front wall, sending the ugly magnificence of the 'Courtenay Heads' to smash on the stone below. The crack widened like an evil grin, and he could see into the heart of the burning manor, like hellfire—of which Sir Victor himself had lit the first avid flame.

CHAPTER NINE

AFTER SOME discussion, it was agreed that they would all go to stay at Astwood House. Although not as large as Courtenay, it would do well enough until the Earl and his retinue left for his home on the outskirts of Bristol.

Once Bethan was safely home, she seemed to grow stronger each day as her aunt plied her with good meaty broth and creamy milk, and ensured that she had plenty of rest. At last she was allowed to leave her bed the day before the Earl planned to leave, when a banquet was to be held in his honour. The dress she and her aunt had chosen for her to wear for the evening lay across the coverlet of her bed—a velvet burgundy with a braiding of gold. She ran her fingers along the exquisite material and then turned to stare out of the window at the lands which seemed to stretch far into the horizon. A thaw had set in, and the snow was melting at last, with the trees dripping water, and white sunshine as the afternoon faded. Her breath trembled as she thought of the evening to come. Not once since they had returned to Astwood had she seen Hugh, and she closed her eyes in frustration. Surely she had not imagined that intense look of desire—of love?—in his eyes. Yet she had been sick, utterly weakened, so perhaps it had all been but a sweet dream . . . Her head went back in silent agony as she remembered how Hugh had touched her with such tenderness. Even speaking his name made her heart lurch. But somehow all the recent past seemed hazy, and much of it she would rather forget. Edward's betrayal was perhaps the worst of all, except that a shadow of guilt made her blush, even now. She tensed, remembering how she had rejected him and wondered again whether her own betrayal had been his undoing. Yet all the events connected with the abbey had started even before Hugh D'Savoury had come into her life, and had she not tried from the very beginning to deny all the furtive feelings that had soared so strongly into her heart? She drew a deep, angry breath. Why was nothing ever straightforward? On the morrow, she could only assume, Hugh would return to London, since there was no reason for him to stay. Except herself. But he had shown quite clearly by his absence that she meant nothing to him. She could only think of the few fleeting times there had been closeness between them, and how, each one of those times, that closeness had gone inextricably wrong. Her lovely face creased into puzzled lines, and she leaned her head wearily against the cold stone of the window frame.

Matilda paced nervously along the long table she had arranged with such loving care. Brass candlesticks were set at required intervals, their gentle light resting invitingly on the food that had already been laid out. Apart from the two venison roasting before the hearth, she had ordered suckling pigs, a dozen plump chickens, two haunches of mutton, a great quantity of smoked fish and salted beef and six great bowls of steaming vegetable broth. Bread was stacked on side tables, as were the tarts, preserves and milk puddings she had prepared with her own hands. It had to suffice! God in heaven, her larders had almost been run dry with the demands of the Earl's household. She was thankful that they were leaving in the morning: enough was enough.

Then she sighed, thinking of her Bethan. She was well enough now, it was true, but her spirits were so low. They had talked at length about all that had happened. She had worried particularly that Edward's unspeakable behaviour might have broken Bethan's heart, but her niece had surprised her by saying that for some time she had known she no longer loved him. So what was it, then? Perhaps only the understandable results of her dreadful ordeal. No, there was more, and she did not want to think about it because there seemed to be no ready answer. It had been easy to see how the mention of Hugh D'Savoury brought a gleam to Bethan's eyes, how her cheeks would suddenly grow pink when she heard a horse come to the house, or the sound of a man's tread on the stair. He seemed not to return her niece's obvious love for him—and yet he was unusually silent, withdrawn, and he had been over nice to herself, as though he felt guilty for his lack of outward care for Bethan, and he had never failed to ask after her every day. Matilda shook her head, once more bewildered by a world that seemed to become more and more complicated.

It had not been like this in Old Queen Catherine's day, she was sure. The King was happy then, and his happiness seemed to filter through to his people. Was it her imagination, or did the long summers of those years she remembered so well seem so much more gentle—

warm and full of peace—and the winters somehow less harsh. Uneasy years had followed, and then Anne Bullen. In the little conversation she had had with the Earl of Somerset during his stay, he had implied that since miscarrying her son, the Queen had almost been ostracised by her husband, and that her enemies, of whom there were many, were saying that her witchery had lost its hold on the King at last. Matilda crossed herself nervously. She had often heard the evil rumour that the King had been seduced by witchcraft—was the stunted sixth finger on Anne's left hand not a sure sign of sorcery? She drew in a sharp, fearful breath, and then swiftly chided herself for her fancies. Anne Bullen was merely a greedy, ambitious woman, and the King a man desperate for an heir—and now, no doubt, a new wife to give him such an heir.

She thought of Bethan then, and how, if things had gone as planned, they would have been making preparations for her marriage to Edward Courtenay. But Edward had gone. They had failed to apprehend him, and in her heart she was glad, for he had lost everything he had ever had in the world and would find fending for himself in a foreign land punishment enough. He could never return to England, and the Earl would see that the Courtenay lands were brought under the crown. So what would become of her lovely niece now? Once the Earl and his retinue had left, they would be on their own again, only more so, because now there was no Edward, no Sir Victor, to call on or to invite for visits. Matilda clenched her fists, rebelling against the inconsistencies of fate. She was old, and Bethan's future would be assured if anything happened to herself, but now all had changed. Well, her sweet niece *would* have a husband, and one of her own choosing! She lifted her head with a touch of defiance as she heard Hugh's deep authoritative voice in the hall. Some men did not know what was good for them, refusing to listen to their hearts—all they needed was a little help, a little push in the right direction! She smiled, a soft, secretive smile that made her old cheeks glow as though she were a young girl again.

The murmur of their voices rose into the rooms above, and Bethan tried to stay a shaking hand as she fastened a pearl collar about her neck. Her hair hung loose beneath a Juliet cap embroidered with seed-pearls and beryls. She was ready now, but torn between wanting to stay and wanting to go. If he had no desire to see her, she had no desire to see him! But she caught an impatient breath, knowing that she wanted to see him more than anything else, but also knowing that that would not be enough. She lifted her chin proudly and moved towards the door of her bedchamber, vowing silently that she would not let him see the want that gnawed at her and that made her heart leap wildly in childish hope at the very mention of his name.

A few men were lingering in the hall as she neared the bottom of the great staircase, and she was rewarded by murmurs of admiration as she passed. A lute-player was singing some bawdy song at the far end of the room, and after her days of confinement, the music and the noise of the company made her cheeks flush with delight. For a moment she stood framed in the doorway, allowing herself to take in the colourful scene.

Hugh had been waiting for her since the first of the retinue had entered the room. It had been a supreme effort to avoid that chamber on the first landing, knowing that she would have expected him to come— even out of politeness—but he could not do it; she could only distract him, destroy his purpose. He reached for another goblet of wine, needing its heady charms to blur his disturbing thoughts. And, after all, were there not many women in the world just as lovely, just as perfect, as Lady Elizabeth Astwood? As he brought the cup to his lips, his eyes strayed over its rim to the door, and there she stood, outlined by darkness and the glow of a teasing candle-flame. He drew a sharp, deep breath as once more her beauty stung him, and he wanted to laugh at himself, at the shallow words that had slid so easily into his brain because he could not imagine that any other woman could be as lovely or as tormentingly perfect as she. And she *was* a woman now—there seemed no trace of the girl he had known only a short time ago. It was as though all the heartache and pain she had endured over the past weeks had given her a glow of wisdom, had turned the rosebud into a rose. His eyes lingered on her form, on the proud, graceful way she moved into the room, the way every man turned to watch her pass.

'So this is the young lady who was saved from certain death!' Somerset's voice cut across Hugh's thoughts. 'My dear, I would raise an army and do the same all over again if I had known what beauty was at stake!' He pulled a cushioned chair out beside him and beckoned to her to sit. Matilda was on his other side, with Hugh beside her.

The Earl had drunk too much, and as Bethan settled next to him, Hugh could hear the wine-soaked slur in his voice praise her extravagantly, slavishly, and he was sickened as a blade of jealousy pierced him. He would have left then if he could, but this banquet was as much for him as for anyone else, and she would know—surely she would know—that he left because of her? He drank another mouthful, hardly tasting the wine as it slid down his throat and then turned to make sweet talk with Bethan's aunt—empty words that held no meaning, only sounds to fill the space between now and the end of the evening. But there would be speeches, comic japes and songs from the lute to pull at your heartstrings before it was over and it was fit for anyone to go to their bed.

Only Matilda was allowed that luxury, but before she rose from her seat to retire for the night, she touched Hugh gently on the arm and he saw that she smiled, a broad pretty smile that by the soft glow of candlelight seemed to repair all the deep lines around her mouth, so that for an instant he saw her almost as she must have been as a lovely young woman. Like Bethan.

'I must go to my bed, or I fear I shall never rise again! But before I do, I would deem it a favour if you allowed my niece to thank you personally for your courage and tenacity in finding her. You have been so busy that she was afraid there would be no time for such a meeting.'

He was glad that in the dim light she could not see the guilt flee across his face. 'There is no need, Lady

Matilda. I am just glad that she has come out of such an anxious time so well...' Liar, liar!

'No, sir, there is every need, and you will offend me greatly if you refuse.' She increased the pressure on his arm as if to add weight to her words, but there was no need. She knew she had left him with little choice, and was rewarded by the curt nod of his head in acquiescence. 'Good! Good, then that is settled—such a little thing to please an old woman.' He laughed silently, bitterly, knowing that his protest had been no protest at all. 'I think the parlour would be the best place for such an occasion, as we seem a little crowded here. Perhaps you would like to make your way there now.' Matilda held her breath, but without a word Hugh obeyed, rising and moving away from the table, walking slowly down the narrow space between the wall and the rest of the revellers, but he was hardly aware of them.

Matilda watched him leave, delighted that her little plan was working so well, and then turned innocently to her niece and the Earl as if to bid them goodnight. She could see at a glance that he was well gone in his cups.

'I am afraid my bed calls me, my lord, but I wonder if you could excuse my niece for a moment while she collects my crochet from the parlour where I left it this morning?' Somerset swayed slightly, and then gave what Matilda took to be a nod of assent. She saw Bethan's look of puzzlement. 'Yes, I know it is a little late, but it is only my bones that are tired, not my eyes,' she added stubbornly. 'I expect I shall be in my room by the time you return, so you may bring it to me there.'

In the parlour, the shadows were deep, long and stealthy. Hugh stood next to the fireplace, the whole of his powerful body shrouded in darkness. Only two candles had been lit, and their light was barely perceptible. Why had he allowed himself to be manipulated so easily into such a corner? He swallowed slowly, and tried vainly to make some sense out of his chaotic and ungovernable feelings. The door behind him was opened almost without a sound, and he turned slightly and saw her lovely head as she came into the room. For a moment she did not see him, and he allowed himself the luxury of watching her unguarded face, saw the pretty lines of puzzlement as she looked about the room, saw the gold from the firelight outline her perfect curves, which made him harden even as he lowered his eyes so that he would not be taunted any longer.

'Hugh?' Her eyes seemed to widen in fear, and he could almost believe that she had not expected him to be there, waiting for her. His gaze settled once more on her face and he saw how the full mouth was parted and still as if all speech had left her. 'I came to fetch my aunt's crochet, but . . . but it does not seem to be here.'

He wanted to laugh then. Did she think him such a simpleton? They had laid a trap, and he had been caught in it just as they had planned! Women were all the same with their little games and schemes to snare a husband, but he had thought Bethan to be different. A shadow of disappointment pierced him for a fleeting moment, but he cast it aside as sudden resentful anger surged.

'Come! Come now, Lady Elizabeth, surely you could have thought of a more original tale?' His lips pursed in a smile that was cold and brittle.

'I don't understand! What do you mean?' Her eyes searched his face, lost and full of confusion.

He sighed impatiently. 'Your games, madam! Silly women's games which would blind any normal man who does not use his wits.'

'I do not understand what games you are speaking of.' Her voice was still soft, still touched with confusion, and he saw that her lips quivered and parted, and he thought he saw a furtive smile tipping the edges of her mouth—wanton, totally, innocently wanton.

'These games, madam...'

She would play with him no longer, because he was not a man to play with! His hands reached out to her shoulders, pulling her roughly against him, his mouth was down to cover hers completely. His arms encircled her so that she could not escape, and slowly, effortlessly, his lips slipped tantalisingly to her neck, her shoulders, and his hands came up to bury themselves in her hair. There had been no more words; she had succumbed to his caress as though it were a spell, and he could feel no protest, only the quickening of her body at his touch, yielding to every practised loving art he had ever used. But there was ruthless vengeance in every kiss, every finger touch, and when he reached the bodice of her gown, he tore it from her shoulders.

He engulfed her. And she felt as though she were drowning, because he seemed to reach depths within her she never knew existed. She wanted to cry out to him that he should stop, but the words would not come, pressed down by soft torturing gasps of delight. But his tearing of her gown pierced the heady quiet that had lulled her so blindly, and she opened her eyes to look into his face. She shivered, seeing only blackness and cold deliberation in his eyes, and wondered if he had closed them once since he had pulled her so mercilessly against him. It was as if he had watched her from the very beginning—using only his hands, his body to seduce her; his mind, his love, remaining like a thing apart. She tried to struggle as he pushed her dress down—down, so that she stood almost naked before him. He seemed to see the sudden fear in her eyes then, but his caresses did not change into gentleness but became more demanding, as if he would flood her with his own lust. His mouth came to suckle so skilfully at her breasts that her head went back in silent torment as she tried weakly to push him away. She felt the sure stealthy path of his hands as they glided down to cup her buttocks and the rustle of her underskirt as it was lifted. God in heaven—no, no! Almost too late she sensed his fingers slide between her thighs and then the shocking, beautiful touch of him graze the plump moist core within. Her throat opened, and she gave a pleading animal-like sound of pure pleasure.

'You see, Bethan,' he murmured, 'this is what you wish, this is what you desire, just like all the others...'

His voice sounded very distant, as if it came from another world, but slowly his words came back, floating, penetrating, and a bitter realisation surged into her heart.

Suddenly and fiercely she pushed him away, so that he fell against the fireplace.

'You are a monster—a cruel, unfeeling monster!' She was trembling uncontrollably, and her hands shook as she lifted her soiled gown from the floor, pulling it up about her so that his eyes could no longer linger on her flesh.

'Come, you are not even honest, Lady Elizabeth! Did you not enjoy my touch? And were those sounds of pain and agony I heard coming from those full, ripe lips? No, I think not!'

His smile was cruel, mocking, and her hand seemed to come from nowhere to meet the broad handsome face, leaving a great red weal that danced in the candle-flame. He seemed to freeze for a moment, but his eyes said everything as they swept insolently over her.

'Goodnight, Lady Elizabeth.'

She bowed her head as he passed her, as he opened and closed the parlour door irrevocably behind him.

The Earl's retinue left just after dawn, but Bethan did not rise to see them off, pleading a sick headache. Matilda worried at her until she had grown unusually irritated and said that she wished to be left in peace. The hurt look on her aunt's face did nothing to help the great bruise that was herself. She had had virtually no sleep, and each time she awoke from some uneasy slumber, the whole sordid episode would come back to her in a painful wave of remembrance. Shame haunted her as she relived each yielding moment in his arms and her belief that he had loved her. Tears stung her eyes, passionate reluctant tears that poured down her cheeks until she had no more to shed. As the dawn began to thread its insipid fingers across the sky, she resolved not to think of Hugh, resolved to cast every furtive thought of him from her mind. It had all been a stupid, girlish dream! He was merely a man who used women. Quite probably he was not capable of real love, and therefore it was completely foolish to moon over him. In any event, how could she have possibly believed that one of the infamous officers of the King could ever have treated her with respect or the sort of devotion she had been led to expect from a husband? Husband? The word had slipped so easily into her thoughts. What a stupid unschooled child she must seem to him! Of course he had never taken her seriously. He never took any woman seriously—so why should she be different? Indignation made her eyes fill once more with tears. He was an oaf—a great, brutish oaf! But she bowed her head wearily as if in submission; if only she could truly believe that . . .

It was March, a timid March that brought with it only a breath of the glorious spring that was to come. Even so, the pink-tipped buds of sycamore trees began showing their wary heads as cow-parsley leaves started to form fresh carpets of deep green beside every hedgerow. Astwood House began to bloom as snowdrops, crocuses and wild primrose flowered in great numbers briefly. Bethan tended the household and the gardens at her aunt's side. She was willing enough, but there was a touch of melancholy that seemed to linger about her every move, that made even one of her tentative smiles seem tinged with sadness. Matilda had never asked her about the meeting she had so carefully contrived with Hugh, but how she had longed to! It had quite obviously gone disastrously wrong, and she felt that the whole blame lay in her own meddling hands. Now it was too late, and he had gone back to the biddings of his master the King. She stood looking through the window at her niece, who was standing next to her horse, stroking the gentle creature's great neck—no doubt she was about to go on another of her endless rides. Matilda drew a deep dissatisfied sigh and muttered a silent prayer to her God, who seemed so busy with other things.

Bethan leaned her head wearily against Tallow's sleek coat before mounting her and riding away from the confines of the house. It had been the same every day since he had left. She could think of nothing else to do, and the long, exhausting rides she punished herself with made her sleep more easily, and at least she could forget him. But that was all. As she rode on to the old bridle path, she wondered if the pain would ever leave her. Time and time again she had berated herself and him, had stripped him of every virtue imaginable, but still that mocking unforgettable face would slip unannounced into her thoughts and she would be back in his arms again, totally submerged by each kiss, each caress; begging.

The air was quite warm for the first time, and she could see tentative buds dotting the naked branches of the trees stretching over the path. Normally she loved this time of the year, but now everything seemed so different, as if it had been spoilt, and all because of one man and the love that lingered like a pain in her heart.

She urged Tallow onward, hoping that the rushing wind could blow all her pain away, but then a small tight smile settled on her mouth as she realised that life would never be simple again—like that of a child whose fears could be hushed away by soft words and a lullaby.

Bethan had decided to visit old Jenna. It had been too long since she had seen her, and perhaps she would make her think of other things, give her heart some other focus, but it was only a small hope.

Jenna was busy. With the first throes of spring, she endeavoured to replenish her stock of herbs and curatives with the freshest roots and leaves, and Bethan watched with an interest she had not felt in weeks.

'I am preparing butter-bur. See the long blackish root, Bethan; it is very good against fevers, and it also works against poison, and kills worms. For those young maidens plagued by spots and blemishes, it will help them, too.' She smiled then, a broad impudent smile. 'But I don't think you have ever suffered from one spot on that pretty young skin, my dear, so I do not need to give you a dose!'

Bethan laughed, feeling her spirits at last begin to rise a little.

'But I think you need something more than butter-bur to cure your melancholy spirits, child,' Jenna said softly.

Bethan lowered her eyes, catching a breath that was not quite a sigh, and then raised her head to stare into the nearby woods now tinged so prettily with green and splashes of spring.

'Is it what happened—and Edward's betrayal?' Jenna ventured. 'You were betrothed for a long time, and no one could blame you for being heart-sick!'

Bethan almost wanted to laugh. 'Oh, no, Jenna! Edward is gone and past, and I rarely think of him.' The words came out too easily, and again Bethan wondered if she had ever really loved him. He seemed like a flimsy shadow compared with the powerful substance that was Hugh.

Nothing was said for long moments as Jenna turned to her brewing, using a great wooden stick to stir the bitter mixture as it bubbled. 'Is it that King's man, the fair one, then, Bethan?' She did not look up, deeming it wiser to keep her stare centred on her brew.

Bethan could not speak; the words caught in her throat. How like Jenna to know, to guess with such accuracy! It was pointless to deny it—and how she longed to unburden the thoughts that had whirled with such painful obstinacy in her head since the morning he had disappeared with such abruptness from her life.

'He has gone...' she said at last. 'There is little point in talking of it.'

'Sometimes it is good to talk, as you well know. How often have I told you that?' Jenna said gently. 'I take it that he is not returning?'

'No, Jenna, he is not.'

She had spoken with finality, and the old woman was taken aback by her tone, which suddenly seemed full of bitterness. It was not like her Bethan. 'Did you quarrel?' she persisted.

Bethan pushed back her hair in a gesture of impatience. 'He is a King's man, Jenna—and always a King's man. Women feature in their lives only as playthings.' She could never tell Jenna what had happened between them, never! Besides, it would serve no useful purpose.

'Yet *he* did not strike me as such a man. Perhaps you have merely misunderstood one another? That often happens when two people are in love and unsure, particularly in the difficult circumstances you found yourselves in.' Jenna leaned forward, her nostrils flaring as she sniffed the pungent smell of the root, but her eyes rested briefly on Bethan's face, where the pain was written clearly.

'I do not think so, Jenna, but it is kind of you to suggest it. In any event, I am hardly likely to find out now. King Henry's court is as far off and unreachable as the moon.'

'Why, Bethan?' the old woman said, lifting her head up abruptly.

'Of course it is, Jenna!' Bethan replied impatiently. 'Not only is it days and days away, but in between there are robbers and rogues to contend with... And you know that my aunt would never hear of it; the very mention of London sends her into a flurry. She believes it to be a brutal, sinful place peopled by murderers and thieves!'

A half-smile tilted the edges of Jenna's mouth. So Bethan had already thought of the journey herself, and was hardly aware that she had done so. 'Come, Bethan! If we believed half of the stories about ghosts, witches and villains, no one would venture out of their homes!'

She ladled a great spoonful of her brew and took a wary sip, anticipating the familiar unpleasant taste, and was not disappointed. She noticed that Bethan had averted her gaze, and her shoulders dropped as if in a gesture of defeat.

'No, it is impossible, Jenna!' Suddenly she added with surprising anger, 'And why should *I* go to *him*! It is *he* who should come to *me*!'

'Men are very stupid creatures, Bethan—you should know that by now! Sometimes you have to lead them to the life-giving water they seem so afraid to drink—like blind horses dying of thirst.'

But Bethan merely shook her head stubbornly in response.

Jenna smothered her impatience and decided that there was only one course of action. 'Go to him!' It was almost a command.

'I cannot,' Bethan replied tautly.

'And why not?' Jenna persisted. 'Pride? Is it pride, Bethan? Because, before God, you will never get your heart's desire if you let that stand in your way.' She took the girl's hand. 'You never have been to the King's court, have you?'

'No,' she answered, hardly able to meet the old woman's gaze.

'Well, then, can you not go there on that pretext? Every young woman of substance should make at least one journey to our great city, so surely that will protect your obstinate pride?' Although, she thought, he would not be deceived for a moment!

'Please, Jenna, let us talk of something else,' Bethan pleaded.

'Only if you promise me that you will at least think a little on what I have said.' For a moment she thought Bethan was not going to respond, but finally her answer came in a soft, small voice.

'Yes, I will think on it.'

Then Jenna smiled with relief, knowing as surely as the sun would rise in the morning that her Bethan would soon be off to King Henry's court.

'It is madness!' Aunt Matilda cried.

'Why is it madness? Many people go to see the King, and I have never been. Surely it is not so much to ask?' Bethan stood defiantly by the doorway; she had made up her mind and would not be swayed, not now.

'It is *everything* to ask! Have you any idea of the dangers we would risk along the way, not forgetting the thieves and rogues who roam the streets of London just waiting to prey on weary, unsuspecting travellers...'

'In that case, I shall go alone. I do not wish to defy you, Aunt—but I *will* go.' And with a curt defiant nod of her head, Bethan left the room.

Matilda's eyes stared unblinking after her. It had, of course, nothing to do with Bethan's desire to see King Henry's notorious court, she knew well enough—it was Hugh. Matilda sighed in weary defeat. She would go, just as she had known from the very beginning. In any event, it was high time she righted the wrong she had unwittingly done, whatever it may have been, when she meddled in their affairs and turned them so unfortunately against one another. She thought of the preparations she would have to make, of the miles they would have to travel, and of London. She shook her head in wonderment, for it was over twenty years since she had seen her sovereign, and he had hardly been much more than a boy...

They did not set out until mid-April. Aunt Matilda had ensured that they would have suitable places to stay at each stopping-point on the journey, so they were unlikely to reach London until early May. Once Bethan had made up her mind that they were to go, every moment seemed precious. She had grown exasperated at her aunt's insistence that they wait for a reply to each of her letters, including that of the Earl of Somerset, who had kindly agreed that they could stay for two days while they rested. Then the weather had delayed them. Rain fell heavily in great sheets making the roads almost impassable, so again they were forced to wait until the ground had dried out enough to bear their horses' hooves. When eventually the day came for them to leave, they were accompanied by an escort of four men on horseback, a serving-maid, and a further two horses to carry baggage. Matilda had been persuaded from taking a small cart to carry more items, as no one could be sure how long the weather would hold, and a cart, however small, would prove a burden if the ground became saturated again, even if the broad wooden wheels were spiked.

The journey seemed fraught with tedious difficulties: a horse would go lame, a strap would loosen, and baggage fall and break open on the wet ground. Rivers were still swollen, so that they had to go further downstream than they had anticipated, delaying them while they found a suitable place to cross. Each delay, each time-consuming halt, made Bethan's temper more and more frayed. She tortured herself with thoughts of Hugh, at court, enjoying himself in the arms of numerous women—sophisticated, beautiful ladies who could outshine her in every way. Doubt in a way of stinging uncertainty assailed her as she wondered at the wisdom of the journey, but then pride and the furtive spectre of her humiliation—and her love—would cast the doubt aside. She gritted her teeth in the face of the cold wind and the persistent showers that April inevitably brought.

They stayed in Bridgwater for two nights, and journeyed with reasonable speed on to Glastonbury and then to Bristol and Bath, where they stayed with the Earl of Somerset for a further two nights. There was gossip to be had at the Earl's table; all the talk centring on the fallen Anne Bullen who was now at odds with the King. Accusations of witchery and of her many lovers, true or otherwise, laced the air. At court, even the mildest of flirtations could be transformed into a passionate affair. It was also said that there was another woman waiting in the wings for Anne's certain demise: Jane Seymour.

By the time the travellers were back on the road again, Aunt Matilda was full of foreboding. The court would be full of evil humour, fostered by the King's ill-temper and his vengeful wrath, notwithstanding the smell of fear that would hang like a pall over everything. They should return to the safety and comfort of Astwood House, which now lay so very far behind. Her hands trembled as she held the reins of her faithful horse. It was too late to turn back now, whatever her fears told her.

Bethan smelt the river long before she saw it. The Thames was enormous, widening slothfully like a great stinking sewer; it was London's refuse-tip, and a safe place to dump bodies and sick animals, should the need arise. The smell grew even worse when they reached the out-skirts of the great city, and the mists from the marshes and the river combined with the smoke from a thousand fires to settle over King Henry's London like a thick layer of grime. As they entered the narrow darkling streets, figures began to emerge out of the gloom, and Bethan realised that the city crawled with life. Her ears were suddenly assaulted by a cacophony of sound as people went about their daily business oblivious of the strangers in their midst. Pedlars and gypsies hawked at every corner with their pies, cockles, charms and sprigs of lav-ender long past their prime. Animals scavenged freely about the streets, adding their own stench and cries to the perpetual din. Children screamed, and fishwives shrieked with the harlots from open windows, carts sank into reeking mud, and cut-throats and thieves seemed to hover at the mouth of each sly black alley. But even through the noise and filth Bethan felt the great city's heart beat, felt its heady excitement. She was enchanted by the variety of unusual goods she saw on display, and the many different shops all crammed with best quality wares, things that she hardly ever saw from one year's end to next—goldsmiths, pewterers, shoemakers, drapers, brewers, lacemakers. She was almost sad to turn away from the frantic bustle of the busy streets, but held her disappointment back as she saw Matilda's ashen face.

'Are you well, Aunt?' Bethan asked, not allowing panic to creep into her voice.

Matilda closed her eyes for a moment, as though she could thus shut out the piercing sights and sounds that had deeply offended her. She was too old for such things, too old to see the raw beauty that so many others seemed to see in this great city. Too old.

'Just tired, child—that is all.' She opened her weary lids. 'I am very glad that the Earl kindly lent us his man, for I am sure we would otherwise have lost ourselves among these narrow streets.'

The mud lay thickly everywhere, and puddles and pits of water littered this crude track called a street. Along its middle ran a shallow channel filled with stinking refuse and unmentionable things that she would not allow herself to dwell on. With an all-consuming relief she realised that the Earl's guide was slowing to a halt outside a large and not unpleasant house. She had arranged to rent the lower rooms at a reasonable price, and understood the owner to be a man of honour and good disposition.

Times had changed since the year she had been here with her dear husband, or at least she thought so, but she was still remembered by her one and only friend who remained alive and close to the court—Margaret, Lady Mascall. Margaret had arranged everything, and Matilda felt she would be forever in her debt. Her gaze shifted uneasily to Bethan's upturned face, and she saw the heady expectation in her bright eyes and the soft curving cheeks pink with the blush of anticipation. Pray God all would be well! Pray God her pretty niece's heart would not be broken again—for even youth in all its fleeting glory and promise was not eternal. And she thought of that sweet promise, of Hugh D'Savoury and all the hope her dear Bethan held so carefully in her heart.

CHAPTER TEN

BETHAN HARDLY slept that night, and when sleep eventually did take her, the dawn broke raucously in on her flimsy dreams. Bells rang from the first cock-crow—church bells and the hollow sound of hand-bells held by muffin-men and milkmaids; cows bellowed and sheep bleated as they were brought in to the daily markets. A thrill of anticipation made her push the coverlets back and run to the window. It had been almost dark when they had arrived the previous night, and although the scores of lighted lanthorns had given her an idea of the crowded humanity which swarmed in the narrow streets, daylight gave everything searing, colourful clarity, even through the thinning smog. So alive! So incredibly different from Astwood, from Somerset, even from any of the towns they had passed through. Her excited eyes scoured the seething mass of faces intent on their daily business. She was astonished to find that if she leaned far enough through the window, she seemed to be able to touch the house leaning almost precariously towards her from the other side. For a time she sat perched in the deep recess of the window, her legs curled beneath her, just watching.

She was aware that she was searching the faces below, no matter how vainly, for the one face she had come all this way to see, and she recalled their last encounter. Her aunt had sorrowfully told her of the little plan she had set which had gone so horribly wrong, but at least it gave her some understanding of his reaction when she had entered the parlour with such an apparently feeble excuse. But his arrogance, his unbelievable arrogance! Whatever happened during her stay in London, she would make him sorry! Drawing in a deep breath, the secret words she had nurtured so carefully in her heart took giddy shape. She would make him want her. She must! Throughout the whole of that day she begged her aunt to be allowed out, but Matilda remained adamant.

'I have been compliant and most tolerant so far, Bethan—even you might allow me that! But to let you wander through these rogue-ridden streets, never! We wait until Lady Margaret arrives. I have already sent word that we have arrived, and I am sure she will not delay in coming to welcome us.' She saw the disappointment in her niece's face, and said with understanding, 'Be patient for once, my child. This is not Somerset, and even there I almost lost you, so please bow to my wishes.' She was rewarded by a reluctant nod, and then added brightly, 'Tomorrow, as we have planned, we go to court . . . and you must look your best, so I am sure that your time would be better spent in ensuring that those lovely new gowns have not been too crushed by the journey.'

Knowing that her aunt spoke her usual common sense and also knowing that she had given the staunch old woman a bad fright when she had been missing at home, Bethan complied, and attempted a gracious smile. It only just failed, but her aunt seemed mollified enough.

The gowns lay in all their glory across an upholstered settle, and Bethan gazed at them in satisfaction. There were three, and each had been especially made for this visit of visits. Aunt Matilda had ensured that her new gowns would measure up to courtly fashion and had asked Lady Margaret to send sketches of what was the current mode; she had done her best with her never-tiring but rather short-sighted dressmaker. However, each one turned out to be a small triumph. There was the deep blue damask bordered with braiding of silver thread, its sleeves fitting to the elbow but gradually falling in great lavish wings of blue and silver-grey, the colour of her eyes. The second was black velvet heavily embroidered with gold and tiny, delicate pearls, its vast flowing skirt inset with a deep V of more gold; her aunt had retrieved a topaz and pearl pendant from her jewellery case and given it to her niece. Bethan lifted the fragile necklet up, letting her eyes rest on the large amber stone that glistened the colour of clear honey, and then replaced it on the black velvet. At the last gown, she drew in a sharp breath, still amazed at its beauty—yards and yards of glorious white satin edged with sleek black fur. The great slanting sleeves almost touched the floor, each was skilfully slashed so that gashes of black satin set off the purity of the whiteness. A small, delicate cap sat beside it—white, trimmed with scores of jet beads and slivers of mother-of-pearl. She had ensured that this particular gown had been artfully cut to reveal her fine shoulders and the silky skin of her upper breasts, the bodice boned and stiffened so that when it was laced, her waist seemed so tiny that it could almost be circled by two firm, strong hands. His hands. She let her fingers linger on the magnificent material, and her thoughts turned inevitably to the following day when they would be taken to court.

She thought of the other ladies in other magnificent gowns that would be there...and of Hugh. He would be in his element, no doubt, and his master the one he had served so irritatingly well—the awesome figure of King Henry himself.

Margaret, Lady Mascall, arrived as the afternoon began to fade and lanthorns were already being lit in the dim narrow streets. She was a gay, tiny little woman and obviously delighted to escort her old friend and lovely young niece to court; it had been a long time since she had anticipated enjoying herself so much.

'Tomorrow you will be presented, and there is a banquet to be held in the evening, so it will be quite a big day.' Lady Margaret's face pulled into a mischievous grin as she saw Matilda pale at her words.

'We are surely not to be the only ones to be presented, Margaret?' she asked anxiously, suddenly picturing the eyes of the whole court on their nervous, provincial figures.

'Heavens no, Matilda! I don't suppose many will even notice two extra faces among all the others—and, besides, most are too busy observing the comings and goings of the King and Anne Bullen.'

'But, as I understand it, she is in the Tower—along with her lovers... Matilda's voice dropped to a whisper so that Bethan's innocent ear would not be a party to such gossip.

'Oh yes, that is true,' Margaret said loudly, 'but she does not give up easily, that one, and will shout her innocence at every opportunity.' She shook her head knowingly. 'It will do her no good, believe me; the King's mind is made up! In any case the young minstrel,

Smeaton, has already confessed to intimacy with the Queen, so it is already too late.'

Bethan gasped with shock. She could still hardly believe that she was now at the centre of England's dilemma, and that the King himself was almost within walking distance of this very house. Her thoughts turned towards his ill-fated wife, and the lover who had betrayed her only through the agony of the rack. She shivered as Lady Margaret continued, realising that the old woman was enjoying herself immensely, and wondered absently what they would all find to talk about once Anne Bullen had been finally quieted.

'...and her own *brother*, Matilda, can you imagine?' Margaret persisted with relish.

But Matilda could not imagine, and then glanced anxiously at Bethan, again praying that her sweet niece had not heard her friend's lurid words. Once more she silently questioned the wisdom of this visit, which seemed fraught with intrigue and corruption. Her niece was sitting with a quiet dignity. She was in love with one of the King's men—was that not really why they had come all this way? Yet how could such a man settle in their country backwater—away from such intrigue and morbid excitement, which was probably like life's blood to him? And what of Bethan—a sweet, country innocent? Suddenly the image she had held of Hugh changed, and she did not like what she saw, or what she imagined she saw. At that moment it seemed to her that nothing good or wholesome could come out of such an unhealthy, shallow place. Yet she knew, stubbornly, that in her heart she had always liked the man who had come so unwittingly into their lives. He had saved her—and her Bethan—

from a man she thought she had known and trusted all
her life. Matilda sighed silently, confusion once more
getting the better of her. Well, it was up to Bethan now,
and God—and, of course, Hugh D'Savoury.

The banquet Lady Margaret had so lightly mentioned
was like nothing Bethan or her aunt had ever attended.
At some moment in the afternoon Bethan had had a
brief glimpse of the top of her sovereign's head, and
their presentation at court, along with scores of others,
was momentarily over. Once the King had returned to
his apartments to rest, the court seemed to breathe a
sigh of relief and look ahead to the evening in a fever
of excitement. There was talk, endless talk, of the unfortunates implicated in the Queen's adultery—all five
incarcerated in the Tower, all including her own brother,
Lord Rochford, tortured until they confessed their guilt.
It was said that they were to be executed in three days,
and then the Queen to follow shortly afterwards. Bethan
heard not one good word said on Anne Bullen's behalf
and she supposed that no one dared; she had not been
well liked, and few would mourn her brief, glittering
passing. But she tried to push the spectre of the Queen's
imminent execution aside and allowed her eyes to scan
the milling crowd of courtiers and ladies who thronged
the court. They were indeed grand, some startlingly so
in their rich dazzling gowns and mantles, but most of
the faces were old, many garishly painted, teeth rotting
behind conspiratorial smiles.

But her gaze swept over them only fleetingly, because
she searched for one face and one face only. Disappointment gave way to anger as she realised that Hugh

was nowhere to be seen, and she wondered if he were not at court at all, or indeed perhaps not even in London. She had not arranged to meet him... Although such a matter should be secondary to being presented to the court and King Henry, her heart told her otherwise. Resentment grew within her as she thought of the long, arduous journey she had borne on his behalf because he had been too proud to come to her. When she happened to look up at a window that overlooked a pretty courtyard, she caught the eyes of a tall, elegant man who had been watching her for some time. He smiled, and dipped his head in a gesture of admiration, and she felt a deep blush creep up from her neck. So, not all the King's courtiers were men past their prime! Some, it seemed, were exceedingly attractive. Hugh would pay dearly for his rejection of her!

The banqueting hall was decorated with all manner of flowers and greenery. Three immensely long tables ran the whole length of the room, with the King's table and enormous chair forming a great cross-piece at the top. Bethan was seated between her aunt and Lady Margaret, at her aunt's insistence, as though she would suddenly be swept off into some unsavoury entanglement, but Bethan was too busy taking note of all the wonders to notice the many glances cast at her.

The tables were covered with a mountain of amazing and mouth-watering delicacies, each having a centre-piece of exotic and magnificent design. A peacock served tail and all and roasted to perfection adorned one table; a second sported a huge boar glistening in aspic, its mouth full of sugared apples and its tail coiled with silver; a third displayed a massive goose, seemingly still fending

off the three wild duck threatening its imagined ter-
ritory. But the King's table was set in white and gold as
two roast swans rose majestically from the centre, their
feathers painstakingly gilded and put back into place,
their proud necks arched in indignant rage as their great
wings stretched out each side in exquisite mantles of pure
white. Bethan's eyes widened in amazement at each new
wonder. Every item which had been prepared with such
consummate skill had been made to eat, but had also
been designed to delight and dazzle the eye—and finally
to please and mollify a King whose vengeful God would
give him no sons, only troublesome wives—and
daughters.

The room hushed, and Bethan felt her heart begin to
pound as all heads turned to the great doors at the far
end, and she saw him: the King. He was tall, and very
well built, but his strong bones were now covered with
a thick layer of fat. Henry walked with a slight limp,
his splendid robes almost concealing the large swelling
in one of his legs. His face was large and plump, the
eyes and finely carved mouth disappearing into pouches
of excess flesh. Bethan stood only feet away as he passed,
and she noted how tightly the lips were closed, how lines
of resentment and disappointment were carved down
each side of his stubborn mouth. He seemed to dwarf
all around him, but it was not merely his enormous size,
it was his air of supreme arrogance, his utter belief in
himself and the power that he wielded that made all lower
their eyes as he strode unheeding through their midst.
Bethan followed him with an awed gaze, unable to look
away until her aunt's nervous fingers pulled her back to
reality, and she returned her eyes reluctantly to the safety

of the flagstones at her feet which peeped so daintily from beneath her gown in their new pretty slippers.

The feasting became raucous, and wine and ale flowed like rivers until everyone, including the ladies, seemed stewed with drink. Spanish acrobats performed in one corner and a man of tricks in another, but eventually the tables and entertainers were swept away so that the company could dance. Bethan did not imagine that the King would dance. She thought he would merely watch, being too removed from mortal man to take a lady to the floor and show her that he had a weakness for such things. But he did, and she was astounded to see that the lady on his arm was the one who waited so patiently in the wings for the death of his Queen. But Jane Seymour was a disappointment; past the prime of her youth, now well over twenty, quite small and pasty-faced, Bethan thought. Even her beautiful gold and ivory silk gown could not gild her plainness. But as she watched them together, the ageing corpulent King and his fragile future wife, she felt only pity and a little fear. She could not imagine how it would feel to have such a man touch her, to have that enormous body crush her as he clumsily endeavoured to plant his seed within her. She shivered and turned her face to the line of people watching their sovereign, and once more caught the glance of the man she had seen earlier. Lady Margaret had pointed him out as he walked into the banqueting hall, almost as though she knew that their eyes had spoken across a room.

Richard Drayton was the son and heir of a rich land-owner—'and a pretty rogue', was all her aunt's friend would say, but Bethan had merely smiled and lowered her eyes. Now, however, with the assistance of some wine, she allowed her gaze to linger on his face so that he moved across the room as if she had invited him. He took her hand to dance, and in her delight she thought she floated round the floor as he held and swung her about the room with practised skill. She felt dizzy with unfamiliar excitement, and the thin, sensuous face that smiled so easily seemed more attractive than ever. She thought of Hugh then, and for a fleeting moment she remembered the heady passion of his embrace... But he had rejected her, and this man who held her so firmly now seemed intent on her only; he had made that quite clear. She allowed her mouth to widen into a broad, inviting smile, and felt his hands tighten over her own in response. She threw her head back carelessly, suddenly drunk with all the giddy sensations she had experienced and with the avid attention of such an elegant and obviously grand catch as Richard Drayton. She had a brief, blurred glimpse of her aunt's worried face as she was swept past the milling people at the edge of the floor, but was then brought abruptly to a halt as Richard stopped in the shadowed curve of an arch. A heavy curtain was pulled half-way across it, and in a shaft of candlelight she could see several couples lingering closely, their hands and bodies seeming almost as one as lips, breasts and legs pressed and intertwined. She looked into the face of the man who stared at her with such open desire; it was as though he were offering her a rare and tempting jewel as his gaze shifted from her face to the couples locked in almost complete abandonment within. For the first time, she felt a vague seed of disquiet—things, events seemed to be happening too fast, so fast that she was almost blinded by their brilliance. She looked briefly to one side, and then back to the now safe arena of the dancers.

There was a movement near the great doors at the far end as a group of people came into the room, and her eyes were drawn by a fair head, by the beautiful breadth of a man's shoulders. Hugh. She felt the breath catch in her throat and her knees go strangely weak as he looked towards her. And it was as if, all at once, they were the only people in the room, as if the touch of their eyes sealed them off from all the surrounding laughter and talk. But then she was aware of the woman on his arm, the pretty pink cheeks and over-generous bosom erupting from a too-tight bodice. Anger like fire surged in her veins and she turned, wounded, to the man who stood so silently waiting beside her. She wanted only revenge now, and to hurt Hugh as he had hurt her. With great deliberation she smiled up at Richard and was rewarded by his long, tapering fingers tilting her chin so that his lips could softly brush her own. She leaned her head back, smiling more broadly, and then laughed as his hands moved to rest on her waist and turned triumphantly to see that Hugh still watched, still stared at her from across the vast sea of people. He would see that she was quite capable of living without him now, quite capable of enjoying the fruits of King Henry's court, just as he was.

Taking her inviting smile as silent agreement, the eager lips moved to the gentle curve of her cheekbone and down the proud pillar of her neck. The hands which held her waist tightened, pulling her sideways into the semi-darkness of the small room beyond the arch. Bethan felt a tremor of panic as Richard Drayton pressed her feverishly against cold stone and his hands reached stealthily up to touch the silvered thread of her bodice. His mouth asked no questions, wanting no answers, no words, just the feel of her soft flesh as they took more and more. It was all a game, a terrible dangerous game for which there seemed to be no rules, only a tireless thirsting for frenzied pleasure, whatever the cost. She thought of Hugh and his ashen face as he had locked her stare across the room, and tears, quite suddenly, sprang into her eyes. This was not how it was supposed to be; these were not *his* hands, *his* lips that burned with such fevered, frightening want, and her head went down in silent, bewildered agony.

So she was here! Hugh sighed as her eyes accused him, as the fine chin lifted proudly and those lovely, full lips he remembered so searingly well parted slightly—or was it his imagination that he could see the moistness, see the soft, tantalising pinkness of her tongue? But her face had clouded with anger and humiliation when she saw the plump loveliness of Kate hanging so covetously on his arm. And did she think to fool him so easily again by turning to the careless arms of Richard Drayton? He knew Drayton of old—an ambitious, depraved fop who favoured virgins and young boys like prey. He could spot the innocent and the guileless as soon as they set foot in St James's... There had been a scandal once, but it had been skilfully concealed by his wealthy and powerful father, and young Richard had been sent to Ireland to cool his heels. Hugh's forehead creased into deep lines as memory prompted him and he recalled how the young

girl Drayton had raped and then flogged to death had
been ill chosen—the illegitimate daughter of the Bishop
of Warwick, not merely an anonymous street wench who
would never be missed. Wolsey had intervened, and all
parties had been made compliantly silent on the affair.
But Drayton had returned like the lost prodigal son, and
now his carefully manicured hands held Bethan! Hugh
had seen the naïve gleam of triumph in her face as she
had fallen so foolishly into Drayton's arms, and although
he had realised that she goaded him—and he should be
beyond goading—jealousy had pierced him. And hate.
For a long time he had waited for the opportunity of
confronting the evil mind that hid behind the sweet,
shallow mask that was Richard Drayton!

Bethan twisted painfully against the crushing, demanding weight of the man whose mouth bruised and
stifled her cries beneath his own. There had been no
gentleness, once the black shadows of the room had
hidden them from prying eyes. He had torn her gown
with ease, and she had gathered her strength to fend him
off, but it was as though he anticipated her every move
and his arm had stretched out swiftly across her body
like a vice, and his mouth had silenced the scream hovering on her lips so that the sound which escaped them
was like a whimpering cry of ecstasy. But when he was
thrust from her by a dark, powerful shadow who
smashed his jaw, she was suddenly unable to move,
hardly aware of Hugh's outraged, glittering stare as his
eyes fell on the blood trickling down her lovely white
breast where Drayton's teeth had left their mark.

'I once said that you were a child playing at women's games, and you are still that foolish, impetuous child, Bethan!' He could not hold the anger from his voice, but it was low and controlled as he saw her deep shame.

Her hands groped nervously for the loose, lost folds of her gown to cover her nakedness, but she was only aware of his gaze as it beat her down and of her own misery and the frightening closeness of him which seemed so suddenly to have made her body stop functioning. The days, weeks and months that had separated them fell away, and her heart seemed to cry out, to shrink and fade from the pain of it.

As her eyes reproached him, all the longing he had held down with such careful deliberation began to rise and engulf him. She, only she, had a way of touching him like a raw open wound, but he had denied the softness she awoke in him, denied the choking desire which surged into his soul each time he saw her. He loved her; he had loved her from the very first—but he had never wanted to! And now, as she stood before him so lost, so vulnerable, so wantonly beautiful, he still felt disbelief and a hollow sickness in his stomach as the weight of that love settled upon his great shoulders with a strange inevitability.

'Hugh! At last! How naughty of you to leave me with such abruptness!'

The affected brittleness of the girlish voice sliced the heady quiet, and Bethan felt the crimson of a blush sweep into her face. The moment was gone. Her shaking fingers gripped the torn flap of material still hanging loose, and she bowed her head, hiding, as if intent on repairing some idle damage.

'Playing the gallant again, Hugh?' Kate persisted, her large blue eyes taking in the situation with unaccustomed sharpness. Her Hugh had not been the same since his return from Somerset, and she had heard of some country beauty he had dallied with during his stay there. But he had come back, so all should be well. Yet it had not been her imagination that had heard the name 'Bethan' slip so softly from his mouth as he had stopped with such suddenness, his eyes dark and fixed on a lovely upturned face which watched him with equal intensity from across the room. Her gaze switched back to the set line of his mouth when he did not reply, and she moved her hand possessively to his arm. 'Come, let us return to the dance.' He still did not move. 'You know you promised that this would be *my* evening, that you would make up for your sullenness of last night.'

Bethan caught a deep, painful breath as each empty word injured her with stinging, surprising ease. Why had she come? Why had she come so far only to be wounded further by him and his pretty painted dolls? Even in her misery she could see that that was all that Kate was, but the knowledge did nothing to soothe her searing hurt. While he was satisfied with the company of such women—and he had given her no sign that he preferred otherwise—why should he bother with her? In her vanity, she had thought to prove him wrong, so she had stupidly come to him. To him! She must have been blind to have come so far for so little, and knowingly. She was foolish, just as he had told her. Biting her lip to hold back the tears which stood waiting to fall, she moved away

abruptly, feeling the touch of him burn her through the
cool silk of her gown. In a moment she was out into the
sudden brightness of the candlelit hall. She felt giddy,
disorientated, and waited for a moment until the dizziness had passed. But he did not come to her, and tremulous hope withered and died in her breast as each tear
fell, half-blinding her to the world which still turned,
still throbbed with life, even as her own stood so achingly
empty.

The following morning she stayed in her bed, pleading
a sick stomach from too much wine, and begged her
fussing aunt that she be allowed some peace. So she was
left with only her wretched thoughts to keep her
company. The day was cool but windless, and her aunt
had opened the windows, only to close them again as
the foul smog and stench from the street began to filter
in. Bethan sighed, all at once hating the sights and sounds
of this place that had so excited her only two days before.
She thought of the clean, sweet-smelling air of Astwood,
and of Tallow, and wondered how she could ever have
found it all so tedious. Her eyes glistened with more tears,
but she blinked them away in angry frustration. She
wanted to go home. She wanted to leave this place and
everything and everyone in it, but knew she would have
to go on with the charade a little longer, otherwise her
aunt would want to know why. Matilda knew nothing
of what had happened the previous evening, and had
not even seen Hugh, thank God. She merely thought
that Bethan had become slightly dizzy with all the rich
food and excitement and had retired to bed early. At
least she could use that as an excuse not to go out today...

But tomorrow! Tomorrow Lady Margaret had arranged for them to take a boat to Richmond, and in the evening they were to attend a masked ball. Bethan wondered how she would endure it. Life was too much, she decided, and thought how much easier it would be to become an old maid, or perhaps go into a convent to get away from the world of men; they seemed to bring nothing but pain and disappointment. Her fingers reached up to the tender spot hidden beneath her nightdress where Richard Drayton had left his mark. Inevitably the vision of Hugh's stony face slid into her mind as he had stood before her, his eyes full of mocking contempt... And she! God in heaven, she was not much more than a trollop—and surely well past twenty-five! Bethan turned with sudden anger beneath the bedclothes, hating her— but hating *him* most of all. Yet the anger was only a tremulous thing as she remembered the longing that had soared into her breast at the sight of him, and a tight knot, like a sob, began to gather in her throat. Closing her eyes tight, she turned her face desolately into the lonely comfort of the feather pillow.

Lady Margaret had arranged an open barge to take them up the Thames. It had been prettily decorated with coloured pennants, and as the day was quite warm and the sky clear, the large piece of red canvas acting as the roof was drawn back so that they could view everything clearly. Even Bethan, for all her sorrow, was aroused by the sights. It had been decided that they should pass beneath London Bridge, and as they approached, she felt her aunt's nervous hand touch her own as they neared the enormous structure that spanned the whole breadth of the river. It was undoubtedly sturdy, but the many arches which supported it had become warped and distorted with age, and the houses built on either side leaned in a most alarming manner. They could just see the narrow dark street that wove its precarious way through the strange tunnel of houses. Lady Margaret giggled maliciously, and pointed to the Southwark end of the bridge, to a drawbridge, and a tower. Bethan looked up at its summit, and there on show for all to see were the heads of those executed for treason, each bloody trophy stuck on the end of a pike.

'Margaret, please!' Matilda cried, her hand reaching protectively to her own neck.

'Oh, come, Matilda, it is only a little jest! God's teeth, these are everyday sights here. You should be less easily wounded and learn to take such things in your stride while you stay at court, or else you will be fainting at every turn!'

Lady Margaret shook her head in a gesture of impatience, and waved the boatman on with an abrupt flick of her hand.

Bethan swallowed hard and tried to shut out the vision of Edward's head stuck on such a pike. For all his betrayal and cruelty, she would not have wished him the agonising and humiliating death that seemed so commonplace in London. Tomorrow Anne Bullen's lovers would all be executed, and two days later, the Queen herself. She closed her eyes in horrified wonder at the lengths to which Henry had gone to rid himself of his troublesome wife—his anger, his vengeance, seemed limitless. Then she thought of the man she had tried so hard to dismiss from her mind, who was at the mercy of his sovereign's terrible disappointment each single day. But Hugh would survive. He would never allow himself to do otherwise!

When they reached Richmond, Lady Margaret had arranged that they should stop and picnic beneath the shelter of some trees if the weather held, and she was not to be disappointed. A pale sun could be seen behind a thin veil of cloud, and while the boat was being tied to the small stone jetty, the sky cleared and a great shaft of warmth pierced the air. Suddenly Bethan was glad she had come. It was a true spring day, and she should be glad to be alive instead of dreaming about someone as blind and conceited as Hugh! Later, when the time was right, she would ask her aunt if they might make preparations to return home. It would not take much persuasion, as she was sure her aunt was as anxious to return to Astwood as she was—and before the nineteenth, because she had no desire to dance at the Queen's execution.

Neither did she wish to see again that blonde strumpet hanging on Hugh's arm—once was quite enough! But tonight she would have to endure. Perhaps he would not come, perhaps she would be free to enjoy herself without his irritating presence. Yet a shadow momentarily dimmed the silver-grey of her eyes as she stared unseeing across the river and wondered if she would ever enjoy herself again.

She wore the white satin that evening. Lady Margaret had brought their masks with barely concealed delight, and Bethan's was the face of an exotic black cat, which went perfectly with her gown. Matilda was wearing pale green trimmed with french blue, and Margaret had concocted a mask of peacock feather for her old friend.

'Far too fancy, Margaret—I cannot possibly wear it. People will think I am trying to be some coy young maid!' Matilda stared anxiously at the artful design that sat so innocently against her dress... But it was quite beautiful, quite bewitching.

'Nonsense! You really are becoming an old fuddy-duddy, Matilda!' Margaret scolded. 'This may be your last evening in London—would it be so much of a sin to allow yourself a little amusement?'

Matilda shrugged, noting the smile touching her niece's mouth and trying to ignore the adamant gaze of her friend who was endeavouring to beat her down. Then she caught her breath sharply in wary admiration—the mask really was quite, quite lovely.

'Then that is settled!' Margaret cried gleefully as she saw a cautious softening in her friend's face, knowing she had won, as she had known from the beginning that she would. 'And I shall wear the butterfly.' From behind her back she produced an exquisite mask in the shape of a gold and scarlet butterfly, wings lavishly outstretched, the thin delicate veins touched and outlined with tiny chips of ruby glass. She held it up to her face by its elegant ivory handle, and sidled wickedly up to Bethan.

'Tonight I shall charm them all behind my naughty little mask! With my stays tightened to perfection, a love-ball perched in my bosom and this lovely butterfly to hide my laughter lines, I shall cause some hearts to pound once again, just as I did in my youth—eh, Matilda?'

Bethan tried to suppress a giggle, despite her melancholy, when she caught the shocked expression on her aunt's face. Matilda, for her part, thought that any man would have to be blind not to see beneath Margaret's very obvious disguise, and she felt once more out of her depth. Dear, wicked Margaret seemed to have an answer for everything!

It was easier behind the mask, for Bethan could observe without others knowing who she was. She was sure that everyone must know about her humiliation of the other evening; gossip fed this place, and she had given them all a morsel to chew. It was easier, too, because Hugh would not know her, either. If he came. She had told herself that she did not want to see him, did not care whether he was present, but it was all foolish, childish nonsense. Tonight would probably be the last time she would ever see him, and she owed herself that, at least. The evening seemed to drag on. Bethan allowed herself to dance with a few fawning men, but then left each one as the music ceased. She had no intention of getting herself into another sordid situation because of her stupid naïvety, yet she could not leave before the King arrived, and he was late.

Even as the thought passed irritatingly through her mind, there was a general hush as people moved back and the great doors were opened. He looked pleased. With a little smile, he walked through the corridor of courtiers—with Jane on his arm. Bethan was astonished at his amazing arrogance; it was as though Anne were already dead, and Jane already crowned Queen. He had no patience, and no one to stay his impetuous hand—

not even able to endure just two more days until his wife's ambitious tongue was quieted.

Bethan's gaze flicked past him to the men following in his wake, all tall, all masked with the heads of animals and birds. It was even possible that Hugh were one of them, but surely he would not deign to come without that empty-headed hussy on his arm! She bit back her anger, hating him again, and then turned impatiently to look for her aunt and Lady Margaret. It was almost true what her aunt's old friend had wished for herself; she did look far younger in her carefully contrived outfit, but only at a distance. As Bethan neared them, it was easy to see the heavy wig covering the sparse white hair, and the thin scrawny neck, like a bird's. Yet Lady Margaret was admirably undaunted, and at least her aunt seemed to be enjoying herself, too, even in the beguiling mask she had thought so vulgar. Bethan attempted to swallow her disappointment at this ill-starred adventure, which had brought her nothing but misery. They would leave tomorrow and she would never come to London again; she would endure her aunt's dauntless efforts at match-making, probably marrying some ageing country squire old enough to be her father. She was jolted out of her melancholy by a hand on her arm, and she raised her eyes into the face of a hawk. It was a clever mask, beautifully made, giving the wearer an appearance of proud insolence—and he wished to dance. She assented, since there was little else to do until they left, which would be a while yet.

The floor was crowded, some dancers carelessly wild, and they became caught in the excitement, their faces flushed with exertion. At the end of the first dance, he

would not let her go, saying nothing, merely assuming
that Bethan would stay with him. She nodded absently.
What did it matter? As they moved over the floor, he
would come close and then draw away, but each time
the gap narrowed between them until his arms came to
circle her and she pulled herself easily away. It was a
game. The next time, his hands settled tightly on her
waist to lift her into the air, only to be gently returned
to the flagstones. The last steps were taken from the rear,
and she could feel the warmth of his breath on the back
of her neck as he crushed her too closely against him.
In spite of herself, she felt her heart begin to race and
a deep blush invade her cheeks. There was something
about this man...but she would not be used again by
some courtly rogue. Not again!

Abruptly she pushed his arms away, protesting, 'How
dare you, sir! I think you presume too much!'

'Do I, Bethan? In that case, you are to blame.'

His voice. She felt her breath stop, shaking in her
throat. He lifted his mask so that she could see his face,
but still she said nothing.

'Yes, you are to blame, Bethan, too lovely for your
own good.' Hugh let his eyes pass over her delightfully
concealed face. He had known her from the first, as he
would know her anywhere.

'It is not I who am to blame, sir, it is you; and other
men like you who only take without giving...' Why did
he always loosen her tongue in this way? Why, just this
last time, could he not be kind?

'Is that what you think of me? A greedy womaniser—
is that what you think, Bethan?'

She could not speak, afraid that her words would be the wrong ones.

'Well, of course you are quite right...' he said slowly.

There was anger now. He was worse than the King with his ill-concealed arrogance—as if he were proud of it!

'You are beyond words, Hugh D'Savoury! Indeed, I wish I had never set eyes on you!' Yet she still wanted him, even as his fierce eyes swept insolently over her and a smile came to rest infuriatingly on his beautiful mouth.

'That is a pity, since I am sure that at various times I have given you some meed of pleasure, or are you too proud to admit it?'

Up came her eyes in outraged disbelief, and he saw how her lips quivered, saw how the full breasts swelled and rose so temptingly as she drew a furious angry breath.

'You are beneath contempt—insufferable! A great brutish oaf who knows nothing of women!' There were a thousand insults she wanted to throw at him, but none seemed vile enough to wound him, and there was that mocking smile on his mouth again.

Suddenly her attention was taken by another, who had come up beside her, and his great shadow fell across Hugh's gilded doublet like a warning. 'Enough, Hugh! Your jesting goes too far.'

Bethan shifted her angry gaze to the other man, and met the eyes of the King. The breath seemed to stop in her lungs. She was dwarfed by him, and her knees grew weak as she endeavoured to give a trembling, clumsy curtsy.

'Well, is it done?' he asked impatiently.

'I do not think she will have me now, your Majesty,' Hugh replied, repressing a grin and bowing his head in a curt nod. The music had died to a murmur, and he knew that all ears were listening, all anxious to sup at the latest scandal. Let them listen, for what good it might do them!

'What!' the King boomed, and turned to Bethan, frowning. He lifted his hands up to remove her mask, and for a fleeting second he allowed the eyes of the man behind the sovereign to take in her fresh young beauty, but then the face of the King slid easily into place. He had heard fragments of their tentative love affair, and had not failed to hear of Drayton's broken jaw. So Hugh had shown his hand at last, and not before time! But there had been scandal enough, now. 'Lady Elizabeth, I grow weary of this handsome rogue who has for so long been in need of a wife to tame him—and I give him to you for safe-keeping.' His lips broadened into a sly lascivious grin, and she saw the shrunken stumps of his teeth. Poor Henry had lost all his mighty beauty, she thought, half-dreaming—for surely this must all be a dream! Then he nodded his great head in a gesture of dismissal and moved slowly away, only to turn back laughing as though he shared some private joke.

'And as I am in such good spirits, you may take advantage of me, my Hugh,' he said. 'Take the Courtenay lands for your valuable services to the crown.' Henry was pleased at his own impulsiveness: there had been few enough times for such giving, and in any event he had done very well out of the recovered treasures from that ill-starred abbey and could afford to be generous. But all at once a brief shadow seemed to flee across his face as he remembered at what cost, and the other souls who were, even now, waiting in the Tower. But that would soon be past, all done with, and he could forget. He glanced over to the other end of the room, to the slight, pale figure who would sit next to him, his Jane.

'Well, have you lost all power of speech, Bethan?' Hugh said gently, amused at the surprise in her face.

'What does all this mean?' Her voice was like a little girl's, afraid.

In one swift movement he lifted her into his arms. 'Did you not hear your King? I am yours for safe-keeping,' he replied, smiling now.

'Put me down, please! I understand none of this.' She was so close to him that she did not want to be put down, did not want to leave his arms, and the people made a path for him to pass through, applauding, as if it were some great joke. Through the clapping, laughing crowd she caught sight of her aunt's shocked and worried face, saw how Lady Margaret touched her arm to whisper in her ear, and then the relieved, tremulous smile—but in a moment she was gone and they were out in the candle-lit corridor.

'You will understand, my Bethan, soon.' His arms tightened round her.

'Hugh, no! Where are you taking me?' But he said nothing.

In a few moments, the sounds of dancing and laughter had fallen behind, and he turned up some small narrow steps. He did not pause as they reached the top, merely slowing before moving forward again and then stopping at a stout wooden door. He held her with one arm as he opened it and they passed through, and closed it quickly with a rough kick.

Bethan looked anxiously to one side, and saw immediately the sumptuous bed that seemed to take up almost the whole room. 'No, Hugh—no! How dare you! Put me down at once!' This was too much. He intended to seduce her, and with full permission of the King, it would seem!

He moved across and put her gently down on the satin coverlet. 'You see, I have done as you asked, at last. I have put you down,' he said, standing over her.

'So that you may ravish me! Just as you have, no doubt, ravished countless other ladies—and harlots—on this same bed!' The coquettish face of Kate slid into her mind, and she wanted to strike him.

'Oh, no, my Lady Bethan, this is a new bedchamber and a new bed. Generally I take my other ladies in their own.'

'You are disgusting! Let me out of here at once—you must be quite mad!'

But he only strode to the door, to turn the key and place it high on the ledge of the lintel so that she could not reach it.

'I must obey my King, Bethan. It is my duty!' He walked slowly over to her.

'But this is wicked... You cannot do it! I will not allow you!' Yet, even in her outraged anger, she did not try to turn away or run from him.

'Is it not a sin to deny your husband your love?' he said, and his voice was low, coaxing.

'But you are not my husband!' What was this hurtful game he played?

'Tomorrow, Bethan, the King has given a special dispensation so that we can be married.' He could not tease her any longer, and he had no desire to. There was only one thing now.

'I do not believe you! This is a cunning jest so that I shall submit to you!' Her heart began to race not with fear, but with joyful hope.

'You do not believe me? Then, if words will not convince you, I must use other means.'

He leaned over her, pushing her back on the bed, moving beside her and then covering her with his body so that she could not struggle. Both his hands pinned her arms as he brought his mouth down to cover her own, kissing any more questions away.

She tried to fight him, but his lovemaking overcame her, obliterating everything. His fingers reached up to the deep neckline of her dress, and pulled it down so that her breasts jutted forth and he could see the bloody bruise where Drayton had left his mark. He kissed it gently, tenderly, until he heard her soft sigh and then moved to her nipples, taking first one and then the other greedily into his mouth. She moaned then, and he felt her hands reach for his in an attempt to push him away.

'No, Hugh, no! You are not my husband, we are not married...' Her words were lost, fading weakly as his skilful tongue took her again.

'You must learn to trust your husband, Bethan.' He pulled her dress further down. 'I give you my word— and that of the King.' Then he moved away so that he stood watching her from beside the bed until his eyes came to rest on the bewildered, lovely face. With great deliberation he began removing his doublet, button by button, so that it lay discarded on the floor; then he reached to his hose and pushed them roughly down so that they, too, lay in a dark circle at his feet.

Bethan lay quite still, unbelieving. Her heart seemed to hammer like a mad thing as she stared up at his powerful naked figure. He deliberately left nothing to her imagination, and waited a moment so that she could see him, see all the hoarded passion he had held so carefully for her. Only for her. She gasped fearfully, as he knelt beside her on the bed, her eyes drawn to the great shaft jutting from his body. His hands reached for her breasts again and he caressed them, kneading them softly, urgently, so that her desire would come to match his. She was a maiden, and he wanted to ensure that her desire would run like a thirsting river so that her pain would drown in it, leaving only pleasure—much, much pleasure.

'I am commanded by my master, by my King, Bethan—and you must know that I never disobey him!'

She could not answer because she had no words, only small inadequate breaths. When he began to unlace her dress, without a protest she let him pull it from her so that the yards of satin sat on the oak floor in a pool of virginal white. For a moment he lingered on her half-naked form, then slowly began removing each one of her undergarments until there was nothing more.

He sighed softly then, and groaned deep in his chest. 'You are more, much more, than I could possibly wish for.' He still knelt, still softly teased her as his hands ran down the silken skin to the soft dark fur waiting at the apex of her thighs.

'No! Please... Hugh!' she pleaded, lost between terrible desire and denial. Yet she wanted him so, wanted him to touch her in all the private places she had dreamed that he touched.

He placed his hand on the velvet softness of her inner thighs as if he had read her thoughts, felt the warmth of her wordless response. 'You still do not trust me, but it will all fall into place, my lovely, just as all our children will fall into place... I want many children, Bethan! Great lusty boys to be my heirs, to follow in their father's footsteps...'

He leaned over her then and gently eased himself down on to her waiting body. No more words. For too long he had waited for this moment—days, weeks, months of denying himself, and her. He abandoned his self-control and plunged deep inside her, and he heard the soft whimper of pain and then a groan as they came together. Her hands came up to slide, asking, across the warm breadth of his back.

Bethan gasped, utterly shocked by the force of love that jolted her interior, flooding her with delight each time he moved inside her. She sighed deeply, pulling him possessively against her, astonished that his body should provide her with such a wealth of pleasure. His arms clasped her against him, his hands moved down to the mounts of her buttocks so that he could pull her more closely to him. But then he stopped, lifting himself a little above her so that he could look down at the lovely flushed face, her eyes shining, her wide mouth avid, beautiful, hungry. And he entered her again, urgently, so that she cried out, so that the pleasure would build and build, feeding on itself until she felt utterly possessed. Her body began to move against him as though he had touched some secret lock, and then they were moving together feverishly, and as their passion rose to new heights she clove to him, abandoning herself to his body and his words, urging, loving, begging...

'My love, my heart's darling, my Bethan...' His voice rose, moaning in strange, pleading ecstasy, and a wave of tingling fire coursed through her limbs, her thighs, flooding her brain like glorious heady wine.

And he was hers. She had come home at last.

SPOT THE COUPLE

AND WIN A

£1,000

REAL PEARL NECKLACE

PLUS 10 PAIRS OF REAL PEARL EAR STUDS WORTH OVER £100 EACH

A

B

No piece of jewellery is more romantic than the soft glow and lustre of a real pearl necklace, pearls that grow mysteriously from a grain of sand to a jewel that has a romantic history that can be traced back to Cleopatra and beyond.

To enter just study Photograph A showing a young couple. Then look carefully at Photograph B showing the same section of the river. Decide where you think the couple are standing and mark their position with a cross in pen.

Complete the entry form below and mail your entry PLUS TWO OTHER "SPOT THE COUPLE" Competition Pages from June, July or August Mills and Boon paperbacks, to Spot the Couple, Mills and Boon Limited, Eton House, 18/24 Paradise Road, Richmond, Surrey, TW9 1SR, England. All entries must be received by December 31st 1988.

ENTRY FORM

Name _____

Address _____

_____

I bought this book in TOWN _____ COUNTRY _____

This offer applies only to books purchased outside the UK & Eire.
You may be mailed with other offers as a result of this application.